Contents

Acknowledgements   ix
List of Illustrations   x

Introduction: Theatre and Diaspora
Nicholas Grene and Chris Morash   xi

Sparks in the Tin Hut
Seamus Heaney   1

PART ONE: THE ABBEY ON TOUR

1 | The Abbey Tours in England
Richard Cave   9

2 | The Abbey in America: The Real Thing
John P. Harrington   35

3 | Lady Gregory:
The Politics of Touring Ireland
Anthony Roche   51

4 | The 'Abbey Irish Players':
in Australia – 1922
Peter Kuch   69

5 | Barry Fitzgerald:
From Abbey Tours to Hollywood Films
Adrian Frazier   89

6 | The Road to God Knows Where:
Can Theatre be National?
Chris Morash   101

PART TWO: TOURING IN AND OUT OF IRELAND

7 | Eighteenth-Century Theatrical Touring
and Irish Popular Culture
Helen Burke   119

8 | Dion Boucicault's 'The Wearing of the Green'
Deirdre McFeely   139

9 | The Gate: Home and Away
Richard Pine   159

10 | Marina Carr in the US: Perception, Conflict
and Culture in Irish Theatre Abroad
Melissa Sihra   179

11 | Druid Theatre's *Leenane Trilogy*
on Tour: 1996-2001
Patrick Lonergan   193

Notes on Contributors   215

Index   219

Acknowledgements

We are pleased to acknowledge the help of the Royal Irish Academy, co-sponsors with the Irish Theatrical Diaspora of the conference in April 2004 with which this volume originated. With one exception, all the essays in *Irish Theatre on Tour* are revised versions of papers presented at that conference. A part of Adrian Frazier's essay appeared first in the *Dublin Review*. We are very grateful for the financial support of this volume by the Department of English, Trinity College, Dublin. For permission to quote from the *Collected Letters of W.B. Yeats*, edited by John Kelly, we acknowledge the Oxford University Press and InteLex Corporation. We have made every effort to trace other copyright holders and can only apologize if there are permissions we have failed to obtain.

In providing illustrations for the book, Charles Benson, the Keeper of Early Printed Books, Trinity College Dublin Library, and Joanna Finnegan, of the National Library of Ireland, were both very helpful. We are most grateful for the careful and diligent copyediting of the manuscript by Deirdre McFeely.

The Irish Theatrical Diaspora project has from the beginning been a collaborative venture involving many col-leagues in Ireland and abroad. We would like to thank all of them for their contributions in making possible this first volume in the Irish Theatrical Diaspora series.

List of Illustrations

Cover Hilton Edwards and Micheál mac Liammóir on tour in Egypt. Courtesy of Richard Pine.

1 Souvenir programme for the 1906 Abbey tour of England:cover. Courtesy of Colin Smythe. [p.13]

2 Souvenir programme for the 1906 Abbey tour of England: inner cover. Courtesy of Colin Smythe. [p.14]

3 Programme for RSC/Abbey production of *Observe the Sons of Ulster Marching Towards the Somme*, 1996. Courtesy of Royal Shakespeare Company. [p.25]

4 & 5 Sheet music for 'The Wearing of the Green'. Courtesy of the National Library of Ireland. [pp.141f.]

6 Playbill for *Arrah-na-Pogue* by Dion Boucicault, Dublin, 1864. Courtesy of Trinity College, Dublin. [p.144]

7 Micheál mac Liammóir in *The Old Lady Says 'No!'* 1929. Courtesy of Richard Pine. [p.163]

8 Garry Hynes in rehearsal. Courtesy Druid Theatre Company, photo by Ivan Kincyl. [p.196]

9 Martin McDonagh in rehearsal. Courtesy Druid Theatre Company, photo by Ivan Kincyl. [p.197]

IRISH THEATRE ON TOUR

IRISH THEATRE ON TOUR

Irish Theatrical Diaspora Series: 1

Edited by
Nicholas Grene and Chris Morash

Carysfort Press 2005

A Carysfort Press Book

Irish Theatre on Tour
Irish Theatrical Diaspora Series: 1
Edited by Nicholas Grene and Chris Morash

First published in Ireland in 2005 as a paperback original by
Carysfort Press, 58 Woodfield, Scholarstown Road, Dublin 16,
Ireland

© 2005 Copyright remains with the authors

Typeset by Carysfort Press
Cover design by Alan Bennis
Printed and bound by eprint limited
35 Coolmine Industrial Estate, Dublin 15

Published with the support of the English Department, Trinity
College, Dublin, and of the Arts Council

Introduction:
Theatre and Diaspora

Nicholas Grene and Chris Morash

Making Ourselves Part of National Life

Yeats, writing to Lady Gregory in a letter of 1907 (mentioned by Anthony Roche in his essay in this collection) makes it clear why he feels the Abbey must tour Ireland: 'We determined', he writes, 'to make ourselves a part of National life'. There is, of course, an obvious logic to the idea that when a theatre company tours throughout its native land, it becomes more fully 'a part of National life'.

And yet, the essays gathered here tell us that the relationship between touring and making theatre part of a 'National life' is not always so simple. If we want to put the issue in historical perspective, we can turn to Helen Burke's essay, where she reminds us that when Dublin's Smock Alley Theatre company rented an old malt house in Cork in the year 1713, they were effectively embarking on the first extended tour by a major company in Irish theatre history. With this as a point of origin, it is worth remembering that even though the Smock Alley company was the official 'Theatre Royal', their reasons for playing Cork had little to do with creating a national theatre culture (arguably an anachronistic notion in the Ireland of 1713 in any case), and everything to do with keeping the company financially afloat during the summer season, when so much of the fashionable Dublin audience deserted the capital for their country homes.

Similarly, when the great touring houses of the nineteenth century were constructed (the Gaiety and Theatre Royal in Dublin, the Opera Houses in Cork and Belfast), they were not intended to be the infrastructure of a national theatre culture, but to bring the big (predominantly English) companies to Ireland (even if at least some of the repertoire was made up of Irish plays, most famously those of Dion Boucicault). When Boucicault opened *Arrah-na-Pogue* in Dublin in 1864, as Deirdre McFeely shows, he was greeted with the enthusiasm of a returning hero. His Irish melodrama of the 1798 rebellion elicited a positive response, with the reception revealing a degree of anxiety in the press about Irish national self-image. However, most of Boucicault's plays were premiered in New York or London, and it appears that the playwright may only have been giving *Arrah-na-Pogue* a provincial try-out in Dublin before revising the play for its London début.

By the same token, if we move forward to the slightly ramshackle descendants of the big touring companies in the years after World War I, such as the much-loved company of Anew McMaster, or The Sparks fit-up company so movingly evoked here in Seamus Heaney's essay 'Sparks in the Tin Hut' as his first experience of theatre, we once again find actors who roamed Ireland in search of audiences and a living, with little thought of creating a unified national culture.

And yet, some time between the building of the Gaiety in 1871, and Anew McMaster's first tour in 1925, people began to think of theatrical touring as a constituent part of 'National life'. What is more, like so much else in that first decade of the twentieth century, the Abbey's Irish tours during those years established a way of thinking about touring as a means of spreading a national theatre culture that would persist for many years. Anthony Roche's essay brings to life the debates that made the early Abbey take to the roads of Ireland in order to justify their claim to be the 'National Theatre'. Equally,

However, his essay reminds us of the perils of such a venture, when Lady Gregory's *The Gaol Gate*, originally performed in Dublin but set in the West of Ireland, took on a different set of meanings for a Galway audience in ways that problematized the concept of an essentially homogenous national audience. If touring was intended to create a unified Irish audience, Roche's essay seems to suggest, in practice it could expose regional and local differences. Indeed, Chris Morash's essay argues that the fundamental experience of theatre-going is so profoundly local, that the theatre can only constitute a national art form when the experience of performance is mediated by print culture, in reviews, the publication of scripts, and, most importantly, through the construction of national theatre histories.

And yet, in spite of such experiences, the equation between touring and a national theatre culture persisted throughout the twentieth century. In the dark days of the 1970s when subsidies were few, only four Irish theatre companies received any worthwhile state funding: the Abbey, the Gate, the Lyric and the Irish Theatre Company, which had been set up as a touring company with the express intention of creating a national theatre culture. Similarly, Druid first began attracting attention in the early 1980s, not just as a company capable of re-thinking plays like *The Playboy of the Western World* but as a company which toured productions to places like the Aran Islands. And, of course, Field Day would bring the logic of touring as the definitive national theatrical form to its most eloquent epitome, finding its elusive Fifth Province (if it were to be found anywhere) somewhere in the back of a van full of actors on the road leading out of Derry. By the time Field Day had become a travelling fixture in theatres and halls around Ireland, arts policy, north and south of the border, was changing, and in the final quarter of the twentieth century there was a proliferation of subsidized and semi-subsidized companies who considered touring to be a part of their remit.

The Real Ireland On Tour

Touring, then, has been at the heart of theatrical activity in Ireland for the better part of three hundred years. And yet, until recently, it has been almost invisible in commentary about Irish theatre. Not that this makes Ireland unusual. Writing in a recent study of national theatre histories, Steve Wilmer observes that 'national theatre historians generally emphasize the main theatre city … and regard the activities outside the theatre capital as of minor interest or of no interest at all'.[1] It was in part to rectify this that the Irish Theatrical Diaspora Project was established in 2002. The aim of the initiative is to research the production and reception of Irish drama throughout Ireland itself and outside the country. The concept of the diaspora, well anatomized in Richard Cave's essay on the Abbey's visits to Britain, was intended to focus both on the literal business of dispersal – Irish theatre spread out across the island and ultimately across the world – and on the conventional demographic application of the term, the pattern of widespread Irish emigration and its consequences. With this in mind, the Irish Theatrical Diaspora Project set out to examine issues such as the extent to which Irish theatre outside the country was conditioned by the existence of diasporic communities abroad. As such, the project brings together a network of scholars in Ireland with associates in Australia, Britain, Canada and the United States committed to exploring such questions among others. A conference in Dublin in April 2004, co-hosted by the Royal Irish Academy, was our first public event; this book is the outcome of that gathering. A second conference, on Irish theatre in England, is being held in London in June 2005 with a second volume in the Irish Theatrical Diaspora series to be published from it.

Even if it were solely the case that touring within Ireland contributed to the making of a national theatre culture, theatrical touring would be a subject worth pursuing. In spite of all of the changes that have taken place in Irish society in recent years, the idea of the nation continues to shape cultural debate in Ireland, its place strengthened rather than diminished by the ascendancy of postcolonial theory in the past decade. However, there is a related, and equally compelling parallel narrative running through these essays. We glimpse it first when Richard Cave begins to consider the souvenir programme of the second Abbey tour of England, in 1906, arguing that there was a conscious attempt to define 'the company's claim to originality as lying in its concern for a scrupulous authenticity'. Purchasers of that early programme were told that W.G. Fay 'has gone direct to the actual scenes' represented in the plays, 'and the interiors used are unique facsimiles of the originals'. Echoing this idea from the other side of the Atlantic Ocean, John Harrington notes that throughout the entire twentieth century, 'there is great emphasis in America on Abbey authenticity'; in short, Harrington argues, 'the Abbey in America has to be "The Real Thing"'. Consequently, a consideration of Irish theatre on tour brings into focus one of the key issues in current Irish cultural debate: authenticity.

We can put this issue in an historical context by reminding ourselves that when it first became clear that cinema was more than a penny-arcade novelty, it became commonplace to ask why anyone would continue to bother going to the theatre: after all, the cinema was cheaper to attend, could do things with spectacle and perspective that were simply impossible on stage, and, perhaps most importantly, could be everywhere at once. An audience in Dublin did not have to wait years after a New York audience for a touring production to arrive in town; they could see a film as soon as a ship could carry a canister of celluloid across the Atlantic. If we remember that cinema as a global art form took shape in precisely the same years that the Abbey came into being and began to tour, it is easier to understand the emphasis on authenticity. 'The situation can be characterized as follows', argues Walter Benjamin in 'The Work of Art in the Age of Mechanical Reproduction': 'For the first time – and this is the effect of film – man has to operate with his whole living person, yet forgoing its aura. For aura is tied to his presence; there can be no replica for it'.[2] For Benjamin, the 'aura' of authenticity is primarily associated with the living presence of an individual person – in the case of theatre, the

presence of the actor. However, when the attraction of a
theatre company (such as the Abbey) was less in its star
performers than in the fact that it was Irish, the aura shifts. The
aura which the Abbey carried with it to London and New York
was the aura of authentic Irishness.

So, when there were plans for the Abbey to tour Australia in
1915, as Peter Kuch reminds us in his essay, the names of the
actors who travelled with the company were less important than
the fact that the company was genuinely Irish. It did not matter,
for instance, that the company who eventually travelled to
Australia in 1922 was not, in fact, the Abbey company, but a
group of ex-Abbey performers. Nor did it matter that none of
the actors who did travel produced star turns (which would
usually be expected of a touring company). 'There is no
"playing up" to one member or star-ordered self-effacement of
others', praised the Melbourne *Age*; it was not the presence, or
aura, of an individual actor that Australian playgoers lined up to
see: it was an authentic Irish performance.

Rather than supplanting the theatre, then, the cinema could
be said to have created a demand for the aura of live theatre;
and, because the reach of the cinema was global (it was, after
all, just a case of bundling up those little canisters and sending
them around the planet), it created a demand for 'the real thing'
that extended around the globe. Further accelerating this
dynamic, as Adrian Frazier's essay here reminds us, was the
extent to which, after the actress Una O'Connor was 'tempted
away' from an Abbey tour of the United States in 1912, there
was a constant movement of Irish stage actors to Hollywood.
As key Abbey actors took up film careers, Frazier argues:

> a certain style of acting … was carried to the world's millions.
> … It is a story, on another level, of globalization, the star
> system, and the triumph of stereotypes in media for the masses.

What is more, it could be argued that the reinforcement
given to the star system by cinema re-animated the demand for
touring theatrical stars in the middle decades of the twentieth
century. It was certainly the case, for instance, that when
Micheál mac Liammóir played Hamlet in London or in

Elsinore, as Richard Pine points out in his essay, audiences did not go to the theatre to see Hamlet; they went to see mac Liammóir play Hamlet – which is not the same thing at all.

There is, however, a fundamental difference between the aura of a live actor and the aura of authentic Irishness. The actor projects an aura simply by being present; the better the actor, it could be argued, the more fully he or she projects that sense of presentness for an audience. A theatrical performance that projects an aura of authentic Irishness, on the other hand, is both Irish in its own right, but is equally a metonymic representation of a larger, distant Ireland. Indeed, that 'real' Ireland need not even be so distant; as Deirdre McFeely reminds us, when Boucicault's *Arrah-na-Pogue* opened in Dublin in 1864, it was advertised in Dublin as 'an entirely new and original Irish drama'. 'The word "Irish"', she notes, 'is predominant in the playbill: "Irish scenery! Irish homes! Irish hearts!" is printed in large letters'. By the same token, when the Abbey company played New York in 1911 they were not simply authentic specimens of Irish theatre; they were also, like ambassadors, standing for an absent Ireland, which, it has been argued, was at the heart of the protests that met productions of Synge's *The Playboy of the Western World*. Later, in the 1930s, when there was an Irish state to regulate the interests of the Irish nation, there would be efforts to control the kinds of representations of Irishness that were carried abroad by the Abbey on tour.

Taking the 'authentic Ireland' on tour, then, was always going to be a task fraught with problems. In 1911, of course, few would have ventured the view that perhaps there was no such thing as an 'authentic' Irishness; however, with the postmodern critique of essentialism that gathered force through the final decades of the twentieth century, the question as to what made an Irish touring production Irish would become increasingly difficult to answer. At the very least it could be argued that the speed at which Irish social change took place in the period from the mid-1980s onwards made it difficult to create plays that were acceptable to audiences in Ireland, and equally acceptable to older diasporic audiences outside of

Ireland. This was certainly the case with the American productions of Marina Carr's plays, examined here by Melissa Sihra, where the authenticity of the representation proved to be a major obstacle for some Irish-American audiences: 'My kind of Irish are not interested in such trash', claimed a Pittsburgh theatre-goer in response to an audience questionnaire after a performance of *Portia Coughlan* in 2000. Pushing the argument a step further, Patrick Lonergan's closing essay suggests that the Druid tours of Martin McDonagh's plays attempted to convey the impossibility of an authentic Irishness to diasporic audiences. Analysing media coverage of the plays in Sydney, Australia, he notes that director Garry Hynes:

> focused more on what the plays might be saying to Australia, than on what they might be saying about Ireland ... when the question of authenticity arose, it was treated as if the reader would understand that the plays are self-evidently inauthentic.

Indeed, Lonergan finds that, at least in the case of the Druid tours, the attraction of McDonagh's plays lay only indirectly in their Irishness; instead, it was the celebrity of their author that gained the most media attention, particularly in England.

It may seem like a long road that carries us from the Smock Alley company making their way to Cork in 1713, to Martin McDonagh and Garry Hynes giving television interviews in Australia in 1999; and, indeed, the contributors here do take us on a long and often fascinating journey. However, along the way increasingly familiar signposts appear as the debate about Ireland's theatrical diaspora begins to take shape. It becomes clear that touring brings into focus for us some of the more important questions, not only in Irish theatre history but equally in the wider Irish cultural debate – questions about the possibilities for creating and maintaining a national culture, both historically and in an increasingly globalized world. In short, the study of Ireland's theatrical diaspora now looks less like an interesting byroad leading away from the main street of theatre history, and more like a path to the heart of some of the most pressing issues facing Irish culture in the twenty-first century.

1 S.E. Wilmer, 'Introduction' in S.E. Wilmer (ed.), *Writing and Rewriting National Theatre Histories* (Iowa City: University of Iowa Press, 2004), p.18.

2 Walter Benjamin, 'The Work of Art in the Age of Mechanical Reproduction' in Hannah Arendt (ed.), *Illuminations* (trans. Harry Zohn) (New York: Harcourt, Brace and World, 1968), p.229.

Sparks in the Tin Hut

Seamus Heaney

Generations of Irish people received their first introduction to live theatre from Anew McMaster and his travelling players, but in my case I have to thank the Ancient Order of Hibernians. Less than fifty yards from the house where I grew up, down a lane parallel with our lane, there was a corrugated iron hut, not much bigger than the wartime Nissen huts only recently erected on Toome Aerodrome. Above the door a small plaque told you this was Hillhead AOH Hall, and here members of the local Hibernian band would assemble to practise for their annual walking days on 17 March and 15 August. And here too The Sparks, a fit-up company that toured the country with their 'plays and sketches, spot prizes and variety', would arrive for a couple of weeks every year, quickening pulses in all the townlands between Creagh and Castledawson.

This was County Derry in the mid-1940s, but it could have been the country of Patrick Kavanagh's poem *The Great Hunger*, 'that metaphysical land,/ Where flesh was a thought more spiritual than music'. The chapel or church or meeting house on Sunday, the fair day once or twice a month, the card school or the public house once or twice a week, the occasional waddle around a waltz floor or wallop round a ceilidh house, that was the extent of most people's mobility and recreation. So when an Irish woman Italianate, rouged and décolletée, fish-netted and full-throated, paraded before them, singing above the glitter and tumult of a piano accordion, she had Circean power.

That particular item always came towards the end of a programme that would have begun with the emergence from behind the curtain of 'Old Sparks' – Mr Lynch Senior, head of the family and of the troupe – to announce the evening's main performance. In a purple velvet jacket and green bow-tie, grease-painted and high-pitched, he would deliver a spiel about the play to come, perhaps a dramatized version of the story of Noreen Bawn, the tubercular heroine who died because of 'the curse of emigration', perhaps another showing of 'The Murders in the Red Barn', or the capture of Robert Emmet by a vividly redcoated and dastardly moustachioed Major Sirr.

Melodrama, music, leg-show, raffle, a general and slightly endangering raffishness – for a couple of weeks The Sparks kept audiences in the company of flesh and blood. Once upon a time Wordsworth had boasted that his poems did the same for readers, but Wordsworth spoke figuratively, whereas the players did it literally, night after night, murder and love scenes, cleavage and slinky silks. In a kind of 'low-life' prefiguring of what should happen at the high-art level, they fulfilled the demands that Yeats once set down for theatre in 'The Circus Animals' Desertion': they managed 'to engross the present and dominate memory'.

When I think of touring theatre companies, I think of Hillhead Hall – the *ad hoc* nature of the event, the intervention it represented, the stir it caused. Not that there were any surface indications of that stir: apart from a few extra people on the Toome Road in the late evening, there was no sign that lives were being affected, yet night after night in the Tin Hut (as our hall was known locally) some strange thing did happen. Once the players stepped out on that cramped stage, a part of our fantasy life stepped out with them. A stealthy suspension of disbelief occurred. Images entered the mind, and for a couple of hours of dreamtime we enjoyed the extravagances that would never have been considered in daytime. It was, in the full and primary sense of the word, glamour, which is to say 'magic, enchantment, spell'.

And, yes, it was all so long ago. There was no electric light in the hall. There were no advertisements for the show on radio or

TV. There were black-and-white posters on gate pillars, and a caravan – silent, huddled, somehow clandestine – parked at the end of the lane. Another world. But a world that had always been (as I recognized a few years later when I encountered the scene in *Hamlet* where the players arrive at Elsinore) and would be again, when Brian Friel and Stephen Rea founded the Field Day Theatre Company in 1980 and toured the country with *Translations*, filling the common mind with the kind of 'fiery shorthand' that Yeats had once commended in the writings of William Carleton, writings which hang like shadowy hand-painted scenery behind the fierce fantasia of Friel's play.

What once happened at parish level with the arrival of The Sparks happened at national level with Field Day's tour of *Translations*. And the name of the company (which was very deliberately glossed in the first programme) indicates that this was exactly the effect the founding directors intended: it stood for 'a day occupied with brilliant or exciting events; a day spent in the field, e.g. by the hunt, or by field naturalists'. A day, in other words, which would engross the present and dominate memory. And a day which would turn into a decade of toured plays, of stirred hearts and minds, of the dangerous intersection of literature and politics.

Whatever attitude people took or take to Field Day, there is no doubt that the plays it toured allowed the preoccupations of the times to strut and fret upon the stage, and to vex and invigorate in equal measure both local audiences and the literati. Obviously, the talents of the writers and the matters they treated were central to the company's success, but equally important was the fact that the plays were taken on the road, that the whole country had a sense that they were part of an action, that a tremor in the audience joined Derry's Guildhall and Cork's Everyman Theatre, Sligo's Hawk's Well and Dublin's Olympia, and put theatrical heart into spaces elsewhere that were not entirely fitted for fit-ups, but all the more vital for that reason.

Just as James Joyce took satisfaction in having a picture of Cork city framed with cork, I take satisfaction (as did Thomas Kilroy) in the fact that the second play Kilroy wrote for Field

Day was *Madam McAdam's Travelling Theatre*. Set during 'The Emergency', this treated of a ramshackle road show on the move through the land at a time of crisis, and was the occasion in 1991 of the annual *ad hoc* itinerary of actors and administrators that had been happening then for more than ten years. During that time, the emergencies of contemporary Ireland, their historical causes and their several refractions had been staged in plays as different as Friel's *Translations* and *Making History*, in Tom Paulin's *The Riot Act* and Stewart Parker's *Pentecost* – to name only the works that directly addressed the matter of Ulster. They addressed that matter, but they were also intent upon glamouring it. It was important that they were not just criticism or history or politics by other means. Ideally, the daytime of the usual would enter the hall and come out of the wings as a play of figures in dreamtime. And theatre on tour is specially framed to effect such a transformation. The come-and-go of the encounter does not mean that the effect is fleeting. On the contrary, as Hamlet's fit-up players quickly demonstrate, the occasional nature of their appearance in a place can be just the thing 'to show the very age and body of the time his form and pressure'.

My own image for this transformation is a heavy crockery mug that once stood on the shelf of our dresser in Mossbawn and now stands on a bookshelf in Dublin. Some time in the mid-to-late 1940s, it was borrowed by The Sparks and used as a prop in one of their plays. I think it was the story of Noreen Bawn, because I remember sitting later that night in the Tin Hut and seeing it raised in a farewell toast by a lover to a weeping maiden who was departing on her fatal voyage to America. Years later, when I was writing the sequence called 'Station Island', I needed something to represent the reality of 'magic, enchantment, spell', something that consumed the ordinary and the ingrained and the dutiful in 'the dazzle of the impossible', something signifying possibility, a farther range – and what appeared in my mind's eye was:

the mug

beyond my reach on its high shelf, the one
patterned with cornflowers, blue sprig after sprig

repeating round it, as quiet as a milestone,

old and glazed and haircracked. It had stood for years
in its patient sheen and turbulent atoms,
unchallenging, unremembered *lar*
I seemed to waken to and waken from.

When had it not been there? There was one night
when the fit-up actors used it for a prop
and I sat in a dark hall estranged from it
as a couple vowed and called it their loving cup

and held it in our gaze until the curtain
jerked shut with an ordinary noise.
Dipped and glamoured then from this translation,
it was restored with all its cornflower haze

still dozing, its parchment glazes fast –
as the otter surfaced once with Ronan's psalter
miraculously unharmed, that had been lost
a day and a night under deep lough water.

And so the saint praised God on the lough shore.
The dazzle of the impossible suddenly
blazed in across the threshold, a sun-glare
to put out the small hearths of constancy.

PART ONE:

THE ABBEY ON TOUR

1 | The Abbey Tours in England

Richard Cave

A perusal of the *Oxford English Dictionary* shows how even in its very roots the word 'diaspora' carries a potential for divergent, antithetical interpretations.[1] The initial meaning offered refers to 'dispersion', dispersal, a thinning out, elimination; by extension it has come to be applied to refugee and migrant communities. In this sense diaspora has a direct bearing on Irish social history: the famine years and the massive depletions effected by the resulting mass emigrations, and the large-scale transportations to serve criminal (usually political) sentences. This tragic dimension of diaspora is reflected in the title of Thomas Keneally's *The Great Shame*, which charts the extent and causes of an Irish presence in Australia. But Keneally takes care to discriminate numerous strands of experience to which that sense of shame might apply: there is what he terms the 'survival shame' of those who outlived the famine; there is the shame that is rightfully attached to British rule for its consistent 'misgovernment of Ireland' and the 'continuing discrimination' against Catholics; and finally shame at the 'failures … to produce by agitation, constitutional or otherwise, a successful nineteenth-century state in a Europe where many other states were emergent'.[2] But the *OED* proffers a further meaning to diaspora, which draws more certainly on the Greek roots of the word: a verb to 'sow' or 'scatter' (in the agricultural sense of a fertilization), which implies not a lack or absence, but a developing presence. Studying the usages of the term in a biblical concordance shows that the first meaning obtains exclusively in the Old Testament, as in Deuteronomy (28:25) where a threat insists that, unless the Almighty is honoured, the Israelites will be routed and scattered before their enemy. The second meaning occurs in the New Testament where (in the opening exordium for the Epistles of both James and Peter) the intended recipients of the letters are addressed as 'dispersed' or 'scattered': they are the missionaries who have gone forth from the homeland to spread the gospel of the new faith. The first use defines a state of being victimized, of being rendered objective, abject; the second honours an active choice, an assertion of subjectivity.

Touring in the theatrical sense embraces an active choice, a going forth with a precise intent. But further study of the *OED* yields some interesting resonances within the words 'tour' (as both noun and verb) and 'touring'. The former is of French origin and appears most frequently in general usage after the (English) Restoration of 1660, when it signified 'a turning around' or 'revolution' (though not perhaps yet in the social and political sense); 'a journey visiting a number of places in a circuit for purposes of recreation or business'; 'a course of engagements'; and also (appropriately in this theatrical context) 'a crescent front of false hair'. It was not until the eighteenth century that the verb carried the specific meaning of 'travelling from town to town fulfilling theatrical engagements' or 'to take a play on tour'. The *OED* also offers insights into the word 'engagement', relevant to the process of touring. Beyond the expected set of meanings relating to betrothal, we find 'a pecuniary liability' (no one would deny that the costs of touring were and are exorbitant); 'a moral or legal obligation' (this admirably summarizes the larger political agenda underpinning the motives of the early Directors for taking the Abbey company on tour); and 'a battle, encounter, combat' (these precisely reflect the tenor of the reception accorded *The Playboy of the Western World* when first performed in a number of English cities, especially where there was a strong Irish community). All three shades of meaning in this instance apply variously to aspects of the history of the Abbey's tours in England.

All the words studied ('diaspora', 'tour', 'engagement') subtly shift their nuances depending on the context of application; but one usage with a dominant significance often brings with it all the panoply of resonances that have accrued over time and determine the word's richness and ambiguity. For the Abbey, touring in England (with or without false hair pieces) did have a moral imperative, which can be seen both as a consequence of and response to negative and positive meanings of diaspora. To put it simply: *how* one interrogates and interprets the various tours over the century since 1904 depends on the composition of the audiences to which the Abbey company was performing, a factor that depends in large measure on the precise theatrical venue of the performances and the precise city. The composition has always varied between predominantly English spectators or predominantly expatriate (immigrant Irish); but always there was a pronounced mix; and this is still generally the case with Irish drama performed on English stages. A postcolonial critique of the situation will need to determine, given the complex spectatorship and every spectator's measure of historical and political awareness, the degree to which ideologically the performance is to be interpreted as combative (anti-British) or reassuring and supportive (pro-Irish). Might there even be a case of the same performances addressing both interests? How were these differing ideological positions negotiated? And how were they received? Crucial information here can best be gleaned from how the Abbey chooses to present its work and itself as an institution on its many forays into England: how, in other words, it prepares its audiences to *read* the performances on offer. Rather than enumerating a check-list of dates and venues to compile a theatre history of facts concerning Abbey tours in England, the focus of this essay will be on a number of specially designed souvenir programmes, which chart a changing relationship between the Abbey and its English audiences since 1904. This essay began with an attention to words and shifting complexities of meaning; it will continue by examining the language that these programmes deploy to negotiate with audiences in the context of a diaspora where, in the final two decades of England's colonization of Ireland, the potential for complexities of shame (as Keneally invites us to interpret the word) for both English and Irish spectators was acute. By the close of the twentieth century, the language of the programmes seems to be endeavouring to establish a wholly new relation between the company and its audiences in England. The change in rhetoric reflects as profound a change in economic as political circumstance: in fact, it pinpoints a decisive change in the very nature of touring between 1904 and 2004, as the economics of cultural transmission have come forcibly into play.

Before the acquisition of the Abbey, the Irish National Theatre Society had visited London in May 1903 and March 1904, sponsored by the London Irish Literary Society; in 1905 Oxford and Cambridge were added to the list of venues visited. On all these visits it might be predicted that their audiences would be informed, liberal and appreciative. The following year the touring was considerably extended: in late April, the Abbey company visited Manchester, Liverpool and Leeds, while from 26 May to 9 July a succession of weekly seasons was given at theatres in Cardiff, Glasgow, Aberdeen, Newcastle, Edinburgh and Hull before returning for a period in London. It was for this second tour in 1906 that an illustrated souvenir programme was first devised and printed.[3] A substantial text outlining 'the origin of the company' and 'the founding of the first National Theatre' with further sections on the playwrights (Yeats, Synge, Boyle and Gregory), the scenery and properties, the plays (*The Pot of Broth*, *Cathleen ni Houlihan*, *Riders to the Sea*, *In the Shadow of the Glen*, *The Building Fund*, *Hyacinth Halvey*, *Spreading the News*) and the music, is accompanied by eight photographs mounted on stiffer coloured paper which alternate with the twelve printed pages.[4]

Illustration 1: Souvenir programme for the 1906 Abbey tour of England: cover. Courtesy of Colin Smythe.

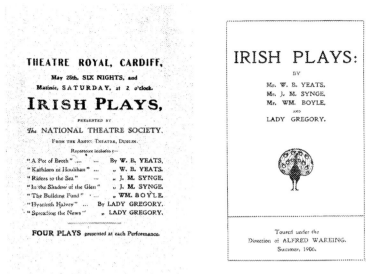

Illustration 2. Souvenir programme for the 1906 Abbey tour of England: inner cover. Courtesy of Colin Smythe.

The programme is a most handsome production, listing on the inside cover the company's repertoire of eight plays ('FOUR PLAYS presented at each Performance'). What is noticeable is that the front cover exclusively and the inside cover and title page by capitalization and size of font give special prominence to the heading *IRISH PLAYS*. This quite dominates the information on the inside cover that the plays are 'presented by The National Theatre Society from the Abbey Theatre, Dublin', and again on the adjacent title page where it tops the list of playwrights, a colophon in the form of a peacock with spread tail, and the information, relegated to lowest position and printed in pale not bold script, 'toured under the Direction of ALFRED WAREING, Summer 1906'.[5]

From the first glance it is not the company (which later in the text is properly lauded as a national theatre whose opening 'marked a new epoch in the history of the Drama') but the wares they offer which command a reader's attention. That the founders of the Irish theatre movement wished to create a stage for playwrights and poets is, seemingly, not being evoked here or not as forcefully as all that is implied by the insistent epithet, Irish.[6] The word recurs throughout the ensuing text: though due acknowledgement is given to Annie Horniman for securing, rebuilding and decorating the Abbey, the sentence about her ends by stressing how the theatre 'with its Irish stained glass, and its Irish copper mirrors from Youghal, and its Irish wainscoating, and its interesting portraits ... has become one of the features of the artistic life of Dublin' (p.4). Equally stressed on the ensuing page is the description of the repertoire as comprising 'only plays by Irish authors ... upon Irish subjects'. Clearly pride is being expressed here through the reiterated epithet, but the repetitions (like the assertion of pride in nationhood) also amount to a challenge in terms of cultural specifics for intended readers/spectators, be they English or expatriate Irish. For them what is being signalled, as the subsequent text exemplifies, is the reclamation of forms of Irish experience (and particularly what passes for Irish experience in plays in performance) as fit properly for modes of representation evolved and practised only by Irish playwrights. Before the text is encountered, the particular title and the way it is presented assert an independence from forms of British hegemonic cultural control. Participating in this theatrical event, it is implied, will be an act of political collusion.

That a political stand is being made over the issue of stage representation becomes clearer as one reads the text: a kind of constellation of specific terms and epithets recurs that steadily defines the company's claim to originality as lying in its concern for a scrupulous authenticity. The oft-reiterated 'Irish' soon attracts into its orbit the term 'national' in respect of the theatre's foundation, though care is taken to discriminate this adjective from 'nationalist', which is characterized as 'antagonistic to art' and as giving 'the National Theatre company a severe trial' (p.5). 'National' quickly brings with it the related epithet 'international' in respect of the recognition that the company has achieved outside Ireland and Britain (pp.5-6).[7] Boucicault and his followers are introduced as promoting conventions for representing the 'stage life of Ireland' from which the company's dramatists have decidedly 'broken away', preferring to take 'their types and scenes direct from Irish life itself' (p.6). 'Direct' is readily transmuted into a preoccupation with studying the 'actual' as the proper basis for the playwrights' dramaturgy and the performers' acting style (p.6). Authenticity is next extended to embrace attempts at realism observable in performance: the wide proscenium openings in the theatres where the company will act will be reduced to 'a width of about 17 feet', as most accurately reproducing the dimensions of 'the interior of a peasant's hut' (pp.6-7). Fay, it is argued, 'has gone *direct* to the *actual* scenes, and the interiors used are unique *facsimiles of the original*' (pp.6-7).[8] One can see from this one sentence how cleverly in rhetorical terms the constellation is built up. A quick glance through the surviving photographs of these recreated interiors shows that they were in practice built by stock means and generally deployed the same items in varying combinations; what gave each particular setting its distinctive quality was the manner in which it was dressed; and indeed the manifesto is on safer grounds when it next turns to discussing properties as 'taken direct from the cottages of the peasantry' (p.7) in Gort, the Aran Islands, and West Kerry.[9] Readers are further instructed of *Riders to the Sea* that 'in dressing this play a young man from the island was brought to the Abbey Theatre to revise all details, so that an exact reproduction of the Aran dress is now given' (p.7).[10] The communal keen, which accompanies Maurya's final speeches, is later described as 'the exact cry still heard at many burials in Ireland' (p.8). The music generally will not be the conventional orchestral accompaniment but will be provided by 'Mr. Arthur Darley, the talented Irish Violinist', playing 'traditional' airs, which he has tramped over Ireland, 'collecting from wayfaring minstrels' (p.11). The final two paragraphs repeat the gist of the argument: that this is a movement which has 'grown up entirely in Ireland' offering plays which are 'portions of Irish life', mounted on stage 'with a care and accuracy of detail that has hardly been attempted before'. The aim is to contest the representation of the Irish peasant as 'a mere merry-andrew' in staging that was barely adequate. What motivates the practitioners of the new movement is 'care' (the noun is twice repeated respecting the scruples of dramatists and actors), most crucially the care the actors take 'to keep close to the actual movement and gestures of the people' from which the company derives 'a style and method of its own' (p.12). The prose is deftly phrased to conclude with a recall of the title but with the addition now of a qualifying adverb, which all the preceding rhetoric has been designed to legitimate: if the company has achieved status as an ensemble, it derives from their continual playing of '*purely* Irish plays'.[11]

Much of this material had appeared of course in *Beltaine* and later in *Samhain*, the theatre's periodical publications, but never so tersely expressed or so pointedly aimed at defining why the founding of the Abbey Theatre was in political terms a recuperative act, a reclaiming of cultural autonomy. Directed at English spectators, the text poses a challenge to cultural and social perceptions and biases formed over several centuries through very different modes of representation, focussed on the stereotype of the Stage Irishman. Given that longstanding stage history, plays that claimed to be 'purely Irish' were inevitably going to be viewed as subversive of traditional theatrical codes, which, it is suggested, becoming moribund, hackneyed and formulaic, offer only travesty of a precise and lived actuality. The stress on the need for care in rehearsing, staging, performing intimates that with the Abbey a new kind of integrity obtains that honours the dignity of Ireland as subject, not the lowness of Ireland as object of a superior (English) gaze.[12] In its covert but calculatedly political approach to English spectators, the programme can be interpreted as defining the concept of a *tour* as designed to promote a revolution in seeing, in reading drama in performance, in discriminating between dubious fantasies of Ireland and an aesthetic governed by principles drawn 'direct from Irish life itself' (p.6). In this context, Yeats's famous, perhaps indiscreet, remark to Lady Gregory about the repertoire of the Abbey ('Not what you want, but what we want') could be viewed not as the expression of arrogance, which it is often interpreted as being, but as an assertion of absolute confidence in a new theatrical gospel. The programme, from such a perspective, emerges as a tool of cultural dissemination aimed at revitalizing theatrical processes. To have succeeded in Dublin, climaxed by the acquisition of the Abbey, was one thing; but to succeed in the larger sphere of Britain was quite another.[13] Audiences needed to be coerced into interrogating their own expectations, into actively engaging with the promotion and reception of drama in performance as ideologically determined and determining. In the incisive simplicity of its stylistic expression the programme is disarming, persuasive and, given its devices of repetition, adamant in asserting a right to occupy the moral high ground. It was making a virtue of *difference*, and rightly so. On previous tours the company had won accolades in the metropolis, the chief centres of learning, and three major industrial centres; and now the Abbey was touring throughout the provinces: there was ample justification for the confidence and rectitude implicit in the tone the programme adopts.

But what of expatriate spectators, who must have made up a sizeable ratio at the venues on this tour? The repetitions, the evolving constellations of related words, are likely to have worked a different line of persuasion. The details defining the degree to which the performances would be 'purely Irish' would promote anticipations of nostalgia, of recognition, a perception again of *difference*, since what the plays would attempt to render was a faithful representation of what to expatriates might well be a remembered lifestyle or one recalled as a subject of family history. The difference was that this representation promised no degree of travesty, no traducing or manipulating of experience to suit a colonial agenda; rather, the company's objective was empowering to an expatriate audience through staging plays with a fit decorum which respected the peasantry as subject. There was an implied promise that there would be no pressure within the auditorium to laugh *at* their lineage and cultural inheritance. The rhetorical structures and the sustained tone of the programme can be read as both reassuring and inspiring from this perspective; there is no hint here of apology for being Irish, since the epithet through its continual repetition is cleansed of the derogatory and revitalized. Repetition for both sets of constituent spectators steadily makes the word *Irish* within the particular theatrical context excitingly *strange* and no longer a comfortable or derided *known*.

The souvenir programme, the only one of its kind produced throughout the first half-century of Abbey touring in England, asserts its imperatives in opposition to established colonial norms. It marked the start of a more adventurous touring policy that by 1921 saw the company visiting twelve venues over several months culminating in a season playing comedies from the repertory nightly at the Coliseum in London. The Irish National Theatre Society made its presence decidedly felt in the English cultural scene, as if that development was a necessary adjunct to being 'national'. While touring continued after the establishment of the Irish Free State in 1922, it was less frequent and more low-key; the Abbey entered a phase of redefining its precise status in relation to the new state at home, and the subversive potential of touring in England was redundant. But actors from the company remained a significant presence on English stages: the famed difference of their simplicity, the freshness of the acting style inculcated by the Fays and Yeats encouraged English managers to seduce them away from the Abbey to perform in the metropolis. This might be viewed as a process of cultural appropriation, except the absorption was not total: the actors retained their difference and were not assimilated into the prevailing English style. The difference was valued, and casting creatively made much of this fact. In his staging of Shakespeare's *Measure for Measure* (Memorial Theatre, Stratford, 1908), William Poel used Sara Allgood's Abbey style in casting her as Isabella to embody a transparent innocence offsetting the prevailing corruption. This pattern continued over decades: as late as 1976 Siobhán McKenna created an Agrippina of monumental stillness and inward strength opposite the Method-school explosiveness and temperamentalism of Jonathan Kent's Nero in Christopher Fettes' production of Racine's *Britannicus* (Lyric Theatre Studio, Hammersmith). That they kept faith with their Abbey training meant that these itinerant actors could always return to the company, and most did on a regular basis: loyalty and integrity were not impaired.

When the Abbey next made a much-publicized tour to England as a company, the nature of touring and of theatre had changed extensively: in 1964 Peter Daubeny invited the company to that year's World Theatre Season at the Aldwych Theatre.[14] They played O'Casey's *Juno and the Paycock* and *The Plough and the Stars* for two weeks alongside visits by the Comédie Française, the Schiller Theatre of Berlin, de Filippo's Neapolitan company, the Polish Contemporary Theatre from Łódź, Karolos Koun's Greek Arts Theatre and the Moscow Art Theatre. The Abbey's reception compared with that for most of the other companies was lukewarm; the work was deemed fusty and dated.[15] They were performing within a new internationally aware theatrical culture and the siting was not to their advantage. The essay on the Abbey contributed by Micheál mac Liammóir to the Souvenir Programme did not help.[16] He stressed the company's style as 'the extremity of simpleness', saw the work as having 'the quality of the Italian or Flemish primitives' and further comparisons were made with Douanier Rousseau and 'the jewels and gold of Byzantium'.[17] He made the Abbey sound naïve and precious; and he served O'Casey no better by likening him to Gorki for celebrating 'the magnificence of poverty [and] the fierce and raw reality of suffering'. This is dabbling in half-truths: crucially mac Liammóir makes no mention of O'Casey's joyous comedy or his highly sophisticated handling of intricacies of tone, which require as sophisticated a handling by actors. The accompanying photographs suggest that the plays are dark, drab and conventional and they contrast markedly with those illustrating the other companies' offerings where experiment, innovation and a challenging theatricality are the focus.[18] Harold Hobson alone amongst reviewers separated praise of the dramaturgical excellence and political acumen of *The Plough and the Stars* from disappointment at the limitations of the production and his sadness 'at the prestige the Abbey had lost by its incompetent *Juno and the Paycock* the previous week'.[19]

Nothing daunted, Daubeny invited the Abbey on a second visit to the 1968 season, where they were now in the company of the Theatre on the Balustrade from Czechoslovakia, Barrault's Théâtre de France, the Teatro Stabile from Rome, Bergman's production of *Hedda Gabler* for the Royal Dramatic Theatre, Sweden, and the Bunraku National Theatre of Japan. The production selected for this occasion was Hugh Hunt's staging of Dion Boucicault's *The Shaughraun* with Cyril Cusack in the title role.[20] In the intervening years there had been a change of personnel at the Abbey with the retirement of Ernest Blythe as theatre manager in 1967; and London reviewers commented on a renewed vigour in the playing and an improved ensemble. While critical response was mixed, it did this time excite greater discrimination than previously.[21] Irving Wardle confidently asserted: 'no Dublin show ... has done more to put over the idea of a dynamic new Ireland than this, which at once rescues a fine dramatist from oblivion and restores the Abbey to its old status as one of the jewels of the English-speaking theatre.'[22] What is remarkable about the Abbey's section of the Souvenir Programme and the publicity flyer is that there is no statement of the company's history or current policy, status or ambitions; the focus is entirely on play, dramatist, and Cusack's career. The entries are curiously self-effacing, as if the Abbey were unsure of its precise identity in relation to the English or to the international cultural scene.[23] Change, however, was imminent.

From 30 September to 8 October 1968, Carolyn Swift organized a seminar in Dublin exploring the concept of national theatres and their relation to the international scene. Irish personnel hosted the event, with representatives from Iceland, the then Soviet Union, the United Kingdom, and Germany (East and West). There had always, of course, been an international dimension in the earlier American tours; but after the seminar the Abbey began cultivating a place in a global international scene; England over the coming decades was now but one possible touring venue.[24] From the 1970s the focus of international touring changed, becoming now a display of the aesthetic criteria governing a country's way of representing itself in theatre and the extent and modes of its funding of stagecraft and the arts of performance. The increasing impact of globalization had to be acknowledged politically and culturally: a national theatrical enterprise had now visibly to justify its status as *national*. The effect of this on touring was radical. Where in earlier decades of the century companies had toured a representative range of their work, the focus after 1968 tended to be on one play as a vehicle through which to demonstrate what was representative of a company's particular initiative, expertise, skill and originality.[25] Nationality was to be defined through one iconic work.[26] Though the Abbey company toured to the National Theatre (then housed in the Old Vic) in August 1970 seemingly as one consequence of the seminar, they chose to offer only revivals of established work (Synge's *The Well of the Saints* and George Fitzmaurice's *The Dandy Dolls*, both directed by Hugh Hunt); distinctive change came with a short run of Behan's *Richard's Cork Leg* at the Royal Court in 1972, followed in 1977 with Kilroy's *Talbot's Box*.[27] Thereafter visits to England by the Abbey have brought only new playwriting.

What is of immediate interest is how the Abbey chose to present itself after 1968. Nothing in fact in the programme for Behan's play indicated that this was an Abbey production (it was described as 'presented at the Royal Court ... by arrangement with Noel Pearson', although there was no reference to his position on the Abbey Board of Directors), while the publicity flyer referred to it as 'one of the highlights of this year's Dublin Theatre Festival', which 'recently completed a record-breaking run at the Olympia Theatre, Dublin'. Only the Court's press handout and newspaper advertisements established the play as an 'Abbey Theatre Production'.[28] While the programme includes substantial material on Behan, there is no statement about the Abbey, its history, or current situation in Irish culture.[29]

Publicity for the Abbey improved somewhat with *Talbot's Box*: it was defined on the programme cover as 'The Abbey Theatre Dublin Production'; listings of the directorial team, described as 'For the Abbey Theatre, Dublin', are placed *above* a similar roster 'For the Royal Court Theatre'; dates are given for opening performances in both the Peacock and the Royal Court; and the programme contains a piece by Tomás Mac Anna (then Director of the Abbey) on the Peacock Theatre, which outlines its size, adaptability, its history and policy since its opening in the 1920s of privileging experimental work.[30] In other words, a challenging, innovative play was situated carefully in terms of Dublin's social and cultural history, and a link was implied between the Peacock and the Court as centres of excellence actively promoting new writing, making the choice of venue for the tour wholly appropriate.[31] The publicity flyer (albeit with the flamboyant rhetoric now expected of such items) further made clear that a pronounced connection existed between the Abbey's history and theatrical innovation: 'Crackling with Irish humour and based in the humane traditions of the Abbey Theatre, this is a fine example of progressive theatre from Dublin.' The rhythms of the prose here bring emphasis to the words 'humane' and 'progressive'; noticeably 'Irish' and 'Dublin' by contrast sustain a marginalized weighting in the sentence.[32] All the material foregrounds the theatre practice of the Abbey as a direct reflection of the particular society in which the theatre is placed.

When Patrick Mason's production of *Dancing at Lughnasa* came to The Royal National Theatre (1990), the accompanying programme had a very different tone and emphasis. The cover was headed by the balanced emblems of both theatres and the credits read: 'From Dublin /British Première /of the Abbey /Theatre Production'.[33] Inside, printed in large font and in white lettering against a darkened ground, is a statement from Noel Pearson (now securely identified as 'Chairman and Director of the Abbey Theatre'), where reference to the 1990 visit of the Abbey to the Royal National Theatre prefaces a list of eleven world-wide venues visited by the company over 'the last three years' to illustrate the Abbey's 'extensive international touring programme'.[34] Brief reference to the strength of the company's 'policy of presenting new Irish writing' ('eight new plays per year') leads to an offer 'to reciprocate this visit by inviting the Royal National Theatre to perform in the Abbey next year'. As a manifesto, this says nothing about the responsibilities of the Abbey as a *national* theatre; the emphasis exclusively advertises the place of the company's work in the global cultural market. There was a certain irony in this boasting. Unlike the pattern followed by most guest companies who brought one or two productions to play on consecutive nights over a short season,[35] Friel's play joined the repertory to play alongside Royal National Theatre productions for three months before moving with a change of cast into the West End. Advertising and programming did not make it abundantly clear whether spectators were maybe watching a co-production; noticeably four out of eighteen reviews anthologized in *Theatre Record* do not mention the Abbey's involvement in the enterprise at all.[36] Was this an instance of negligence on the part of the Abbey's publicity staff? Or was an English institution quietly appropriating Irish cultural excellence yet again? Pearson's statement is not given a dominant position in the programme but noticeably relegated to the closing pages *after* the material that audiences are most likely to give attention to before a performance.[37]

By comparison, the programme for the tour of the Abbey's production of Frank McGuinness's *Observe the Sons of Ulster Marching Towards the Somme* under the auspices of the Royal Shakespeare Company to the Barbican Theatre in March 1996 was altogether more subdued; but again there is more than a hint of appropriation in the way that the information is ordered.

Illustration 3: Programme for RSC/Abbey production of
Observe the Sons of Ulster Marching Towards the Somme,
1996. Courtesy of Royal Shakespeare Company.

The cover sports a fine photograph of Peter Gowen as Pyper, beneath which comes the statement 'The Royal Shakespeare Company /by arrangement with Thelma Holt /*presents* the Abbey Theatre, Dublin production'[38] Below this in an appropriately larger font comes the title and dramatist's name, while above both it and the photograph in heavily bold font is the Royal Shakespeare Company logo, the formal name of the company and reference to the sponsor for the current season, Allied Domecq. The information about the Royal Shakespeare Company and Thelma Holt's involvement with the Abbey is repeated on the central pages along with the cast list. At bottom right is listed the directorial team while opposite (in minute font) appear details of the original performances of the play at the Abbey (1985) and the Hampstead Theatre Club (1987). Further reference to this as an Abbey production is found only in the small print after the cast biographies, where under 'Production Acknowledgements' the Abbey Theatre records its thanks for various kinds of assistance, concluding with '*the Cultural Relations Committee of the Department of Foreign Affairs, Dublin, Ireland* for their support of this tour'.[39] This production had toured extensively abroad and was to visit four other venues in England, but there is no vaunting rhetoric about international cultural exchange. Was a repetition of Pearson's manifesto considered tactless to accompany a play about the ravages of a World War? References to this as a *state-funded* touring production seem underplayed to the point of near-invisibility: of twelve reviews of the performances included in *Theatre Record*, two make no mention of the Abbey's involvement and two refer to it as 'a new RSC touring production'.[40] These might appear merely crass errors, but the appearance of the whole programme does look like an RSC take-over. Clearly cultural exchange can quickly transmogrify into appropriation. It was some seven years since the RSC had commissioned *Mary and Lizzie* from McGuinness. Did they still consider him a house-dramatist?

What gives added strength to the argument supposing that these are instances of appropriation of an Irish product by two monolithic English institutions is a statement that graces the programme for the touring of the Peacock Theatre production of Marina Carr's *Portia Coughlan* to the Royal Court. This opened on 9 May 1996, within weeks of the staging of McGuinness's play at the Barbican. The programme offers the customary phrasing on the title-page: 'The Royal Court Theatre presents /The Abbey Theatre production'; and performance dates for both venues are recorded.[41] After suitable preliminaries explaining the special commissioning of the play, a whole page is given to 'The Abbey Theatre Dublin'.[42] The anonymous text is an altogether more sophisticated manifesto than Pearson's. It tells what seems the conventional Abbey history (the founding, the riots, American touring, the fire, the new theatre and its succession of directors) except for certain emphases, especially the detail that state provision in 1925 came in response to recognition of the theatre 'as a cultural asset'. Later claims for the Abbey's award-winning potential, culminating in the listing of all twelve citations garnered by *Dancing at Lughnasa*, is seen as 'affirm[ing] the aspirations of its founders'. The ideology underlying the whole article is revealed in a final, isolated sentence: 'The Abbey Theatre remains Ireland's foremost cultural ambassador'.[43] Claiming diplomatic immunity (as ambassador) is a wily move to subvert further appropriation. What is original is the rhetorical strategy whereby the imperatives of current practice (the need for world-wide recognition) are seen as fulfilling the intentions of the founders. This is to claim that an economy-driven revolution in theatre practice is but the turning of a wheel that is coming full circle. Only by being visibly a part of the globalized cultural market can the company now demonstrate its credentials as representative, national. To find an identity as 'purely Irish', the Abbey has seemingly embraced diaspora as one necessary condition of its being.

Globalized theatre takes the edge off national conflicts. It was easy for London critics to see *Dancing at Lughnasa* in a haze of nostalgia with its pretty tourist-board setting and wild dancing and ignore the darker heart of the play that examines the social and cultural circumstances of a particular loss and betrayal. If the production was appropriated, so too was the

play in this act of simplification.[44] *Portia Coughlan* was readily
containable too, but within the category of 'new writing', which
patronizingly relegated Marina Carr to the category of 'a
dramatist to watch', as if she had not quite made the grade by
the English gold standard. McGuinness's play by contrast
escaped such belittling critical tactics; noticeably reviewers
focussed less on the acting and production than an (often-
grudging) admiration for the dramaturgy and respect for a
Catholic dissecting Orange experience with such intense
empathy.[45] The very subject-matter of *Observe the Sons of Ulster* (at
once deeply inward yet socially subversive) resists all processes
of subduing or simplification in its concern with the specific
relation of past with present experience in the shaping of
Northern Ireland as a No-Man's-Land, an enduring 'great
shame' within Britain and Europe. And that shame has been
situated firmly in the international arena: written with a
sympathy disciplined by moral scruple, McGuinness's play
invites as stringent a rigour and conscience in the viewing. In
touring the production, the Abbey introduced a political sore
into the soothing complacencies of the globalized market. It
was an act of daring wholly in line with the values, ambitions
and originating manifestos of the founders of the Irish National
Theatre: cultural assertion, not submission.

---

[1] The Shorter Oxford English Dictionary, Third Edition (Oxford:
Clarendon Press, 1973).

[2] Thomas Keneally, *The Great Shame* (London: Chatto and Windus, 1998),
p.636.

[3] I am grateful to Colin Smythe for allowing me access to his copy of this
programme (one of the very few extant). He published the text only
and without commentary as an Appendix to Ann Saddlemyer (ed.),
Theatre Business: The Correspondence of the First Abbey Theatre Directors
(Gerrards Cross: Colin Smythe, 1982), pp.316-21.

[4] Three of the eight photographs show scenes from *Spreading the News*,
The Pot of Broth and *Riders to the Sea*. These are the now familiar
images of the cast line-up before a wall covered in posters for
Gregory's comedy; the Tramp seated with an intense, almost
mesmeric gaze as with hands spread before him he weaves his tale to
the impressionable (unseen) Sibby in Yeats's play; and Maurya and
her daughters seated or kneeling at the hearthstone in *Riders to the*

Sea. The remainder include portraits of Yeats and Synge as sketched by J.B.Yeats and conventional studio shots of Gregory, Boyle and W.G. Fay, who is described as 'Producer and Stage Director'. As the image for *The Pot of Broth* is of Fay in character as the Tramp, he appears twice: in and out of character, showing his skill in transformation.

5 'Direction' here is misleading, since the direction of the plays was in the hands of Fay and the dramatists; Alfred Wareing, who had been Beerbohm Tree's business manager, was appointed to manage this long tour, thereby relieving Synge, who represented the Directorate throughout, of the more arduous duties involved in advertising the company and its repertoire.

6 This technique of giving major billing to the phrase 'Irish Plays' was copied the following year when the company performed at the Great Queen Street Theatre, London, throughout the week beginning 10 June 1907. Even though the format of the programme was much simpler (a single printed sheet folded in two), 'Irish Plays' alone appeared on the front beneath the Abbey Theatre's emblematic logo (Elinor Monsell's woodcut of 'Queen Maeve with her Wolfhound'), while on the inside, opposite the day-by-day listing of performances, 'Irish Plays' has pride of place and font-size so that it dominates the ensuing information about the company, the venue, the times of performances, the orchestra and ticket sales.

7 'the plays have been translated and produced at the Deutsches Theater, Berlin, and at the National Bohemian Theatre, Prague' (pp.5-6).

8 My emphases.

9 That the Abbey Directorate were anxious to promote as authentic a mode of realistic representation as possible is evident from the letters that passed between them in the weeks prior to this tour's opening in Cardiff. On 7 May 1906 Synge wrote asking Lady Gregory to find an appropriate spinning wheel, as the current one 'has practically given out'; and, to combat any hint of staginess in their performance, he recommends that Sara Allgood should learn 'to spin so that there may be no fake about the show'. The programme noticeably records: 'The spinning wheel... was in use near Gort for over a hundred years till it was bought by Lady Gregory' (p.7), which shows she responded promptly to his request. For the full text of Synge's letter see Saddlemyer (ed.), *Theatre Business*, p.122.

10 'Dressing' and 'dress' in this quotation refer to costuming and not to the arrangement of props and stage furniture within the setting, which is also known technically as 'dressing the stage'.

[11] My emphasis. The text of the programme is anonymous but the masterly structuring suggests it is the work of Yeats, conceivably with some input from Lady Gregory.

[12] Lady Gregory's oft-repeated justification for her involvement in the theatre movement that 'we work to bring dignity to Ireland' can be sensed behind, even if it is not stated within, every paragraph of the programme.

[13] Significantly, though Annie Horniman is justly given her due, at no point is it mentioned in the programme that she is English. Noticeably too, the verbs chosen to describe the nature of her aid are 'secured' and 'obtained' (p.4) and not 'bought' or 'financed', an actuality which might have been seen as compromising the rhetorical preoccupation with a 'purely Irish' venture.

[14] The Aldwych had at this time recently become the London home of the Royal Shakespeare Company, which was undergoing a major overhaul at the instigation of the artistic director, Peter Hall. For periods of around eight weeks in the early summer of each year (while the Stratford company prepared to bring the previous season's work to London and the London company rehearsed new work for Stratford) Daubeny brought theatres from around the world to play to English audiences. It was an annual festival of international theatre-making.

[15] It did not help that the company had received considerable press coverage prior to opening on account of the actors using the occasion of the London visit, which was also deemed by many to be an act of reconciliation between the Abbey and O'Casey, to threaten a strike over better pay. O'Casey sided with the players and the situation was eventually resolved to their financial betterment; but the whole, much publicised wrangle meant that first-night audiences and critics went with overly high expectations and were inevitably disappointed. Perhaps the kindest criticism came in a summing up of the whole season in the form of a discussion between the two reviewers for the *Daily Telegraph* (W. Darlington and Eric Shorter) in which Shorter's comments while trying to be kind succeeded only in being patronizing: he deemed them 'a lively and experienced company of about our repertory standard and they managed quite well, especially in "Juno"' (undated and unpaginated press cutting, World Theatre Season/Aldwych Theatre holdings, file for 1964, in the collections of the London Theatre Museum). In all subsequent notes reference to the Theatre Museum is to the London Theatre Museum.

¹⁶ Noticeably there was no contribution from any member of the current Directorate. Did they or Daubeny organise the compilation of the programme?

¹⁷ The Souvenir Programme for the 1964 World Theatre Season is unpaginated. The section devoted to the Abbey contains (beside mac Liammóir's essay) the Abbey emblem of Maeve and the Wolfhound, a short paragraph on O'Casey accompanying a photograph, brief synopses of the two plays with cast lists, six photographs of the plays and three woodcuts by mac Liammóir. The whole section covers some five pages in all. *Juno and the Paycock* played from 21-25 April 1964 and *The Plough and the Stars* from 27 April-2 May; Frank Dermody directed both plays with a cast that included such admirable veterans as May Craig and Eileen Crowe.

¹⁸ The photographs appear to have been taken during rehearsals (Frank Dermody, the director, appears in one of them) and most lack any hint of the dramatic. Two of the three dark woodcuts by mac Liammóir have a decidedly cartoon-like quality, as if slyly making fun of O'Casey's plays.

¹⁹ *The Sunday Times* , Harold Hobson, 'Who'd be a patriot?', 3 May 1964.

²⁰ The choice of play excited criticism in Ireland and some bafflement amongst English critics, amongst the majority of whom the play encouraged an unpleasant superiority. One unidentified press cutting amongst the materials in the World Theatre Season/Aldwych Theatre holdings in the collections of the Theatre Museum is typical: 'I cannot imagine why the Abbey brought Dion Boucicault's *The Shaughraun* to the World Theatre Season unless it is to prove that even a relatively good Victorian melodrama isn't really worth reviving except as a curiosity.'

²¹ The response of Philip Hope Wallace in the *Guardian* is typical: 'The production is jokey and spirited but without any kind of style or delicacy', while J.W. Lambert in the *Sunday Times* considered that, despite the fun of it all, 'the drama is skimped'. (He instances the lack of tension in the wake over Conn's supposed corpse and how the mob's hounding of Harvey Duff, the informer, seemed an embarrassment rather than an occasion to 'set our nerves jangling'.) The general view would, however, support Darlington's claim in the *Daily Telegraph* that Cusack 'was strongly supported by a very level company'. All these quotations are taken from press cuttings included (often unidentified) in the World Theatre Season/Aldwych Theatre holdings in the Theatre Museum.

²² *The Times*, Irving Wardle, 'Abbey restored to old eminence', 21 May 1968.

[23] Noticeably, no new writing was included in the selection of plays performed at either World Theatre Season. On its first visit to England in 1903, the company's repertory was entirely of writing new to English audiences and on subsequent visits for many years at least one new play was included or familiar works were seen in new stagings. Both tours for Daubeny 'played safe', though it is not clear how much influence he exercised over choice of productions.

[24] It is not absolutely clear where the impetus for the seminar came from or to what degree it may have been prompted by the critical reaction to the Abbey's visits to Daubeny's World Theatre Seasons or to the steady changing of the old order on the Directorate.

[25] The Abbey, for example, at the Great Queen Street Theatre, London, in the week beginning 10 June 1907 had given eleven plays over eight performances. A change in the advertised schedule allowed for a performance of Yeats's *The Hour Glass* to be included. This meant that a substantial ratio of the company's current repertoire was on show in the one week.

[26] It is not to be supposed that the seminar was uniquely productive of this change, but rather that discussions there brought more prominently into consciousness amongst delegates the need for decisive action to combat globalization.

[27] In 1973 the Royal Court Theatre mounted its own productions of Friel's *The Freedom of the City* (February) and Wilson John Haire's *The Bloom in the Diamond Stone* (October).

[28] Even then the ordering of the billing and the deployment of capitalization places the Abbey in a decidedly inferior position; the advertisements read: 'By arrangement with Noel Pearson /The Royal Court Theatre presents /THE DUBLINERS / in The Abbey Theatre Production of…'.

[29] The programme contained a photograph and biographical sketch of Behan, a discussion of Behan's creative relationship with Alan Simpson (the director of this and other works by the dramatist), and an essay, 'The Importance of Being Brendan' by mac Liammóir. The production played throughout September 1972, following after the run of Wesker's *The Old Ones*, while in October the Court was to stage Edna O'Brien's *A Pagan Place*. (All the material referred to regarding *Richard's Cork Leg* comes from the Royal Court holdings for 1972 in the collections of the Theatre Museum.)

[30] The programme in the form of a folded sheet opens out into three columns: to either side of the centrally placed cast and directorial listings and a photograph from the play in performance, there are short articles on Matt Talbot by Kilroy and biographical details of

Thomas Kilroy to the left; and to the right an appropriate extract from Emmet Larkin's biography of James Larkin (headed 'The Slum Jungle') and Mac Anna's statement about the Peacock.

[31] Ironically this linking was not on this occasion to the advantage of the Court as host institution. The reviewer in *Country Life* (29 December 1977) noted tartly: 'Visiting productions like this one from Dublin may well do something to revive the fortunes of the Royal Court.' (Press cutting in the Royal Court holdings for 1977 in the collections of the Theatre Museum.)

[32] Programme and flyer for this production are both in the Royal Court holdings for 1977 in the collections of the Theatre Museum.

[33] The contents include a four-page essay by Mary Holland on 'The Abbey Theatre'; extracts from *The Festival of Lughnasa* by Maire MacNeill and; an oral account of 'Lughnasa Customs in Co. Armagh, 1941' transcribed from the Archives Department of Irish Folklore at UCD; and biographical details of Friel accompanying his photograph. The (unpaginated) programme for the production is in the writer's own collection, but examples can be found in the Royal National Theatre Archive and the collections of the Theatre Museum.

[34] The venues referred to are Moscow, Leningrad, Washington, Hong Kong, Adelaide, Perth, Wellington, Montreal, Paris, Edinburgh and New York.

[35] Strehler, Bergman, Ninagawa and Planchon, for example, had brought their companies to perform there in the format of the short season described.

[36] See *London Theatre Record*, 8-21 October 1990, pp.1384-95. The four reviews in question were from the *Spectator*, *What's On*, *City Limits* and the *Financial Times*.

[37] It was situated above the first of the cast biographies. The positioning reduced the tone to bathos.

[38] The italics are a part of the original presentation. The programme is in the writer's own collection, but examples may be found in the collections of the Theatre Museum and in the archives of the Royal Shakespeare Company in the library of the Shakespeare Centre, Stratford-upon-Avon.

[39] Italics as in original document. This information is given no larger prominence than the thanks expressed to Faber and Faber as publishers of McGuinness's play text.

[40] See *London Theatre Record*, 26 February-10 March 1996, pp.303-5. The reviews that fail to mention the production as deriving from the Abbey are in the *Daily Express* and the *Sunday Express*, while the

reviews recording the work as an RSC affair appear in the *Spectator* and *Time Out*.

[41] As is customary with all productions appearing at the Royal Court, the programme also contained the Faber text of the play.

[42] The project was designed to celebrate the centenary of the National Maternity Hospital, Dublin.

[43] See Marina Carr, *Portia Coughlan* (London: Faber and Faber, 1996). The section of the publication constituting the programme is not paginated.

[44] Nine of the reviews anthologised in *Theatre Record* evoke the name of Chekhov (in Friel's favour: it is intended as a compliment, despite the number of heavy-handed jokes about renaming the play, 'Five Sisters'). Both playwrights were being honoured as poets of decline and enervation and in the process subdued and simplified, rendered appealing to an England mourning its own political decline. This was a disservice to the complex realism of Friel's play. For a fuller discussion of this muting of the play's anger, see Richard Allen Cave, 'The City Versus the Village', in Mary Massoud (ed.) *Literary Inter-relations: Ireland, Egypt, and the Far East* (Gerrards Cross: Colin Smythe, 1996), pp.281-96.

[45] The *Spectator* considered the play to be 'more of a poem or novel than a play', while *The Times* found it at times 'dauntingly dense and "poetic" [here used pejoratively]'. The one wholly negative response was from Neil Smith in *What's On*, who dismissed the play's 'highly schematic structure' as 'primitive to say the least'. See *London Theatre Record*, 26 February-10 March 1996, pp.303-5.

2 | The Abbey in America: The Real Thing

John P. Harrington

America has been the beneficiary of Abbey Theatre tours since 1911, and an American tour was again in the centenary programme of the company in 2004. Touring is a consistent part of the history of the National Theatre of Ireland, though general perceptions of the Abbey at home and abroad have never really confronted and analysed the nature of the International Theatre of Ireland. This neglected part of the Abbey identity has been there since the founding productions of the Irish Literary Theatre in 1899, which were based on international models, especially Scandinavian. Later, Lennox Robinson's wonderful pitch in 1922 to the provisional government for a state subsidy was argued on the basis of French, Russian, and German precedents. It is wholly appropriate, then, that the centenary anniversary of the national theatre was international in scope.

As in many other cultural, political, and economic matters, America has been a favoured trade partner with Ireland in theatre. For many, the history of transatlantic cultural commerce represents Irish artists and American hosts at their mercenary worst: Irish performance standards eroded by the influence of American 'entertainment', and American com-modification of an artistic heritage. However, I believe that this part of Abbey history can be seen as a mutually enlightening transaction. The record of the Abbey in America is not representative of its entire history, but it is a significant and potentially revealing dimension of it. The centenary was an especially appropriate time to assess its significance, because in 2004 the Abbey chose largely to repeat its first trip to America – to take *The Playboy of the Western World* to several of the original cities, including Boston, New Haven, New York, and Chicago. Though this plan was criticized by some in America for choosing repetition over artistic innovation, I want to use the history of the Abbey in America to argue that this form of celebration was well chosen, that it highlighted dimensions of Abbey identity worth preserving in its second century, and that *The Playboy of the Western World* in America was a good thing for the company and for audiences.

The result of nearly a century of touring is a quite specific American notion of the Abbey. To see how specifically and persistently 'branded' the Abbey Theatre is in America, which is, of course, a superpower of branding, we can begin in 1914. More particularly, January 1914, which would be after the first two tours of America by the Irish Players, a convenient corporate entity adopted to counter well-founded criticism of the company for diversion of national resources to foreign audiences. At the beginning of 1914, just before the third tour in three years by the Irish Players, mainstream New York press turned to a new art theatre. It opened at the Henry Street Settlement on the Lower East Side of Manhattan, and it was called The Neighborhood Playhouse for its ambitions to cultivate masses of East European immigrants on the lower East Side. The Neighborhood Playhouse was doing a stage adaptation of Tolstoy, about the liberation of serfs, for a solely Jewish audience, and doing it with production values the press called 'deficient in all the spectacular allurements which "the uptown crowd" is accustomed to take for granted'. By that they meant small stage, minimal set, no real lighting at all, and direct rather than stylishly melodramatic acting. There was an available term for this, 'Little Theatre', but the press adverted not to that but to the Abbey. The headline in the New York

Evening Sun was: 'At the Henry Street Settlement You will find the Irish Players of New York – They May Be Russians, but What of That?'[1] Even at the outset, the Abbey was a distinct identity that could be applied opportunistically, and very unscientifically.

A more recent example can further frame the topic, which is the consistent presence of the Abbey Theatre in America and the kind of expectations the National Theatre of Ireland generated there and at various times satisfied or, perhaps when the company was most artistically successful, failed to satisfy. Ninety years later, at the end of 2003, the American press covered the announcement of the Abbey centenary in 2004. In New York City, the launch of the anniversary was a quite wonderful evening of readings at the Metropolitan Club (founded in the nineteenth century by J.P. Morgan when he was not yet a Brahmin and could not get into the Union Club). But press coverage was a little discouraging. It kept referring to the Abbey as a theatre known for productions of W.B. Yeats, James Joyce, and Samuel Beckett. *Playbill*, perhaps *the* New York theatre periodical today, headlined the presence of 'leading Irish actors' associated with the Abbey, including 'The Celtic Tenors'. The *New York Times*, self-declared protector of responsible journalism opened its story with the words, 'Ah yes, the whiskey was flowing like buttermilk' and throughout conflated the Abbey and James Joyce, as in its headline, 'Another Round of blarney? Yes I Said Yes I Will Yes'.[2] The authorities quoted on the importance of the event were the brothers McCourt.

That usefully frames the question of, 'What does the Abbey Theatre mean in America?' In America, the Abbey is very well recognized as one singular sensation, an exceptional production company very unlike New York uptown or down, and it is warmly welcomed as an alternative that is at once exotic and reliable. In this perception it is quite different, for example, from the Royal National Theatre of Britain, which now comes to New York to do *Oklahoma!* – better than us, to many minds, but *Oklahoma!* nevertheless. However, at the same time, that exceptionality is of somewhat indeterminate purport: a haze of literary and popular culture associations. Throughout the century, there is great emphasis in America on Abbey authenticity, as in programme imprimaturs certifying that this really is 'the official national theater of Ireland.' The Abbey in America has to be 'The Real Thing' with all the complications collectively brought to bear on that phrase by Henry James and Tom Stoppard.

In America, some of the associations created around that brand, Abbey Theatre, over nearly 100 years derive from two underlying factors, one from the Irish side of the Atlantic and one from the American. First, America is green with envy over the idea of a national theatre, something it has failed to create for more than a century. Second, as national theatres go, the Abbey is unique, is perceived as such by foreigners, and has chosen for itself a particularly difficult enterprise, at least when abroad.

Other models may help us understand what America expects to find in a national theatre and why the Abbey does not conform to it. By coincidence, on the eve of the first Abbey trip to America in 1911, no less than Henry Arthur Jones, playwright of sixty London hits, was in New York, at the podium, at Columbia University, lecturing on 'The Aims and Duties of a National Theatre', with Brander Matthews in the Chair. For Jones, who never referred to the Irish National Theatre Society by any name, the purpose of a national theatre is to foster a national dramatic literature by subsidizing a production company that can keep the literature on the stage. He talked about how he had recently offered 'to wager fifty to one that America would be the first to have what may be called a National Theatre'. And he congratulated the New Yorkers for constructing 'a beautiful, dignified building that is an ornament to your city, and a testimony to the princely munificence of its founders'. 'Unfortunately', he added, 'a National Theatre is not a National Drama', and so he sadly told the Americans that they could not have a national theatre because they did not have any plays for it to stage.[3] True enough of America at the time.

This helps to us understand something about the domestic context from which America would perceive the initial visits to its shores by the National Theatre of Ireland. The Henry Arthur Jones anecdote and commentary underscores the desire in America for a model of national theatre, which was also evident in the ready application of what was known about the Irish Players on their first visit to other performance practices not customary in New York, such as that of the 'Russians' at the Henry Street Settlement. At the same time, the disapproving Jones lecture illustrates an initial general confusion in America about what a National Theatre might be. A century of reinforcement has largely resolved the confusion, but a trace of it survives in *New York Times* publicity over the Abbey centenary in 2004. It is also worth noting that Americans accepted the admonishment of Jones and others and left establishment of a true national theatre to some unidentified future date when the requisite dramatic literature would be sufficiently available. That is a great reminder of the boldness of the future tense that runs through the Yeats-Lady Gregory-Edward Martyn prospectus for an Irish Literary Theatre in 1897. Rather than wait for the dramatic literature, they chose to provoke it: their vow was not to stage but to generate that national literature that would constitute 'a Celtic and Irish school of dramatic literature'. [4] They had no counterparts in America.

There are many notions for a national theatre, and they run a full gamut, from Granville Barker (for whom it was mostly a business plan) to today's Costa Rican National Theatre (whose mission is to be an inspiring building). One indication of what America might expect from a national theatre during the Abbey's first visit was one of its own experiments, the Drama League of America, a short-lived venture founded in 1911 during the Abbey's first visit. Though its founding documents evoked the Irish precedent, its vision was to have a decentralized membership of 100,000 to distribute scripts and to stage productions in small towns and villages – the national theatre as provincial performing arts. Later, the American National Theatre and Academy of the 1930s was conceived principally as a school, and Eva La Gallienne's Civic Repertory was conceived as showcase of nationally important productions

of work from anywhere, with an emphasis on Chekhov for
Americans. Like the more recent visits of the Royal National
Theatre to New York, these promised qualitative improvements
over performance standards in America, which have always and
deservedly been criticized for vulgarity, commercialization and
general allegiance to entertainment values over art values.

Hence, on arrival in 1911 to a country conscious of,
experimenting with, and confused by ideas about national
theatres, the Abbey company was immediately perceived as
unique because it presented something very different from
qualitative improvements. Instead, it represented content: an
artistic expression of national sentiment in the form of
repertory drama delivered to foreign audiences in their home.
John Quinn, the lawyer and art collector so ubiquitous in Irish-
American cultural relations at this time, introduced the
company in these terms and even quoted the Yeats-Lady
Gregory prospectus: 'this little company of Irish players', he
wrote in 1911

> have succeeded because of their courage in keeping to the road
> they have chosen, by nationality in keeping to the narrow limits
> to which they bound themselves – works by Irish writers or on
> Irish subjects.

In other words, a content, a repertory. Even Theodore
Roosevelt, at the time an ex-President looking for a role, not
only wrote about the Abbey in national terms, ('like every
healthy movement of the kind, it has been thoroughly
national'), he also turned the moment into a kind of national
drama arms race (the members of the company 'have done
more for the drama than has been accomplished in any other
nation of recent years').[5]

It is worth remembering that the Abbey never got
unqualified or uncomplicated applause in America, and in this
initial trip the relation of nation to Abbey was itself occasion
for critique as well as praise. An unsigned 1911 editorial in a
newspaper coincidentally named *Nation* stated that the
company:

may be said to constitute the beginning of a national theatre, inasmuch as they are, in the main, Irish representatives of Irish life, but they are not representatives, in the broad sense, of Ireland or the Irish.[6]

During the first Abbey company visit to America in 1911, the interesting points made in positive or negative criticism were that the national theatre of Ireland had chosen a narrow and difficult course, that it was very effective in it, and that it somehow was more real when it was less real. This interesting conception of the enterprise was much more provocative than most of the rhetoric of early *Playboy* riots in Dublin or in America. The American conception seemed to recognize that the dramatic literature was Irish even if its patrician caretakers, such as Yeats and Gregory, were not typical: the repertory was representative, even if the producing directors were not, and so artistic success was not confused with the documentary truth of reality. Of course, this left behind the Irish nationalist audience that desired documentary authenticity for ennobling images of their heritage. As we shall see, this American audience has never been placated. However, the broader American conception of the Abbey was from the start much more complex and accommodating to ideas of authenticity based more on artifice than on anthropology. A mainstream newspaper critic at the Abbey opening in New York in 1911 cited the company for providing 'intimate glimpses of their interesting propaganda', and he meant that as praise.[7]

There was complexity on artistic as well as national criteria, and it is remarkable how consistently that complexity depends on conception of the 'real'. One of the most famous expressions of praise was Eugene O'Neill's in these words, on his experience in 1911: 'the work of the Irish Players on their first trip over here, was what opened my eyes to the existence of a real theatre, as opposed to the unreal . . . hateful theatre of my father'.[8] By 'real' he certainly meant the direct rather than the melodramatic style of presentation associated with his father, the great actor James O'Neill. The same directness and

realism was the sense of praise by Susan Glaspell, who saw the
company in Chicago with Jig Cook. She wrote years later:

> Quite possibly there would have been no Provincetown Players
> had there not been Irish Players. What [Jig] saw done for Irish
> life he wanted for American life – no stage conventions in the
> way of projecting with the humility of true feeling.[9]

It helps to remember the James and Stoppard anatomies of the
word 'real' when trying to understand the 'real' in this context.
It is a difficult four-letter word. Ludwig Lewisohn, then perhaps
the most influential academic critic, attacked the Yeats works in
the repertory as, in his words, 'not only unreal but, if one must
be frank, puerile'.[10] For Lewisohn, the real is the most adult
and, for O'Neill, the most adult is the most unreal.

One result of the first Abbey tours was inspiration of
imitators, all of them determined to become more real than the
competition. A good example is Whitford Kane, from Larne. A
great actor himself, he spent years touring in England with Iden
Payne's Repertoire Company, mostly in Shaw roles, and then
worked in Miss Horniman's company in Manchester. He came
to America in 1912 and toured to great success in Rutherford
Mayne's *Drone*. The Irish Players had hardly left in 1912 when
Kane, seeing a market opportunity, opened The Irish Players of
America, because, he said, there would be 'demand for our
product, as we had seen so-called Irish plays done so badly that
we could not believe the public would unresistingly swallow
such travesties of Irish life'. He was wrong. He opened the
company with Mayne's *Red Turf* and ended up, in performance,
in a shouting match with the audience, who believed that they
alone had the map coordinates of the real real Ireland. In
Kane's account, they shouted him down on the stage and told
him:

> if you want to see a real Irish play, why don't you go over to the
> Lexington Opera House to see *Hearts of Erin*? There, we were
> informed, we would see a play about the real Ireland that
> everybody loved, not a sordid story of bickering farmers.[11]

Soon after, Kane changed course entirely and starred in a David
Belasco spectacle about bickering saloon-keepers called *Dark*

Rosaleen, no doubt convinced that in it, at last, he had discovered the real Ireland.

Throughout the 1920s, in the absence of any Abbey presence, imitations such as 'Irish Theatre, Inc.', filled the market, and self-appointed guardians of the real Irish drama, such as Ernest Boyd, proliferated. The imitators and the guardians were respectively greedy and protective of a national image and a stage style that were both recognized, American-style, as assets. However, the full dynamics of the cultural transaction can also be seen in 1927, to my knowledge the first time America sent an inspector to Dublin to monitor Abbey productions of American plays. In that year a programme of Glaspell's *Trifles* and O'Neill's *Emperor Jones* was produced under the auspices of the Dublin Drama League. The American in Dublin, J.J. Hayes for the *New York Times*, wrote that Rutherford Mayne in the O'Neill role sometimes 'came nearest to the real negro', but in the end 'ceased to be a negro and became the white man playing the part of a negro in the white man's way'. His verdict: very good, or at least very nearly very good, but just not real. Incidentally, Hayes also reported then that for the first time the Abbey season would begin in July 'for the benefit of Americans'.[12]

After a period of open market on Irish drama in America, the Abbey, in its second series of tours from 1931 to 1935, was understandably careful to guard its authenticity as the real Abbey Theatre. The souvenir programme from the last cycle, ending in 1935, identified the company as 'The Official National Theatre of Ireland'. In fact, the programme copy went further. It insisted that:

> there have been plays presented in America, from the Abbey Theatre Repertoire, by companies containing former members of the Abbey Theatre Players, but none of these organizations were official Abbey Theatre companies from the Abbey Theatre, Dublin – the National Theatre of the Irish Free State.

In a display sidebar the programme warned that 'this is positively the last opportunity you will have to see this distinctive national organization in America for years to come'.[13] In this rationale, what gave the Abbey authenticity and separated it from other touring companies was its repertory. This was quantified: the Abbey declared that it had a repertory of 300, that it came with 27, and that it preferred to perform 12. This was the real thing.

Two business arrangements were unique to the Abbey tours in America in the 1930s. The first was that they were considered on 'concert management': rather than playing a theatre for a percentage, the Abbey worked under subcontracts to seven commercial bureaus which were responsible for selling dates to venues in seven separate areas. In this way potentially spectacular but unpredictable profits were sacrificed for predictable income: the bureau rather than the Abbey lost if a house was empty. The second unique business arrangement was that the audience could choose from the repertory. A *New York Times* correspondent travelling with Lennox Robinson in advance of the company reported how in Walla Walla, Washington, the local audience saw advance notice that the programme would be *The Rising of the Moon* with *The Playboy of the Western World*. They demanded that the opener be changed to *Riders to the Sea*. The company obliged. Similar arrangements were made in places like Wyncote, Pennsylvania; Pocatello, Idaho; Hattiesburg, Mississippi; and Nacodoches, Texas.[14]

It is fortunate that the Abbey did establish its authenticity in America on its repertory and not on a more qualitative dimension of performance style, because style shifts far more than content. As it had lost its American nationalist audience after the first cycle of tours and the American equivalent of *The Playboy of the Western World* affair in Dublin, it generally lost its high art audience in this next interregnum following the 1930s tours. At the very least, publicity about the Abbey's reputation, and so American expectations of it, changed for the worse. In 1937, from Pittsburgh, George Jean Nathan filed his story on the latest tour under the title 'Erin Go Blah'. Of course, this was not a particularly strong period for the Abbey, and Nathan's loyalty to O'Casey probably affected his perspective, but Nathan did report that the Abbey, 'not so long ago one of the finest acting organizations in the world, is now a caricature of its former self'. He faulted it for direction, for mugging to the audience, and for shouting 'lines like college yells'.[15] That negative critique was repeated fifteen years later by an equally influential critic, Eric Bentley, when he, like J.J. Hayes in the 1920s, went to the source to slake his thirst for real Abbey productions instead of American productions of Irish plays with semi-retired Abbey émigrés hoping to be called to Hollywood. For Bentley, provoked by Peter Kavanagh's Abbey history:

> An integral part of the Irish legend is the Abbey Legend: the Abbey as the Globe Theatre of our time. What a comedown for the visitor to Dublin to see performances that would scarcely pass muster in a provincial German Stadtheater!

Again, there are many qualifying conditions to note, especially the burning of the original Abbey building, the move to the Queen's Theatre, Ernest Blythe's policies, and the impact of all those on production standards. Though he was at pains to make allowances, in the end, echoing O'Neill, Bentley reported that previously 'people found the Abbey performances "real" in contrast to the unreality of current theatre, and one is sure they were right'.[16] But not anymore. Like Nathan, Bentley wanted the real Abbey artistic performance and could not find it. Of course, both were looking for an Abbey style and not a content. Neither commented on the Abbey repertory, its most reliable product and ultimately a much more substantial dimension of its identity than the mythic 'Abbey style'.

The real solidification of this notion in America – Bentley's term as well as O'Neill's – of an Abbey 'reality' superior in its way to the general 'unreality' of familiar theatrical practices helps explain one of the most negative episodes in Abbey visits to America, one which illustrates the strength and the limitation of an identity based on repertory. In 1988, after an intercontinental tour, the Abbey brought to New York Tom MacIntyre's *The Great Hunger*, that great performance piece about repression and self-destruction, with Tom Hickey in the lead. Naturally, it disappointed some Americans who were expecting something in the Cecil Woodham-Smith vein. But most of the substantial portion of the audience who walked out in real anger were more sophisticated and literate than that. All publicity for this New York visit emphasized that this was the 'real' Abbey, as in the press release from David Rothenberg Associates: 'Ireland's national theater will make its first appearance in Manhattan in fifty years'.[17] The Abbey had, in fact, been in New York over the previous half-century, most recently at Brooklyn Academy of Music with *The Plough and the Stars* in 1976. In this case, Manhattan was able to project its blinkered view of New York City just as the publicists were able to project an image of the Abbey inconsistent with the nature of MacIntyre's work. It is also interesting to note that MacIntyre and Hickey's work had previously been very well received in New York, but under auspices other than 'Ireland's national theater'.

The very negative critical and popular reception of *The Great Hunger* was based on disappointment that this was not the 'real' Abbey at all. Expectations had been encouraged that were entirely inappropriate for the production, which was further handicapped by being scheduled for the height of New York City's peculiar St Patrick's Day rituals. New Yorkers are very sensitive to feeling that they have been the victims of fraud, and that was the sentiment not only of an Irish-American audience that still, long after the American *Playboy* affair, demanded uplifting versions on stage of the land of their increasingly distant ancestry. The disappointment that a different product had appeared under the rubric 'Allied Irish Bank presents the Abbey Theater' also came from the mainstream press reviewers. The notice from Mel Gussow of the *New York Times* is a representative example. It opened with regrets that 'the play seems to contradict the founding principles of the Abbey Theater as a home for eloquence', and then went on to explain that 'the primary difficulty with *The Great Hunger* is not so much with its dearth of poetry as with the familiarity and the ingenuousness of the performance techniques'.[18] Mel Gussow is no philistine, and he is quite familiar with forms of eloquence that are not textual. But here, for the case of the Abbey alone and not, for example, in his many notices on innovative productions of Beckett, he seems to demand unfamiliarity and not confirmation of accepted performance standards and conventions. He wanted an Abbey that was unique, consistent, exotic in America, and not doing what he can get from Beckett, MacIntyre, Hickey, or anybody else under any name except 'The Real Abbey Theater'.

This view was shared by all other reviewers in New York. Many added a 'Coals-to-Newcastle' complaint that on this occasion the strangers came from afar bearing what America already had. Even a very progressive theatre professional like Gordon Rogoff wrote that 'for the Abbey, no doubt, all this removal from the traditional verbal fuel must seem like revolution [but it's] not so daring' here and now.[19] MacIntyre's work was linked to Jerzy Grotowski, Robert Wilson, and Peter Brook, three people whose work in one way or another actually was on the New York stage in the same week. On this occasion, the wittiest critic was Clive Barnes, who in disappointment observed that 'the Abbey certainly seems to have a new Abbott'.[20] Barnes characteristically welcomes novelty, but apparently not from the national theatre of Ireland, sole source for him, as previously for Nathan and Bentley, of a certain prized product. The interesting lesson is that while reductive identity, restricted repertory, and narrow expectations can reasonably be associated with diminished artistic merit, in this singular case, the Abbey in America, breaking the template in fact diminishes artistic merit because the result becomes from the local New York perspective more conventional and more familiar.

That certainly seems counter-intuitive, and it may be only a local phenomenon of little import or an aberration of a single time and place. However, this conception of a 'real' Abbey consistent with the identity defined and reinforced over nearly a century was recently confirmed. Until the centenary tour of 2004, the last time the Abbey visited New York was in 1999, with the *Freedom of the City* production directed by Conall Morrison. That was part of a summer season with exports from the previous year's Dublin Theatre Festival. The Irish contributions were *Freedom* as produced by 'The Abbey Theater presented by Lincoln Centre Festival "99"', *Aristocrats* as produced by the Gate, and Friel's *A Month in the Country* as produced by the Royal Shakespeare Company. It seemed to many commentators disappointing that the Abbey was offering the play most literally associated with the Ireland of sectarian violence American audiences knew from television news. *Aristocrats*, in particular, seemed to be more challenging and potentially rewarding for an audience unaccustomed to images of Ireland outside a very narrow stage repertory including many dramatizations of 'the troubles'.

Freedom of the City was very well received and drew larger audiences than the companion productions, despite drawing the least attractive venue, a college theatre close to but not within the Lincoln Centre. At an interview event, Ben Barnes and Thomas Kilroy articulated for Lincoln Centre audiences ideas about a national theatre that were, in comparison with most of the customary pre-performance and post-performance events in New York, much more devoted to issues surrounding public and cultural identities. This led to an active discussion with general audiences – neither the old nationalist audience nor the more recent and equally estranged art theatre audience – that was certainly very rare in New York. The choice of play may have seemed narrow, but the challenge to American audiences proved broad, invigorating, and novel. It was an effect that depended on the persona of the 'real' Abbey Theatre. Previously, *Freedom* had opened on Broadway in 1974 as produced by others and closed in a week. There were many other differences between the productions of 1999 and 1974, but one undeniable and significant factor of difference between them was the Abbey identity as foundation for audience expectations and platform for performance interaction. In 1999 even New York's ever dour *Irish Echo*, which had an uncomplex editorial position on Northern Ireland, was as positive about *Freedom* as it could be; it grudgingly described the production in terms such as 'nearly seamless' and 'almost uniformly excellent'.[21] The Gate and the Royal Shakespeare did less well in reception, as their identity was not as well-defined, and, coincidentally, they had no public interview events at all.

This record of Abbey reception in America wholly justifies the somewhat surprising decision to build the first Abbey tour of America of the twenty-first century around *The Playboy of the Western World*, which was at the centre of the repertory the company brought to the same cities – Boston, New Haven, New York, Chicago – in 1911. In Dublin, a different degree of imperatives may apply, but given the extent to which the Abbey reputation and the institutional history is international, the transatlantic experience must have some relevance to discussions of the Abbey prospectus for its second century. The basis for the Abbey reputation in America has been difference: difference from the very broad spectrum of work to be found in American theatres, difference in maintenance of a distinct repertory, difference in surviving the expectations of the lost audiences, and above all difference in choosing from many models for a national theatre a singular and demanding one and then remaining true over time to a founding vision. These are distinctions on which a future can be constructed. These make the Abbey different from the Gate or the Druid or whatever other company from Ireland that might tour America. The 'real' Abbey Theatre, whether or not it ever found the 'real' Ireland certainly found the real role of a national theatre. Examination of the company history outside Ireland leads to the surprising conclusion that in America the Abbey chose a narrow repertory and that was a good thing for the company and for its audiences.

---

[1] 'At the Henry Street Settlement You Will Find the Irish Players', *Evening Sun* (New York), 12 January 1914 (clipping, Lillian Wald Papers, Columbia University, Box 61, Reel 75).

[2] 'Bold face Names', *New York Times*, 24 December 2003, B2.

[3] The Aims and Duties of a National Theatre: A Lecture by Henry Arthur Jones, Delivered in Early Hall, Columbia University, on the Afternoon of Thursday, January 26, 1911 (New York: Columbia University Press, 1911), p.2.

[4] Lady Augusta Gregory, *Our Irish Theatre* (New York: Oxford University Press, 1972), p.8.

[5] John Quinn, 'Lady Gregory and the Abbey Theatre', and Theodore Roosevelt, 'Introduction', *Outlook*, 16 December 1911, pp.919, 915.

6 Editorial, *Nation* (New York), 30 November 1911, p.528.

7 Louis V. De Foe, 'Visitors from Across the Sea', *New York World Sun*, 26 November 1911, M6.

8 Edward L. Shaughnessy, *Eugene O'Neill in Ireland: The Critical Reception* (New York: Greenwood Press, 1988), p.36.

9 Susan Glaspell, *The Road to the Temple* (New York: Frederick A. Stokes, 1941), p.218.

10 Ludwig Lewisohn, *The Modern Drama: An Essay in Interpretation* (New York: B. W. Huebsch, 1916), p.269.

11 Whitford Kane, *Are We All Met?* (London: Elkin Mathews and Marrot, 1931), pp.175, 176.

12 J.J. Hayes, 'An Irish Emperor Jones', *New York Times*, 13 February 1927, section 4, p.1.

13 Abbey Theater Souvenir Program, 1932, Billy Rose Theater Collection, New York Public Library.

14 Jack Quigley, 'Dublin's Abbey Theatre Rediscovers America,' *New York Times*, 13 March 1932, section 10, p.1.

15 George Jean Nathan, 'Erin Go Blah', *Newsweek*, 27 December 1937, p.24.

16 Eric Bentley, 'Irish Theatre: Splendeurs et Misères', *Poetry*, January 1952, pp.217, 220.

17 Press release for *The Great Hunger*, 1988, Billy Rose Theater Collection, New York Public Library.

18 Mel Gussow, '"Great Hunger", A Dearth of Words', *New York Times*, 18 March 1988, section C3.

19 Gordon Rogoff, review of *The Great Hunger*, *Village Voice*, March 1988; reprinted 'The Abbey Theatre: Speechless at Last' in *Vanishing Acts* (New Haven: Yale University Press, 2000), p.161.

20 Clive Barnes, 'Abbey Goes Avant-Garde', *New York Post*, 17 March 1988, p.37.

21 Joseph Hurley, 'Friel's Vivid Bloody Sunday Tableau', *Irish Echo*, 21 July 1999 (clipping, Billy Rose Theater Collection, New York Public Library).

3 | Lady Gregory:
The Politics of Touring Ireland

Anthony Roche

When they presented their plays to an indifferent or hostile Dublin audience or to the outside world, Yeats, Synge and Lady Gregory – the Abbey Theatre's three directors – maintained a united front. But when they turned to the task of touring Ireland, suppressed or hidden conflicts emerged which were as much political as personal. Not only did the differences between the three directors and the two Fay brothers widen to the breaking point, but internal tensions between Yeats, Synge and Gregory also became more pronounced. If Yeats and Synge shared some ambivalence on the score of touring Ireland, Lady Gregory declared herself unequivocally in its favour. And yet when her plays toured from Dublin to her home place of Galway in January of 1908, her reaction proved the most complex and contradictory of all.

A National Institution?

Touring Ireland was not an initial priority of the Abbey Theatre. For over a year after the December 1904 opening, the Abbey's programmes were played exclusively in Dublin. But from February 1906 onwards the company began to tour around Ireland. The tours which have attracted most attention are, of course, those of the United States because of the controversy generated there in 1911 by Synge's *The Playboy of the Western World* and in the 1930s by O'Casey's *The Plough and the Stars*. The Abbey Theatre's tours around Ireland are less well known but no less deserving of attention. For one thing, as the directors themselves realized, without a serious effort to perform before the entire country, the Abbey could scarcely claim to be a national institution. Yeats addresses this issue in a letter to Synge of 15 August 1907, written from Coole and hence dictated to Lady Gregory:

> We did not expect to make at present by the country tours, but we determined to spend £50 of Miss Horniman's £150 [*recte* £250] on Irish tours, to make ourselves a part of the National life. There is always the remote chance of money coming to us from some other quarter at the end of the Patent period, and that chance would be much better if we have made ourselves a representative Irish institution. A Theatre with an uncertain hold on Dublin and a much stronger hold on London and the English provinces would have less chance of being capitalized than if it were a part of the public life of Ireland.[1]

Yeats's letter discloses that the principal site of touring since the Abbey's opening had been London and the English provinces, with a positive reception in England bolstering both the theatre's financial and cultural capital back home. Such positive critical re-enforcement became particularly important in the wake of the Dublin production of *The Playboy* in 1907 – not that it was guaranteed an easy or unproblematic reception on the English tour. But the Abbey's performing of *The Playboy* in London within four months of its Dublin premiere was a calculated move to enhance its positive reputation. On the Irish tours undertaken in the same year (1907), Synge's play made no part of the programme offered in country towns – hardly surprising at a time when, according to Lady Gregory, she heard that in Clare and Kerry 'all the District Councils are passing resolutions against the Playboy' (p.217).

'The People' – Rural or Urban?

This rural opposition raises the second issue in relation to the Abbey touring the country. Although two of its three Protestant

Ascendancy directors and almost all of its Catholic actors were born in Dublin, the main theatrical fare offered by the National Theatre was what came to be termed the 'peasant play' – a representation of rural people. The term 'the people' itself came to be much invoked during the early years of the Revival as the idealized prototype of the represented subject and as the ultimate court of appeal and judgement for what was so represented. These terms received their fullest airing over *The Playboy* controversy. The issues were not exclusively those of class, however, as an exchange between Lady Gregory and playwright Padraic Colum in January 1906 revealed. Gregory responded to Colum's charge 'that we are becoming less and less a theatre of the people' by proclaiming:

> We cannot let our work stop – we must look for the best plays we can find, write the best we can write, get them acted as well as is possible. We must go on with our Dublin programme. We meant to go to the country (my own chief interest in the scheme from the beginning) and to this end we must pay actors who will be free to go there (p.105).

Any sense that Gregory might be playing up to Colum's preferences in her assertion that taking plays around Ireland was her own chief interest in the Abbey scheme from the beginning are scotched by the letter Colum wrote to Willie Fay when he received Lady Gregory's:

> Now I don't want a country audience (you know them) nor I don't want an English audience. I want a Dublin audience … My ideal is a people's theatre, and I'd rather work for the Gallery of the Queen's than for a few people in the Halls (p.108).

For Colum, 'the people' are to be found in the working-class theatres of Dublin; his democratic urban view has no place for the country in its theatrical vision.

Lady Gregory's exchange with Padraic Colum occurred during the first major secession of actors and writers from the newly opened National Theatre. It was a political rift, between those who favoured a more democratic approach (to the selection of plays, for example) and Yeats's determination to establish a hierarchy in which he, Synge and Gregory would wield control. It can also be seen as a split between two kinds of actors, between those who wished to retain amateur status, holding down day jobs while acting at night, and those who could be hired and remunerated as professionals, who were making the theatre their life's work. Only with this professionalization, as Gregory's remarks make clear, would touring Ireland become a real option. The decision to make the Abbey a joint stock company in November 1905 led to a mass defection of actors, who went on to found the Theatre of Ireland; by Mary Trotter's reckoning, 'all but four members of the original Irish National Theatre Society resigned from the Company'.[2] A great deal of scrabbling around ensued to assemble virtually a new company of actors so that the Abbey players were able to travel to Wexford on the first Irish tour of 26 and 27 February 1906, accompanied by Synge. As Gregory wrote to him, 'I am longing to know how Wexford went off, or is going off. If we capture the country towns we shall be independent of everyone' (p.116). This is not only a tilt at Annie Horniman and her resented patronage but at the nationalist actors who had left the company over the previous six months.

'Too much country about the country'?

Yeats and Synge in their plays take the countryman and woman as their dramatic object and leave no ostensible trace of the urban (or, indeed, the suburban) in their plays. They operated, in other words, at a considerable geographic distance from the people they represented. This distance comes through in their attitudes towards touring Ireland. Yeats is drawn between encouraging and deploring the idea of touring Ireland, but is particularly concerned that they avoid booking a town like Dundalk in 'race weeks when there is too much country about the country' (p.124). Synge describes the Dundalk audience in mainly positive terms as 'very intelligent, ready to be pleased, but very critical' (p.121). He adds a shared assumption of cultural inferiority – 'and, of course, not perfectly cultured' – to which Yeats readily assents. But Yeats responds in terms which are more extreme and offensive than Synge's:

> The country towns in Ireland are mainly animal, but can sometimes be intoxicated into a state of humanity by some religious or political propagandist body, the only kind of intellectual excitement they have got used to (p.124).

Synge was the only director of the three who travelled frequently with the company, not only throughout Ireland but also to England and Scotland. This may well reflect the temperament of someone who sought out the remoter areas of the west and south-west of Ireland; but his mingling with the actors was no doubt encouraged by the fact that he was in love with one of them, Molly Allgood, sister of Sara, who (to avoid confusion) acted under the stage name of Maire O'Neill. Molly Allgood was enabled to pursue the profession of actress through the changes that had just taken place at the Abbey. As W.J. Mc Cormack puts it:

> The secession of Máire Nic Shiubhlaigh and others from the Abbey to form the Theatre of Ireland resulted in the promotion of "bit players" like Molly to the security of a contract and twenty-five shillings a week.[3]

Synge withheld news of his relationship from his fellow directors for quite some time, since he could imagine how they would react to his breaching of class and religious boundaries.

Lady Gregory was the most unequivocally positive of the Abbey's directors about the issue of touring Ireland, as has been seen. Though she travelled to Dublin on a frequent basis to witness productions of her plays, she did not join the company in their travels around Ireland. Her social class would have prevented that. She came into her own in this respect in the several months she spent with the players in the United States in 1911 and 1912, effectively taking over from Synge.[4] This is only one of the many contradictions and complexities one encounters in relation to Lady Gregory — between her political awareness as director and playwright for an Irish National Theatre of the importance of touring Ireland, and her socially immuring herself within Coole Park. A primary focus of

this essay will be Gregory's own different and sometimes
contradictory claims regarding how her plays were received by
Irish audiences. The argument will finally focus on Willie Fay's
decision to include Gregory's political tragedy, *The Gaol Gate*, as
part of the programme to be performed in her native Galway in
January 1908 and the internal dissension this artistic decision
provoked.

Gregory as Playwright: More than a Writer of Comedy?

Distance from the subject matter is a characteristic Thomas
Kilroy has seen as shared by Anglo-Irish playwrights; and it is a
useful means of connecting the London expatriates Wilde and
Shaw with the Dublin Abbey playwrights Yeats and Synge. All
four were born and (mainly) raised in Dublin; their plays are set
in and focussed on societies (London, the west of Ireland) from
which they are removed. Kilroy considers this geographic
distancing as enabling in turn a creative distancing which
'involves some movement towards abstraction and the
perfection of the idea'. The result is 'a theatricality of imagined
space between the mind of the playwright and the material on
which he is working'.[5] The 'he' here and the playwrights
mentioned are all male. But Lady Gregory confounds the
distinction, since she combines the distance (of social class)
with the geographic closeness of her being from Galway. Her
plays distinctively combine the working out of a theatrical idea
with a strongly particularized sense of locale and history. Colm
Tóibín quotes Yeats's rather damning judgement on Gregory as
a playwright, but the terms can be read more positively in the
now of a century later:

> Being a writer for comedy, her life as an artist has not shaken in
> her, as tragic art would have done, the conventional standards.
> Besides, she has never been part of the artist's world, she has
> belonged to a political world, or one that is merely social.[6]

When it came to discussing her own plays, Lady Gregory
was modest and reticent. She claimed that she began her career
as a playwright by supplementing (usually) the plays of Yeats:

> I began by writing bits of dialogue, when wanted. Mr. Yeats
> used to dictate parts of *Diarmuid and Grania* to me, and I would
> suggest a sentence here or there. Then I, as well as another,
> helped to fill in spaces in *Where There is Nothing*.[7]

This concept of supplementarity is also evident in the myth of
Lady Gregory as 'a writer for comedy'. In order for audiences
to attend to the verbal demands of the verse plays of Yeats, a
less demanding theatrical entry was required for the evening's
programme; so, she writes:

> Comedies were needed to give this rest. That is why I began
> writing them, and it is still my pride when one is thought
> worthy to be given in the one evening with the poetic work.[8]

However, the absolute distinction between Lady Gregory as the
writer of comedy and Yeats as the writer of tragedy breaks
down in practice. For one thing, it is contradicted by the
principle of collaboration in the writing of plays that she has
already enunciated in relation to her dramatic beginnings. The
extent of her collaboration with Yeats on plays which were
allegedly solely by him, most famously his one popular play
Cathleen ni Houlihan, has been authoritatively established by
James Pethica.[9] And while Gregory's comedies are themselves
accomplished, what is so striking about her dramatic output is
its range: comedy, tragedy, history, romance, adaptations and
translations. When she arrived in New York in 1911, Yeats
revealed that she had written a '"comedy [*Hanrahan's Oath*] on
shipboard." "No, no, it isn't a comedy," insisted her ladyship'.[10]
And the play I will be discussing in this essay, *The Gaol Gate*, is a
sombre tragedy. Even in regard to one of Gregory's very first
and most enduringly successful plays, the comedy *Spreading the
News*, she first conceived its central situation – in which a
person's good name was taken away by local gossip – 'as a
tragedy ... But comedy and not tragedy was wanted at our
theatre to put beside the high poetic work ... and I let laughter
have its way with the little play'.[11] Tragic elements still lurk
within *Spreading the News*, and few of Gregory's plays lack a
complex hybrid. Neither did she regard a high degree of
laughter as sole dramatic reward or justification. When visiting

an Abbey production of her play *The Workhouse Ward* with Ibsen's translator, William Archer, in November 1908, she noted 'it was a good [i.e. well-attended] house, over £11, and applauded everything in Workhouse, so he [Archer] would get an impression of a large popular appreciative audience'. But she herself was dismayed by the quality of the performances: 'I thought the performance no better than before, but the audience was very cheery' (p.294).

When the Abbey toured the rest of Ireland, Lady Gregory's comedies bulked largest in what was to be offered. Synge fared worst, with *Riders to the Sea* the only one of his plays ever considered for performance outside Dublin. In August 1906 he was shown a touring programme for Galway, Mullingar, Athlone and possibly Tuam which contained none of his plays among the six being offered. Yeats fared somewhat better, but inevitably those plays of his selected for touring in Ireland tended to be those in which Lady Gregory had a fair share, notably *The Pot of Broth* and (inevitably) *Cathleen ni Houlihan.* The preferred Lady Gregory plays were the comedies, especially *Spreading the News* (which was always a draw) and *Hyacinth Halvey*. In one of her few positive remarks about Lady Gregory, Annie Horniman insisted that her 'work must be well treated – she is the best "draw" of the lot of you. I am so proud of her because she makes the people laugh in a witty manner' (p.162). In general, Lady Gregory did not object when her comedies were foregrounded, but she did continue to maintain that the poetic plays were her preference. However, the great exception to this rule is the programmes the Abbey Theatre proposed to offer on their two tours to Galway, on 15 and 16 September 1906 and for the week beginning 6 January 1908.

The White Cockade: History Over Comedy?

It was decided that Gregory's *The White Cockade* would play in Galway on the first visit in 1906 . This was a highly unusual play to choose, not least because it ran to three acts, so upsetting the range of one-act plays on offer, and also because of its greater number of parts. A letter from Yeats to Synge on 17 August

1906 revealed that the insistence on playing *The White Cockade* in Galway had come from Gregory herself:

> Fay is very doubtful of getting a cast that can tour White Cockade, and if he cannot get it Galway had better be put off, as Lady Gregory doesn't want to go there till we have historical or romantic work (p.141).

The White Cockade is a historical play, set during the Battle of the Boyne, one of the most deeply divisive events in Irish history. The Catholic King James is portrayed as a vainglorious coward, anxious only to return to France, while King William of Orange conveniently remains offstage. The Williamite soldiers lack any real conviction. The only leadership on either side is provided by Patrick Sarsfield, who articulates the play's governing thesis that the Irish will only be free when they band together and cast off foreign domination (implicitly, subjugation by Rome). Colm Tóibín puts a rare foot wrong when he claims that the plays Lady Gregory 'and Yeats had written had not been a direct celebration of recent rebellion; they were rooted in history and could be read as metaphor'.[12] This echoes Yeats's statement that *Cathleen ni Houlihan* should be read as metaphor. Most audiences persisted in reading it as political, not least because of the emphasis in Irish history on cyclic recurrence. And if *The White Cockade* was 'rooted in history', the same could not be said of the recent controversial events represented in *The Gaol Gate*.

As he feared, Willie Fay was unable to secure a cast for *The White Cockade*, in particular because professionalization at the Abbey only extended so far, and part-timers were taken on when large casts and/or touring were involved. The newcomers had an inflated sense of what they might be paid, while the company regulars nursed a sense of injury at being paid so little. As Willie Fay reported:

> More trouble in Ireland. The man I had playing Carter struck yesterday for money he wanted to be paid, he said. … That's Carter off. The genius I had playing the Soldier has not turned up either so there's no chance of getting White Cockade to Galway by the 17th September. I don't know where the Dickens to look for people. You see it got round town we are paying people, and that we did well on tour, so that every sundowner

that turns up expects to be paid, and it's perfectly absurd the cheek they have. They can't speak King's English, walk or do a thing. One has to begin at the very beginning with each of them and waste the time of our own people.[13]

The programme which was finally confirmed for Galway differed in no way from the norm, with Gregory's history play removed and her comedies *Hyacinth Halvey* and *Spreading the News* restored. Yeats wrote separately to Synge about his concern over Fay repeatedly playing a broadly comic repertoire:

> I don't think it wise to let Fay go round with that old farce programme. He has got to despise it and to play with it, to overact abominably … I am sorry at even Spreading the News having to do. But there is nothing to put in its place, and it is [our] most certain success with country audiences (p.145).

The Gaol Gate: 'A Direct Incentive to Crime'?

When the Abbey returned to Galway sixteen months later in January 1908, relations with Willie Fay had deteriorated considerably. In many ways it suited Fay well to tour Ireland in the more broadly popular of Gregory's comedies, since it increasingly resembled his early theatrical experience of touring popular melodramas in the fit-up companies. As Yeats had warned earlier:

> It will be a mistake to go on touring indefinitely with a practically comedy programme, for if we don't get an audience for the work more burdened with thought pretty early we will make our audience expect comedy and resent anything else. Comedy must make the ship sail, but the ship must have other things in the cargo (p.126).

Having witnessed Fay's management of the players in England and Scotland in the interim, Annie Horniman was outraged at what she perceived as his slovenliness and encouraged Yeats to sack him. Fay was courting the actress Bridget O'Dempsey, an extremely young member of the Company, but matters were not aided by Synge's canoodling with Molly Allgood. Horniman knew Yeats would hear nothing said against Synge so she redoubled her fire upon the hapless

Fay. Efforts were made to restrict him to peasant plays, while bringing in English theatre people to handle all other productions. In the fraught weeks leading up to the second Galway tour Fay reacted against his recent sidelining by issuing a list of proposals in which he was to be made top dog, insisting 'that there shall be no appeal to any other authority than mine by the people employed by me on all matters dealt with in their contracts'.[14] The issue was one of authority and at the directors' meeting held on 4 December 1907 it was made clear where the authority lay. The first sentence declared unequivocally 'That we could not agree to his proposal about dismissal of the Company and re-engagement by him personally'(p.246). Concern about the direction of the company and a clear articulation that it was a theatre for intellectual drama were expressed: 'That it be explained to the Company that this Theatre must go on as [a] Theatre for intellectual drama, whatever unpopularity that may involve' (p.246). Having put the company in their place as to the kind of work they were involved in, the rest of the proposal constituted an ultimatum that politely but firmly showed Willie Fay the door:

> That no compromise can be accepted upon this subject, but that if any member find himself unable to go on with us under the circumstances, we will not look upon it as unfriendly on his part if he go elsewhere, on the contrary we will help him all we can (p.246).

It was in these charged circumstances that the second tour to Galway was organized. On this occasion, Lady Gregory's comedies did not exclusively fill the bill; rather, they shared the two programmes which the Abbey offered for the week with her political plays, *The Gaol Gate* and *The Rising of the Moon* (and *Cathleen ni Houlihan* which was at least partly hers too, if the truth had been known). Contrary to the usual practice, the selection was not agreed in advance by all parties involved. In Dublin Willie Fay made the selection, with what consultation with Synge one cannot tell, but without reference to Lady Gregory. The response from that quarter was thunderous. Gregory wrote to Synge on 26 December 1907:

> I am afraid from a letter from Fay Yeats sends me, that a break
> up must come. He has put on Gaol Gate for Galway (which I
> was particularly against for local reasons) and says he was given
> leave to choose the Galway programme – which he *never* was
> (p.261).

In her letter to Yeats the same day, Gregory was more detailed
and explicit about why she so vehemently opposed one of her
own plays being staged locally:

> I particularly didn't wish to have Gaol Gate there in the present
> state of agrarian excitement; it would be looked on as a direct
> incentive to crime … I am not, as I first intended, wiring you to
> stop Galway – I wouldn't like his going to be based on that
> (p.262).

Ann Saddlemyer's note to this letter reads:

> The programme finally offered at the Galway Court Theatre
> January 6 to 10 [1908] was *Riders to the Sea*, *The Rising of the Moon*,
> *The Hour Glass* and *Hyacinth Halvey*.

But an advertisement for the 'enormous attraction' of the
forthcoming 'Irish Plays' in the *Galway Pilot and Galway
Vindicator* of Saturday 4 January 1908 reveals that the touring
Abbey players presented not one but two programmes in the
course of the week. The one outlined by Saddlemyer played the
Monday, Wednesday and Friday. But the programme
announced for Tuesday and Thursday confirms that *The Gaol
Gate* was indeed played in Galway, over Lady Gregory's
objections, along with *Cathleen ni Houlihan* and two plays from
the first programme. A local story in the week the Abbey played
Galway in September 1906, headlined 'Agrarian Outrage in
Clare', gives some sense of what she had in mind in speaking of
'the present state of agrarian excitement'. It tells of a near fatal
shooting of a young man who had gone out in the woods
'picking hazel nuts'. His family looked after a farm which had
been the scene of an eviction some time earlier and the arrested
man was a herdsman who had been put out of possession of
the holding as a consequence. The primary political concern of
The Gaol Gate rests with the question of whether the prisoner,
Denis Cahel, had informed against those others with whom he

was imprisoned. His mother and daughter arrive at the prison gate to inquire of his fate, only to learn that he has already been executed (the day before) but that his name was vindicated. The crime for which the young men have been collectively charged is described on the play's first page as 'moonlighting': 'What call had he to go moonlighting or to bring himself into danger at all?'[15] Chambers defines the term (in a specifically Irish context) as 'a person who committed agrarian outrages by night about 1880, in protest against the introduction of the land-tenure system'.[16]

  The Gaol Gate was a recent play by Lady Gregory. It had received its premiere in Dublin at the Abbey fifteen months earlier on Saturday 20 October 1906 when Joseph Holloway recorded in his journal that it played to a crowded house and was well received. Although pausing to question 'the excellence of its dramatic quality', Holloway's praise for 'the excellence of the playing' – Sara Allgood as the mother, Molly Allgood as the daughter and Frank Fay as the gaol porter – shows a grudging admiration for the play itself, as he describes how the actors 'entered the spirit of the terrible situation, and made the intense grief of the women appear almost real to us'.[17] At its close, 'rounds of applause followed, and the actors took their calls in artistic attitudes in keeping with what had gone before'. Throughout, Holloway discusses the play exclusively in aesthetic and generic terms, as a 'tragedy of humble life'. In so doing, he shows that for all his jibing at Yeats, Synge and Gregory, he was the true Abbey habitué suggested by his constant attendance there and that he absolutely accepted their emphasis on art to the exclusion of politics, since there is no detail in his assessment of *The Gaol Gate* sufficient to uncover or draw attention to the play's politics.

  During the Abbey's five-night run in Galway in January 1908, Lady Gregory did not appear at the theatre until the Thursday and Friday nights. As her correspondence with Yeats reveals, she did not 'go before plays because it is such a nationalist programme'.[18] And while she had encouraged nationalist friends to attend, she felt that she 'could not ask "the classes" to come', given the content of the Abbey programme.[19]

'Some had asked for [The] Canavans, and some for the Doctor [Lady Gregory's version in Kiltartanese of Molière's *Le Médecin Malgré Lui*], and all for Spreading the News, so it is annoying.' She also wanted to keep her distance from the company of actors, given the coming break-up with Willie Fay, and expressed her annoyance at the position they had adopted: 'I don't think any of them have behaved well if, as Synge says, they "were all against Fay!" and could not stand him, and then will not support us openly.' The equivocal status of Synge in all of this, where he is neither clearly making one with the actors nor siding with his fellow directors, provokes Gregory: 'I cannot speak to him [Fay] or to any of the company without knowing if you and Synge will back up what I say, and yet I don't like to leave Galway unwatched.' She is clearly torn between a desire to keep an eye on developments and the fear that if she goes in too soon, she may 'hasten a crisis'. In the end, she only ventured in on the Thursday night, the second of the two performances of the *Gaol Gate* programme.

In a puff piece on Saturday 4 January, the *Galway Pilot* had drawn attention to the forthcoming local appearance of 'the popular plays of the National Theatre Society', and predicted that, as 'some of these plays are set in Galway [no mention is made of their author], we are sure they will be an enormous attraction, and we expect crowded houses'. There was no follow-up piece in the following Saturday edition. Molly Allgood, playing one of the key roles in *The Gaol Gate* and featuring prominently in the rest of the Galway programme, reported back to Synge in Dublin by the Wednesday that the company had 'bad houses', to which he replied on the Saturday: 'Lady Gregory told me how bad the house was on Friday, you seem to have had ill luck'.[20]

The Parting of the Fays

On Monday 13 January, three days after Galway, on foot of the ultimatum from the directors concerning control of the company, William G. Fay, his wife Bridget O'Dempsey and brother Frank Fay formally resigned from the National Theatre

Society Limited. As Willie Fay reveals in his autobiography, the director who delivered the final challenge in person was Lady Gregory: she 'came to me to say that they were not disposed to make any changes, and what was I going to do about it? I did the only thing that was left to me – I resigned on the spot'.[21] Following fast upon the heels of the resignation, he wrote to Lady Gregory requesting permission for the Fays' new company to perform certain of her plays in London; the permission was immediately forthcoming, as the directors had indicated it would be. Almost four years later, Lady Gregory went out on tour with the Abbey Theatre Players in the US and, during the first touring engagement at Boston on 27 November 1911, happily included *The Gaol Gate* in the evening's programme. As she wrote of it later in *Our Irish Theatre*: 'The *Gaol Gate* was put on first which, of course, has never offended anyone in Ireland'[22] – with the notable exception of its author when it played in her home town. In *Lady Gregory's Toothbrush* Colm Tóibín has described Lady Gregory as occupying two worlds – that of the Galway landowner and that of the Abbey Theatre writer of rebel plays – and managing them with some equanimity. Or rather, one might say, recalling Thomas Kilroy's remarks on the Anglo-Irish theatrical imagination, that she was able to manage them when some necessary distancing of one role from another was concerned. But when the two coincided and collided, as on the occasion of the Abbey's visit to Galway, the politics of touring Ireland may have proved more than even the redoubtable Lady Gregory could handle.

---

[1] Ann Saddlemyer (ed.), Theatre Business: The Correspondence of the first Abbey Theatre Directors: William Butler Yeats, Lady Gregory and J.M. Synge (Gerrards Cross: Colin Smythe, 1982), p.236. All further citations of the correspondence of Yeats, Gregory and Synge are from this volume, unless otherwise noted, and will be incorporated in the text.

[2] Mary Trotter, Ireland's National Theaters: Political Performance and the Origins of the Irish Dramatic Movement (Syracuse, NY: Syracuse University Press, 2001), p.119.

[3] W.J. Mc Cormack, *Fool of the Family: A Life of J.M. Synge* (London: Weidenfeld and Nicolson, 2000), p.288.

[4] For a comprehensive account, see Paige Reynolds, 'The Making of a Celebrity: Lady Gregory and the Abbey's First American Tour', Special Issue: Lady Gregory, *Irish University Review* 34.1 (Spring/Summer 2004), pp.81-93.

[5] Thomas Kilroy, 'The Anglo-Irish Theatrical Imagination', *Bullán: An Irish Studies Journal* 3.2 (1997-8), p.9.

[6] Colm Tóibín, *Lady Gregory's Toothbrush* (London: Picador, 2002), p.108.

[7] Lady Gregory, *Our Irish Theatre: A Chapter of Autobiography* (Gerrards Cross: Colin Smythe, 1972), p.53.

[8] Ibid.

[9] See James Pethica, '"Our Kathleen": Yeats's Collaboration with Lady Gregory in the Writing of *Cathleen ni Houlihan*', *Yeats Annual* 6 (1988); reprinted in Deirdre Toomey (ed.), *Yeats and Women* (Basingstoke: Macmillan, second edition, 1997), pp.205-22.

[10] 'Interviews with Lady Gregory 1911-1912', *Our Irish Theatre*, p.164.

[11] Ann Saddlemyer (ed.), *The Collected Plays of Lady Gregory, Volume One: The Comedies* (Gerrards Cross: Colin Smythe, 1971), p.253.

[12] Tóibín, *Lady Gregory's Toothbrush*, p.92.

[13] Richard J. Finneran, George Mills Harper and William M. Murphy (eds.), *Letters to W.B. Yeats, Volume One* (London and Basingstoke: Macmillan, 1977), p.189. Fay's letter is dated '22nd August 1907' but, as Ann Saddlemyer has pointed out (p.142), this is a misdating and should read '1906'.

[14] Fay Brothers' Manuscripts f. 92, National Library of Ireland.

[15] Ann Saddlemyer (ed.), *The Collected Plays of Lady Gregory, Volume Two: The Tragedies and Tragic-Comedies* (Gerrards Cross: Colin Smythe, 1971), p.5.

[16] *The Chambers Dictionary* (Edinburgh: Chambers Harrap, 1998), p.1046.

[17] Robert Hogan and Michael J. O'Neill (eds.), *Joseph Holloway's Abbey Theatre: A Selection from his Unpublished Journal* (Carbondale and Edwardsville: Southern Illinois University Press, 1967), p.73. The remaining references to Holloway's remarks on *Gaol Gate* are from the same page and will not be individually footnoted.

[18] Letter from Lady Gregory to W.B. Yeats, 8 January 1908. This, and the other letters cited in this paragraph, are from the forthcoming *Collected Letters of W.B. Yeats Volume Four* (Oxford: Clarendon Press). I am grateful to the General Editor, John Kelly, for supplying me with copies of the relevant correspondence.

[19] John Kelly thinks that Lady Gregory 'means her class by "the classes" – the landed gentry, etc. She uses it in this context in some of her other letters. There were intermittent problems with the grass farmers at this time, so they were particularly sensitive to any plays

with a political dimension.' Personal correspondence, 22 September 2004.

[20] Ann Saddlemyer (ed.), *The Collected Letters of J.M. Synge Volume Two: 1907-1909* (Oxford: Clarendon Press, 1984), p.129. He remarked in his reply to Molly on the Thursday, 9 January: 'It is queer that Lady G. hasn't turned up'.

[21] W.G. Fay and Catherine Carswell, *The Fays of the Abbey Theatre: An Autobiographical Record* (New York: Harcourt, Brace and Co., 1935), p.231.

[22] Gregory, Our Irish Theatre, p.112.

4 | The 'Abbey Irish Players' in Australia – 1922

Peter Kuch

Ireland and Australia share a rich theatrical history that stretches back over two centuries. The first play ever staged in Australia was a 'fit up' of George Farquhar's *The Recruiting Officer* (1706), performed on 4 June 1789, barely eighteen months after the founding of the new colony, by a troupe of convicts before the Governor, Captain Arthur Phillip, and his fellow officers. Staged in a wooden hut near the newly-constructed Government House, the performance was the highlight of the second anniversary of official colonial celebrations of the birthday of His Majesty, King George III.[1]

The ensuing centuries were to see a succession of Irish playwrights, actors, managers and theatrical companies – particularly following the Australian gold-rushes of the 1850s – as Sydney and Melbourne joined an international circuit that typically originated in Dublin, gained its credentials in London, toured America, went on to Australia, and then returned to London or Dublin. As Christopher Morash has emphasized:

> From the 1830s, a London production was no longer the only or even the most important prize for an aspiring Irish actor or dramatist. There was a new world to conquer – a world increasingly populated by an Irish diaspora.[2]

Of no other country was this more true – per capita Australia has more people of Irish descent than anywhere else in the world.[3] So, given the establishment of such a recognized theatre circuit and the networks of personal links between Ireland, England, America and Australia, it is not surprising that a tour of Australia was first broached in 1915 – barely eleven years after the Abbey Theatre was founded.

Yet it was not the Abbey which first came to Australia but a group of leading actors from the Abbey who had formed themselves into a break-away company called the Irish Players, though in the event the distinction between the two companies, at first jealously guarded,[4] was considerably blurred, firstly by the six-or-so years that passed between the split and the Australian tour, and secondly by the way the Australian press progressively elided the two. For example, one of the earliest notices, in *Stage and Society*, announced the tour as 'The Irish Players from the Abbey Theatre, Dublin' (28 April 1922); a review of the opening season in *The Sydney Morning Herald* carried the headline: 'The Abbey Theatre Players' (8 May 1922); while a notice in the Melbourne *Age* toward the end of the tour simply announced the Irish Players as: 'Abbey Theatre Co.' (24 July 1922).

Abbey plans 1915-16

The idea of touring Australia seems to have originated with W.B. Yeats and Lady Gregory, and appears to have arisen from their desperate attempts throughout 1915 to stave off yet another financial crisis threatening the Abbey, a financial crisis that would in part lead to the secession of the Irish Players. The first reference to an Australian tour that I have been able to locate occurs in a letter to Lady Gregory *circa* 9 June 1915 where Yeats advises that A.P. Wilson, the Abbey manager:

> is at the table behind me making out his calculations of the expense to keep the company till word comes from Australia. Of course we can hardly decide without the Audit as the winter's loss has to be thought of.[5]

That there seems to have been an earlier approach is evident from a letter written a week later advising Lady Gregory that he has been visited by the London agents of Australia's major impresario, the J.C. Williamson Company, and has subsequently been advised that J.C. Williamson's 'bookings for 1915 are "quite complete"' but that the agents 'have asked for full particulars of the company, with a view to arranging a tour in 1916'. The London agents, he assures her, are 'of the opinion that the Australians mean business this time'.[6] Yeats then goes on to reassure Lady Gregory that he has sent the particulars of the company to Australia and that he calculates, having consulted Wilson, that the Abbey can undertake the tour for £100 or less.

But there was still the problem of the company's finances, the audit that would show whether or not there was sufficient money to pay the actors until they heard from Australia, a problem compounded by the fact that the audit had been mailed to the wrong address and that mails to Australia were at worst irregular and at best took six to seven weeks one way. The company did have an engagement at the London Coliseum, but even that might have been insufficient given the twin tyrannies of time and distance and the engulfing uncertainties of the War. We need to remember that these negotiations to go to Australia were being conducted barely seven weeks after the landing at Gallipoli, while the second battle of Ypres was still being fought, and only thirty-nine days after the sinking of the *Lusitania* in which Hugh Lane had been drowned.[7] For Lady Gregory to be asked to focus on the needs of the theatre at a time when she had lost her nephew and was beginning to discover the complexities of his will must have been extremely difficult for her. 'You may however feel very decided one way or the other', Yeats concluded, 'I have no clear idea as yet'.[8]

But it was money problems that continued to press. On 22 June 1915 Yeats wrote again to Lady Gregory that he would be wiring her for the audit. Wilson, he advised, had drawn his attention for the second time to a very serious matter:

The company & staff (with the exception of those who go to
Coliseum) are only paid up to end of this week etc on present
contracts. We must therefore make an immediate decision
about the future. Are we to keep all or none and at what
salaries. We must decide at once. I am in the dark, not having
seen audit. I conclude we are holding on till we hear from
Australia.[9]

In the meantime Yeats busied himself with negotiating a further
interim measure. As he explained to W.F. Bailey, one of the
Abbey's most influential supporters:

We are trying now to arrange an American tour at the Music
Halls, for our principal people. To begin when the Coliseum
tour finishes, and to go on till the players must return for the
Australian tour if that comes off. We have had a definite offer
and have sent out our terms to the States. We don't want the
players to know this for the present as it would cause discontent
among those not chosen. We may be able to weather the storm,
as the American tour, like that of the Coliseum and that to
Australia, will contribute substantially to the Abbey.[10]

By 25 June 1915 Yeats had begun to finalize a detailed plan. He
wrote again to Bailey:

We have decided to dismiss all extra people from the list of
actors as from the staff … We shall pay them from week to
week until we hear from Australia. If we get a refusal from
Australia, there will be nothing for it, I believe, but the dispersal
of the Company … Should we get a favourable telegram from
Australia, the problem will arise of keeping the Company
together until February … The Australian contract so far as
terms, are concerned, will I imagine, be the same as a proposal
we discussed with the agents a few weeks ago? In that case the
Abbey will receive a minimum of £20 a week, and its whole
company will be supported for months.[11]

Complications, however, continued to multiply. At the end of
the month Yeats received a second enquiry from Australia. This
new company – most likely the Tait Brothers – want to know,
he advised Lady Gregory:

(1) if complete company numbers sixteen (2) if we bring forty
plays including one act (3) if we bring our own scene, &

costumes (4) if we will accept £250 a week to include all the
[?]sailing on the water (5) can we start at once. I have sent
Wilson a wire asking him to come here. If he gets it in time I
will probably write before post & give scheme. The wire has to
be sent on Friday to Australia.[12]

But before Yeats and Lady Gregory were able to respond, the
entire project began to unravel. Kerrigan and O'Donovan, two
of the senior players, alarmed by rumours that the company was
in financial difficulty, asked Udolphus 'Dossy' Wright, the
veteran Abbey actor and stage electrician, to see Yeats on the
players' behalf. In the course of their discussion it emerged that
the rumours about the financial difficulties seemed to have
originated with the leading actor Arthur Sinclair, who had
already taken it on himself to seek alternate engagements. Yeats
suspected that Wilson had talked to Sinclair, a suspicion that
was confirmed when he discovered that Wilson had been
negotiating on his own behalf with the agents acting for both
the American and the Australian tours. It also emerged that for
at least the previous two months Wilson had been urging the
players to permit him to negotiate more lucrative engagements
for them. Such uncertainty, Yeats was to discover, certainly
unsettled Sara Allgood for shortly after his discussion with
Wright, she signed a contract with Alfred Butt for a tour of J.
Hartley Manners' *Peg O' My Heart* commencing at Blackpool on
26 July.

For Sara Allgood this decision was to prove momentous. *Peg
O' My Heart*, which Manners wrote in 1912 for his actor wife
Laurette (Cooney) Taylor, was first toured in America and
England and then brought to Australia by the Tait Brothers in
1915. As Ann Saddlemyer has pointed out:

few scholars ... seem to be aware that ... Sara Allgood ... was
stranded in Australia during the first world war while touring ...
Peg O' My Heart ... married her much younger leading man;
settled in Mosman; gave birth to a daughter, who lived for only
one hour; and then, while touring New Zealand, lost her
devoted husband during the influenza epidemic. On Sally's
return home to Ireland, she never again referred to this double
tragedy, though knowledge of it makes one appreciate even

more her performance as the grieving mother in *Juno and the Paycock*.[13]

Australia, however, would not have held many mysteries for J. Hartley Manners, for though he was born in London of Irish parents, he had begun his career as an actor on the Melbourne stage in 1898. And he would have been delighted to secure such a talented and versatile actor as Sara Allgood. Her decision however placed Yeats's and Lady Gregory's plans in jeopardy. Understandably, Yeats was for dismissing Wilson immediately, the more so when he discovered from Bailey that 'Wilson some months ago said to Miss Allgood "The Abbey is going smash. I mean to make all the money I can out of it"'.[14] Despite a petition from the company to retain Wilson, Yeats dismissed him and appointed Dossy Wright manager.

Money continued to be a problem, though not an overwhelming one, for when a new offer from another company for a tour of Australia came in late November 1915, Yeats was reluctant to accept it without considerable re-negotiation as the agent could not offer a financial guarantee.[15] He was however overtaken by events, and events that were to lay the foundations for the first tour of Australia, a tour that at that point was still six years away, and a tour that in the event would not be undertaken by the Abbey Theatre but by a group of its leading actors – disenchanted with its management, fearful of its financial viability, and convinced that their careers could only prosper if they managed themselves.

The Irish Players split 1916

In the immediate aftermath of the Easter Rising the Abbey suffered its own revolt. Throughout May 1916 the disaffection that had complicated plans to tour America and Australia the previous year was further aggravated by the extreme unpopularity of the current Abbey manager St John Ervine, with the result that murmurings and grievances erupted into open warfare. Gathering themselves around Arthur Sinclair, and hiring Wilson as their business manager, the seceding actors formed a company called the Irish Players. In July 1916 they played two weeks in Belfast and then toured England and the Irish provinces, before appearing in Dublin in October.[16] And though their secession deprived the Abbey of many of its best actors and though they took audiences away, the Irish Players, it seems, did not pose the terminating threat that it was first thought they might. As Hogan and Burnham have pointed out: 'Although Sinclair's group toured successfully for a number of years it was basically an actors' company, it had no permanent base, and it really initiated no new scripts of merit'.[17] On the other hand, the Abbey did. On 13 December 1916, the Abbey presented Lennox Robinson's *The White-headed Boy*, a satiric comedy that was to become a minor classic of the Irish theatre, and was to be purportedly the sole work that the Irish Players would bring to Australia for their 1922 tour of Sydney and Melbourne. A brief account of the fortunes of both the Irish Players and the play between 1916 and 1922 formed part of the Australian pre-season promotion.

What remains a mystery is the way the Irish Players, a break-away group, subsequently managed to acquire rights in the Abbey's plays. It would seem that Lennox Robinson retained the rights in his own play. By 1922 he was again managing the day-to-day running of the Abbey and as one of its three directors would have felt at ease granting rights to *The White-headed Boy*. Also by 1922 neither Yeats nor Lady Gregory were as actively involved in the Abbey as they had been in 1916, when they had taken out an injunction against the Irish Players to protect the Abbey repertoire. It could also be that in negotiating the tour the J.C. Williamson management and subsequently the J. and N. Tait management insisted on the right, if need be, to use the Abbey name and draw from the Abbey repertoire. Both companies were sufficiently powerful to make such demands. Finally, it might have been the case that once in Australia the Irish Players discovered that certain plays were not protected there and that they were free to perform them without permission and without financial penalty.

Sydney publicity

The Australian public first learned about the tour from the 'Music and Drama' columns of the *Sydney Morning Herald* of Saturday 15 April 1922:

> The Irish Players, a Dublin combination from the famous Abbey Theatre, which has remained intact for five years, is now on its way to Australia, and will open in Sydney about three weeks hence. The date at present proposed by the J.C. Williamson management is May 6. This company is on a world tour with a single play *The White-headed Boy*. It possesses a great repertoire, but no other play has so far been required since the original production of this three-act comedy at the Abbey Theatre on December 13, 1916. ... [Following] the Abbey Theatre success they toured the [Irish] provinces, and then achieved an unbroken run of 300 nights at the Ambassadors' Theatre, London ... On the strength of its London success Mr Nevin Tate, after prolonged negotiation, secured the attraction ... The piece has now stood the test of a long tour of the USA ... and Canada ... Australia will be the sixth country in which this delightful Irish folk comedy has been performed by the Irish Players, and if their triumphs continue they will have circled the theatrical globe before they reach Dublin again ... With three minor exceptions the original company will appear here. There are no star parts, but Maire O'Neill (sister of Sarah Allgood) as the whimsical, shrewd spinster Aunt Ellen, and Mr Arthur Sinclair as Postmaster Duffy stand out.[18]

A fortnight later under the headline 'A Company with a History', *Theatre Magazine* offered readers some additional detail about the negotiations in a feature article on the impending tour. It was reportedly Charles Dillingham who saw the production in London and who arranged the tours of America and Canada; while the Players' Australian representative, Phil Walsh, who had been associated with the Company in Dublin in 1912 and again in New York in 1917, is quoted as saying; 'their acting is along the lines followed by the French ... in the one word – naturalness'.[19] *Theatre Magazine* further reassured its readers that the main feature 'does not contain a single political allusion'.[20]

Three days before, the magazine *Stage and Society* had carried a leading article illustrated with a scene from *The White-headed Boy* also emphasizing the play's apolitical nature by pointing to its universality. The emphasis in both cases, it would seem, was probably intentional and almost certainly conceived in the best interests of the players and the play. For in 1922 in Australia there was still a considerable amount of anti-Irish sentiment lingering from the Easter Rising. Furthermore, such sentiment was being fuelled daily in the months preceding and during the Players' visit by graphic and detailed accounts of the murders, atrocities, bank robberies, burnings, assassinations, bombings and shootings that were being committed during the civil war and that were reported in lurid detail in all the state newspapers[21]:

> Mr Robinson has written a comedy of life rather than of Ireland, for his "White-headed Boy" is the favorite [*sic*] son of the universal mother, petted and made much of at the expense of his brothers and sisters, but eventually triumphant, despite the fact that he has failed to make a way for himself in the world. The piece is saved from the slightest suspicion of dullness both by reason of the sparkle of the lines and by the cast to which these lines are entrusted.[22]

Characteristically, the *Bulletin* – known locally as *The Bushman's Bible* and a fervent campaigner for White Australia – was as crisp as it was colloquial in reassuring its readers with clichés and stereotypes:

> The Irish Players – the original Abbey Theatre Company – open at the Palace Theatre under the management of J. and N. Tait on Saturday. They have captured England, the U.S. and several other countries with Lennox Robertson's [*sic*] *White-headed Boy*, and Sydney will see him whiter and brighter than ever. Knowledgeable critics have acclaimed the play as the last word in drollness and whimsicality.[23]

The final sentence is not only revelatory of what Australian audiences expected from Irish humour, but is also revelatory of what many of them saw as appropriate for comedy. In the event, both sets of expectations were to have a determining influence on the fortunes of the company down under.

Sydney reception

The tour began with a public reception hosted by the Lord Mayor of Sydney accompanied by the Lady Mayoress and various dignitaries, who reassured the Irish Players that 'Australians loved art, and theatres, and entertainments, and would, doubtless, show their appreciation of the players in the usual way'.[24] The claim was more than just an effusive welcome. In talking about his experience of the theatre in Australia in the early 1920s, the eminent Canadian journalist, John Willison (later Sir John Willison), informed the Empire Club in Toronto:

> The best plays run for months in the theatres of Sydney and Melbourne. The average production is of higher quality than we get in Canada. For that there is a reason. It is a long and a costly journey to Australia. A failure in Sydney or Melbourne means disaster. Hence only the best actors with the best companies can risk a season in the Commonwealth. When we were there Dion Boucicault, Seymour Hicks, Oscar Asche and Gertrude Elliot were playing nightly to crowded houses. Melba, with a wonderful company of artists, recruited in Europe, was just closing twelve weeks of Grand Opera in Melbourne, and during all those weeks there was seldom a vacant seat or a vacant box in the theatre in which the company appeared, although it had an actual seating capacity of four thousand. It must be remembered, too, that Sydney is a city of only a million people and that Melbourne has a population of only 800,000 … Australia is distinguished for its love of music and for the generous patronage which it extends to the distinguished artists of other continents.[25]

Yet, the opening fortnight in Sydney proved rather slow for the Irish Players, doubtless because of the strong competition from the cinema and from other theatrical productions. In the first week, for example, *Pollyanna*, starring Mary Pickford, Charlie Chaplin's *The Kid*,[26] D.W. Griffiths' *Way Down East*, and the Australasian Films' production, *Snowblind*, starring Pauline Stark, all opened.[27] The front cover of *Everyone's Variety and Show World* that carried the announcement of the opening of *The White-headed Boy* proclaimed that *The Sheik*, starring Rudolph Valentino, was now in its twelfth week.[28] Competing theatre attractions included Emilie Polini in *My Lady's Dress* at the Criterion, Rene Maxwell in *The Little Dutch Girl* at Her Majesty's, and the return of Gladys Moncrieff in *Maid of the Mountains* at the Theatre Royal.[29]

Reviews of opening night, given prominence in all the dailies and the magazines, provided detailed plot summaries, were respectful of the Abbey tradition, emphasized the universality of the work – perhaps to combat prejudice and to reassure patrons that *The White-headed Boy* was apolitical – remarked its accessibility, and without exception wrote long and, for practically the entire cast, glowing analyses of the style of acting. The *Sydney Morning Herald*, for example, reassured its readers who were yet to see the play:

> [It] has in it none of the mystic, ethereal beauty of Yeats's plays, nor is it concerned with the grim realities of life in the peat cabin so dear to Synge. It is a comedy of rural Ireland, a charming study of life in a modern Irish home, with clever satire upon the idiosyncrasies and traits of a very lovable race. It has, too, another merit, and one of inestimable advantage in view of present-day events. With neither politics nor religion is it concerned. Republicans and Diehard, Protestant and Catholic, can meet here upon common ground in the enjoyment of much wit and drollery.[30]

The analysis of the acting by the theatre critic of the *Green Room* is typical of the high praise that was clearly the consequence of close and appreciative observation:

> We speak of the 'acting' of the Abbey Theatre players, but it does not appear to be the studied gesture and movement of the theatre, it seems to be absolute naturalness just put upon the stage where we may view it … Witnessing their performance was like sitting in the corner of the room with them, taking in all they said and did. Every one of the twelve persons in the play is a character study, clearly cut, well defined, and having characteristics differing from those of the rest.[31]

By the end of May 1922, having played for three weeks, it had become clear that both the Irish Players and *The White-headed Boy* had won an audience – the 31 May issue of *Everyone's Variety and Show World* observing:

The White-Headed Boy is holding a nice share of public patronage, and there is every reason to believe that this delightful little play will run much longer than was anticipated after a somewhat unobtrusive opening. The story is one of the most natural ever written, and is a plain and unvarnished narrative of what actually happens in many Irish households.[32]

Whether success came as the result of the Sydney public feeling more comfortable about an 'Irish' play, or whether the company and the audience had adjusted themselves to one another's expectations, or whether the company in courting controversy had won a following, it was clear that by the end of the month that neither the Irish Players nor *The White-headed Boy* could be called apolitical. In its issue of 1 June, *Theatre Magazine* noted:

Denis is likened to Ireland in his desire to live his life his own way, John Duffy adding, 'And we are like the British Government offering him every damn thing but the right one!' The comparison is unduly stressed, and the inevitable applause so waited for that it sounds like an unnecessary introduction into the original script.[33]

For their final week in Sydney, the Irish Players decided to stage Synge's *Playboy of the Western World* – this piece, *Everyone's Variety* noting:

having commenced to please patrons last Monday at the matinée. This delightful company of theatrical folk deserves all that is best, in the way of encouragement, for their very natural work so ably demonstrated in *The White-Headed Boy*'.[34]

But if the patrons were pleased, the critics were not. Though they again stressed the 'universality' of the play it clearly left them flummoxed and irritated:

The Playboy of the Western World – is a very unusual type of drama – in Australia at all events. The mentality evidenced in the play, and the ethics of most of the characters therein, cannot, surely, be generally typical of the peasantry of Ireland.

The most charitable assumption is that the easy toleration – in fact the awed admiration – for a self-confessed murderer who boasts of slaughtering his own father, is the condition of things in some wild, isolated region in Western Ireland; or, again, it may be an overdrawn satire on the wild, hot-headed boasting that characterizes certain members of segregated illiterate communities not only in Ireland but all over the world.[35]

Praise was again accorded the acting, though this was salted with advice:

> Arthur Shields cleverly succeeded in making Christy Mahon a possible reality. Sydney Morgan imparted much realism to the character of old Mahon, the 'murthered' father ... Interesting as the production of this drama may be from the literary point of view, the Abbey Theatre Company must surely have plays in their repertoire that would make a much stronger appeal to Australian audiences than Synge's *Playboy of the Western World*.[36]

Melbourne and Adelaide

In the second week of June 1922 the Company travelled 650 miles south to Melbourne, a stately Victorian city rich in theatre history since the gold rushes of the 1850s – Dot Boucicault, son of the famous actor and playwright, managed the Bijou Theatre there – and a community openly more 'Irish' than Sydney.[37] Again *The White-headed Boy* was the feature, though the season booked for the Theatre Royal in Bourke Street was almost a fortnight shorter than the Sydney season – 17 June to 6 July. Again the critics gave high praise to the acting, the drama critic for the *Age* seizing the opportunity for some pointed sermonizing about thespian obligation:

> The Abbey Theatre Company is one of the famous institutions of British drama. It adheres to the principle that the purpose of a theatrical entertainment is to present a play as the author intended it to be presented, and not to regard the 'book' supplied by the author as a medium for a series of self-advertising vaudeville turns by the players ... The result ... is a revelation of how drama can be made to live upon the stage. Every character in this play is real and convincing. There is not a hint of aggression or exaggeration anywhere. There is no unnatural manoeuvring so as to arrange the cast 'in an order of importance'. There is no 'playing up' to one member or star-ordered self-effacement of others.[38]

Compared with their Sydney counterparts, the Melbourne critics provided their readers with briefer summaries of the 'plot', more analysis of the structure, and a truer image of the play's Irishness:

> Lennox Robinson's much-travelled play of provincial Irish life … [is] … ingeniously Ibsenite in construction, though *The White-headed Boy* has no lines and picturesque incidents that haunt one's memory like the best in *Bunty Pulls the Strings*. Less concerned about dramatic effect, it is more open to convincing representation than *Bunty* was. Of course the story isn't *all true*. The drollery of the *dénouement* is achieved by the Bernard Shaw device (Shaw, by the way, is Irish) of introducing the impossible in a matter-of-fact manner. … The comedy makes certain of success by becoming farcical and funny. Your impression of quiet realism in the earlier scenes, wherein Duffy's masterful wooing of Aunt Ellen is the most realistic of all, are somewhat clouded by recollection of biting satire in the farcical finale. But you have been thoroughly entertained.[39]

And, as with Sydney, the Company won an audience, though *Everyone's Variety and Show World* reported of the penultimate performance on 5 July that '*The White-Headed Boy*, as presented by the Abbey Theatre Players is meeting with a fair amount of success at the Theatre Royal'.[40]

With their next engagement, at the Theatre Royal in Adelaide, the capital of South Australia, at that time the only colony founded by 'free settlers' and at that time (and still) the least Irish in complexion, 'a fair amount of success' would have been welcome. This section of the tour seems to have been a disaster. The Theatre Royal was booked for the week Monday 10 July to Friday 14 July, with advance notices having been run in the *Adelaide Advertiser* from Thursday 29 June. The sole review, again in the *Adelaide Advertiser*, was a grab-bag of cliché and stereotype:

> *The White-headed Boy* represents Lennox Robinson at his best, and into the three acts is crammed a wealth of homely Irish wit, and a big slice of the pathos always associated with stories of the Emerald Isle … The natural Irish brogue of the players, the homely cottage, with its homely people, and the delightful humor [*sic*], gave the comedy an irresistible appeal … Mr Arthur

Shields, the 'white-headed boy', won all hearts with his breeziness and independence, while the old Irish mother was perfectly portrayed by Miss Maureen Delany, who shone in the scene in which she appealed to Denis not to go away from her.[41]

By Thursday evening, after a run of barely four nights, the play was pulled, a small notice edged in funereal black in the top corner of the Entertainments page advising intending patrons that:

IN CONSEQUENCE OF THE EXTENSIVE
PREPARATIONS IN CONNECTION WITH 'THE PEEP
SHOW' THERE WILL BE NO PERFORMANCE OF THE
WHITE-HEADED BOY TONIGHT .[42]

The *Bulletin*, the 'voice of democratic Australia', could barely conceal its scorn for the City of Churches, and in a brief notice of the Adelaide season sharply observed:

The White-headed Boy has found heavy support in cultured Adelaide before being literally pushed out of the Royal by preparations for a first-in-Australia revue. Maire O'Neill is the popular success of the Irish comedy, and her frequent appeals to the Deity are always (for some obscure reason) received by the house with delighted laughter. Equally acceptable in a different way are the quiet women who fit into their dull-grey characters as if they were not acting at all, notably Maureen Delany and Nora Desmond. The men are Irish types finely differentiated.[43]

Drawing to a close

By now the entire tour was drawing to its inevitable close, partly for financial reasons and partly because the Company had by then been on tour abroad for almost a year. Returning to Melbourne, and to the Theatre Royal, the Irish Players presented a triple bill from 24 July to 28 July 1922, comprising William Boyle's *The Building Fund*, Synge's *In the Shadow of the Glen*, and Lady Gregory's *The Workhouse Ward*. The single notice in the *Age* predictably praised the acting, commended the clever bitterness of *The Building Fund*, agonized over *In the Shadow of the Glen*, and simply noticed *The Workhouse Ward*. From Melbourne

the Company returned to Sydney for a brief season
commencing 8 August at the Palace Theatre with a triple bill
comprising Synge's *In the Shadow of the Glen*, Boyle's *The Building
Fund*, and James Bernard Fagan's *Doctor O'Toole: a farcical Comedy*

> Three plays which will introduce the company in a series of
> character roles that will enable the performers – not only to
> indicate the genius which has made their fame world-wide – but
> to display their remarkable versatility and consummate skill.[44]

Again, as with the triple bill in Sydney, Synge's work was
criticized for demeaning characterization, flawed construction,
sordid subject matter, and disgusting language – all criticisms
levelled at the original productions by Irish audiences, critics
and reviewers. To encounter these reviews is like going back
fifteen years and returning to the other side of the world. The
reviewer for the *Green Room* even went so far as to suggest that
such people and circumstances, if they did exist, were not fit
subjects for drama:

> Many Australians would like an authoritative pronouncement
> from a fully qualified independent authority as to the
> authenticity of Synge's delineation of the characteristics and
> mentality of those Irish portraits that he presents to us in
> certain of his dramas that we have seen. They seem to be
> distinguished by a sordidness, an unreal atmosphere, a distorted
> mental perspective, a callousness in the presence of death, and a
> soulless bargaining in connection with marriage that are
> revolting and, running through them all is a thread of mournful
> Celtic poetry expressed in inverted English, and in fantastic
> Irish idiom that seems unreal to the direct, terse, sun-baked
> Australian.[45]

For the most part two articles – the first published in the
Bulletin on 27 July and the second published in *Everyone's Variety
and Show World* the previous day – sum up the Irish Players
1922 tour of Australia. The *Bulletin* article linked the tour's lack
of financial success to the plays that were offered. Not only did
they not conform to local images of Irishness, the article
argued, but their 'universality' leeched them of colour,
significance and energy:

> Had all the scoffers at 'commercial' drama gone to *The White-headed Boy* it would at least have been a fair success in both cities. One such play, anyhow, should have been a success of curiosity, although a succession of them might have palled on intelligent understanding. The Irish play has no variety in it, no pleasantly humorous picture of outdoor life … Not that there is any insult to Oireland [*sic*] in it, to explain the want of enthusiastic Irish support. Change the accent and it would do for a comedy of English village life. Deck it in a brighter raiment, and substitute the name of some other capital town for the Dublin they talk about, and this might, presumably, be a comedy of Roumanian or Bulgarian life. Provincialism is the key-note in *The White-headed Boy* and the sentiments of provincialism are pretty much the same in many countries.[46]

The article in *Everyone's Variety and Show World*, while acknowledging the tour's lack of financial success, chose rather to emphasize the great skill of the actors, their evident professionalism, and the subtle synergies that existed between players and play:

> Those enthusiasts who anticipated seeing the Irish Players in a brief return season are doomed to disappointment, and the company will leave for South Africa as originally planned. The Australian tour of this unique combination cannot truthfully be said to have been anything like a financial success, nor did the public quite realise the quality of the fare provided. Nevertheless, the story of *The White-headed Boy* was one of the most natural ever told. Perhaps because of its simplicity and fidelity it failed to reach the heights anticipated by the local playgoers, who would have preferred a more 'stagey' presentation; but to many, the memory of the very faithful interpretation of a unique little company, will long be cherished.[47]

In fact the company did not immediately leave for South Africa. It seems that they either re-negotiated or temporarily suspended their contract with the J.C. Williamson company and then set out for an extensive tour of Queensland – but that is an aspect of the 1922 tour that will have to be explored elsewhere. What remains certain however is that with the departure of the Abbey Irish Players, or the Abbey Theatre Co. as they had misleadingly come to be known, for South Africa towards the end of 1922, Australian theatre audiences lost the opportunity to explore images of Irishness that for nearly two decades had generated responses in Ireland itself ranging from subtle smiles of recognition to outraged denunciation.

When the 1916 Abbey split that produced the Irish Players occurred, a Dublin critic, suspecting that the departure of so many accomplished actors would see the end of genuine theatre, exclaimed: 'when the Abbey is gone the mirror of Ireland is broken'. In the event, the Abbey survived the 1916 split, and both the Abbey and the Irish Players continued to perform throughout some of the most turbulent years of Ireland's long history. But it was not so for Australia. After the Abbey's abortive plans of 1915 and 1916 and the fraught visit of the Irish Players in 1922, it seems that neither the Abbey nor the Irish Players considered touring Australia for another sixty-eight years – but then, with a touch of irony that cultural history so often produces, when the Abbey finally did come it was to Adelaide, to its internationally renowned Festival of Arts.[48]

---

[1] Robert Jordan, *The Convict Theatres of Early Australia 1788-1840* (Sydney: Currency House, 2002), p.29: 'Since the prologue specially written for that production spoke of the "novelty" of the occasion, there can be little doubt that it actually was Australia's first full-scale theatrical event'.

[2] Christopher Morash, *A History of Irish Theatre, 1601-2000* (Cambridge: Cambridge University Press, 2002), pp.86-7.

[3] Patrick O'Farrell, *The Irish in Australia* (1986; rev. ed., Kensington: New South Wales University Press, 1993), p.318: 'At the time of the Bicentenary in 1988, when the crowds gathered to watch the re-enactment of the landing at Sydney Cove, the demographer C.A. Price estimated that there were nearly 3 million (2,810,430) Australians of Irish origin – that is 17.24% of the then population of 16.3 million, by far the largest minority in relation to an English majority group of 43.92%'.

[4] Robert Hogan and Richard Burnham (eds.), *The Modern Irish Drama: A Documentary History, V: The Art of the Amateur, 1916-1920* (Dublin: Dolmen, 1984), p.47.

[5] John Kelly (ed.), *The Collected Letters of W.B. Yeats* [electronic resource] (Charlottesville, VA: InteLex Corporation, 2002–), accession number

2661, to Lady Gregory, c. 9 June 1915. Quotations from the *Collected Letters* appear by permission of Oxford University Press.

[6] Kelly 2002: acc. no. 2674, to Lady Gregory, 16 June 1915.

[7] Allied landing at Gallipoli, 25 April 1915; second battle of Ypres, 22 April to 25 May 1915; sinking of *Lusitania*, 7 May 1915.

[8] Kelly 2002: acc. no. 2674, to Lady Gregory, 16 June 1915.

[9] Kelly 2002: acc. no. 2679, to Lady Gregory, 22 June [1915].

[10] Kelly 2002: acc. no. 2684, to William F. Bailey, 23 June 1915.

[11] Kelly 2002: acc. no. 2690, to William F. Bailey, 25 June 1915.

[12] Kelly 2002: acc. no. 2694, to Lady Gregory, c. 28 June 1915.

[13] Ann Saddlemyer, 'John, Willy, Lily, George, Gilbert... and Arthur: My Australian Connections', in Peter Kuch and Julie-Ann Robson (eds.), *Irelands in the Asia-Pacific* (Gerrards Cross: Colin Smythe, 2003), p.204.

[14] Kelly 2002: acc. no. 2718, to Lady Gregory, 18 July [1915].

[15] Kelly 2002: acc. no. 2821, to Lady Gregory, 1 December 1915.

[16] Hogan and Burnham (eds.), *Modern Irish Drama*, p.47.

[17] Ibid.

[18] *Sydney Morning Herald*, 15 April 1922, 'Music and Drama', p.8.

[19] *Theatre Magazine*, 1 May 1922, 'A Company With a History', p.9.

[20] Ibid.

[21] There were many leading articles on the situation in Ireland from 21 December 1921 to 11 April 1922 and an editorial on 13 April 1922.

[22] *Stage and Society*, 28 April 1922, p.34.

[23] *Bulletin*, 4 May 1922, p.34.

[24] *Green Room*, 1 June 1922, p.25.

[25] 'Australia as I Saw It', an address by Sir John Willison, LL.D., F.R.C.S., delivered to the Empire Club of Canada, Toronto, 2 October 1924. Accessed 22 February 2004 at :
http://www.empireclubfoundation.com/details.asp?SpeechID=2851

[26] *Everyone's Variety and Show World*, Vol. 3, No. 114, 10 May 1922, p.17.

[27] *Everyone's Variety and Show World*, Vol. 3, No. 112, 3 May 1922, p.619.

[28] *Everyone's Variety and Show World*, Vol. 3, No. 114, 10 May 1922, front cover.

[29] *Everyone's Variety and Show World*, Vol. 3, No. 112, 3 May 1922, p.619.

[30] *Sydney Morning Herald*, '"White-Headed Boy": The Abbey Theatre Players', 8 May 1922, p.5.

[31] *Green Room*, 'Plays of the Month, The Irish Players', 1 June 1922, pp.5-6.

[32] *Everyone's Variety and Show World*, Vol. 3, No. 112, 31 May 1922, p. 19.

[33] *Theatre Magazine*, 'From a Spectator's Point of View: Performers on and Off the Stage', 1 June 1922, p.11. See Lennox Robinson, *The*

Whiteheaded Boy: A Comedy in Three Acts (Dublin: The Talbot Press Limited, 1922), p.158: 'DUFFY: Free?... Bedad, isn't he like old Ireland asking for freedom, and we're like the fools of Englishmen offering him every bloody thing except the one thing?'

[34] *Everyone's Variety and Show World*, Vol. 3, No. 118, 7 June 1922, p.20.

[35] *Green Room*, 'The Playboy of the Western World*: Synge's Interpretative Drama', 1 July 1922, p.8. Those critics who had denounced the original production as a 'slur on Irish womanhood' would probably have been just as outraged by the half-page advertisement for Solyptol Soap printed beside the review featuring an endorsement by a leggy 'Miss Nora Delany' – photographed in such a way as to be a 'specimen of winsome Irish girlhood as one could wish to see'.

[36] Ibid.

[37] Dot Boucicault – the nickname of Dionysius George Boucicault (1859-1929), actor and dramatist, son of the playwright and husband (1901) of the actress Irene Vanbrugh. For the Irishness of Melbourne in the 1920s see O'Farrell, *Irish in Australia*, pp.156-7 *et passim*.

[38] *Age*, 'A Real Live Drama: *The White-Headed Boy* at the Theatre Royal', 19 June 1922, p.13.

[39] *Bulletin*, 22 June 1922, p.34. Graham Moffat's stage farce, *Bunty Pulls the Strings*, was first produced at the Haymarket Theatre, London, in 1911. In 1921 it was made into a movie directed by Reginald Barker, and starring Raymond Hatton, Leatrice Joy, Cullen Landis, and Russell Simpson.

[40] *Everyone's Variety and Show World*, Vol. 3, No. 122, 5 July 1922, p.25.

[41] *Adelaide Advertiser*, 'The *White-Headed Boy*: Whimsical Irish Comedy', 10 July 1922, p.8.

[42] *Adelaide Advertiser*, 14 July 1922, p.2. See also *Everyone's Variety and Show World*, Vol. 3, No. 125, 26 July 1922, p.25.

[43] *Bulletin*, 20 July 1922, p.34.

[44] *Theatre Magazine*, 1 August 1922, p.7.

[45] *Green Room*, 'The Abbey Theatre Company', 1 September 1922, pp.6-7.

[46] *Bulletin*, 27 July 1922, p.36.

[47] *Everyone's Variety and Show World*, 'Abbey Players for Africa', Vol. 3, No. 125, 26 July 1922, p.27.

[48] Adelaide Arts Festival in 1990; Sydney Arts Festival in 1993; Festival of Perth 1995; Melbourne Arts Festival in 1999; Brisbane and Sydney in 2004.

5 | Barry Fitzgerald:
From Abbey Tours to Hollywood Films

Adrian Frazier

1

In March 1933, the Abbey Theatre company was in Chicago. Barry Fitzgerald was playing Captain Boyle, a spluttering, five-foot-two, profane Jupiter, in *Juno and the Paycock*, the world's favourite Irish play since its 1924 début. The play was still a money spinner in Chicago. Since embarking at Galway on 1 October 1932, the company had played in New York (four weeks), Pittsburgh, Philadelphia, and Baltimore; after Chicago, they would head for Washington, DC, before returning to New York. They would not be back on the Dublin stage until July 1933.

This was one of three long tours of North America by the Abbey players in the years following the onset of the Great Depression. The Abbey Theatre itself was left dark, or occupied by the starless 'Second Company'. The Abbey directors – W.B. Yeats, Lady Gregory, Lennox Robinson, and Walter Starkie – were in a bind. If the company did not tour, its actors could only just afford to live in Dublin on the proceeds of the box office (small audiences paying low prices) and the £1,000 per year state subsidy. The best actors would soon be whisked away by Hollywood agents and London producers, leaving green understudies behind.

In the long run, would American tours solve the Abbey's problems? As a side effect, they showcased potential stars to those cherry-picking Hollywood and Broadway talent-scouts the Abbey management was trying to keep at bay. In the mid-1930s, half of the total population of the USA went to the cinema every single week. In Ireland, 1,271 films were screened in 1935, the majority from Hollywood; over eighteen million tickets were sold in the Free State, even though the Pope, Pius XI, declared moving pictures an evil worse than books, temptations sufficiently pernicious in themselves. The world's money, scarce everywhere, was flowing as rapidly into Hollywood as bathwater into a drainpipe, and soon enough, would the actors not follow it?

2

In March 1933, while in Chicago, Udolphus Wright, who had joined the Irish National Theatre Society in 1903, gave a backward-looking interview to a reporter for the Chicago *Sunday Times*, mostly consisting of reminiscences of those actors who had left the Abbey over the years and made good in other countries.[1]

A first wave of departures came shortly after the foundation of the Irish National Theatre Society in 1902. P.J. Kelly, Dudley Digges and Maire Quinn, three of the ten founding members of the company that was to become the Abbey, their idealistic patriotism already rattled by Synge's *Shadow of the Glen* (1903), left to put on Irish plays at the 1904 St. Louis' World Fair. Thereafter, Digges married Maire Quinn, became a big shot on the Broadway stage, and, in recent years, had moved to Hollywood. In the 1933 cinema sensation, *The Invisible Man*, Digges plays the chief detective.

Other departures from the Abbey company were consequences of the first North American tours. Una O'Connor was tempted away after the second Abbey tour in

1912. Along with Digges, she was seen in *The Invisible Man*, as the innkeeper's wife.

In Sara Allgood's case as well, touring with the Abbey led to breaking from the Abbey. From 1904 Lady Gregory felt that the success of her plays depended on Sara Allgood taking part in them. By 1916, however, Allgood had become a bankable star – too plump and plain by movie standards for an ingénue role, but charming and deep in every other respect. With the Abbey's profits dropping from the start of the First World War, then plunging steeply after the Easter Rising, Allgood received an offer to star in a production of *Peg O'My Heart* touring to Australia, and she snapped the offer up. Several years later, after her marriage and then the deaths of both her husband and child, Allgood returned to the London stage and then finally to the Abbey. Then, however, her triumph in *Juno and the Paycock* (3 March 1924) led to offers to revive the play with a different cast in London, it in turn bringing an offer from Alfred Hitchcock to star in a film of the West End hit – his first 'talkie' – released in 1930.

3

Yet there were advantages to being in the Abbey that might be lost outside it. In the same month that Udolphus Wright was being interviewed by the *Sunday Times*, Barry Fitzgerald was talking to a reporter for the *Chicago Daily News*. Yes, he had done a spell on the London stage, with vast crowds, and a big pay cheque, but still Fitzgerald wanted to go back to the Abbey:

> There was such a difference in rehearsals. In London the directors told every actor just what to do, with the result that the cast could get no further than the limitations of the one director. I'd no liking for the commercial theatre … Mind you, I like money too, but I like the Abbey style better. There every actor, once he has shown himself to be one of the company, is allowed to develop his role with more liberty than anywhere else … We don't make the money [they] do in commercial theatre, but we're more secure.[2]

What is more, Fitzgerald made it clear that intellectually he was interested in great drama and in Irish cultural nationalism. From the time he was a young man, just starting as a civil servant in the Department of Unemployment, Fitzgerald was caught up in the enthusiasms of the Irish Literary Revival. He and his brother, Arthur Shields, revered Yeats; in time they both became friends with Sean O'Casey and Lennox Robinson. Shields had been doing walk-on parts since 1912, when he was just 16 years old.[3] In the years before 1916, Fitzgerald went to the Abbey every night. Sara Allgood, Maire O'Neill, Joe Kerrigan, and Arthur Sinclair were his idols, and he thought that the plays in which they appeared – the works of T.C. Murray, Lennox Robinson, Lady Gregory, and Synge – were important to the emergent nation.

When actors resigned *en masse* after 1916 in protest against the management of St John Ervine, Fitzgerald got his chance. Seeing Fitzgerald as the Captain trying to say a polysyllable was like watching a man struggling to keep a slippery eel in his mouth: eyes bulged, spittle flew, and his jaw nearly unhinged. The character was apparently based on a real-life acquaintance of O'Casey's, one of many work-shy layabouts, but this one claimed, falsely, to have been a sea captain. Barry Fitzgerald was just the man to impersonate him, but not because Fitzgerald was like the man in question. No one could be less so Fitzgerald was a man who spoke slowly, measuring his words; he worked constantly; he earned a good deal of money; he liked to play golf on Sundays; his best friend was J.J. O'Leary, owner of a printing works. But Fitzgerald had a talent for 'taking off' Dublin's dissolute and eccentric characters, those rich in personality and in nothing else.

4

O'Casey's great Dublin plays of the mid-1920s held the stage throughout the 1930s wherever English was spoken. Yet something seems to have happened to the Abbey productions of these classics, quite apart from bowdlerization of the Abbey acting-version of *The Plough and the Stars*. In *Juno and the Paycock* and *The Plough and the Stars*, speech after speech became a set-piece, like arias in an opera. Character was everything to the Abbey players, plot and atmosphere nothing, a New York critic observed.[4] The performance of *Juno* was 'more an exhibition than a play'. But the exhibition was that of a half-dozen maestros. Barry Fitzgerald 'fairly SMELT his part of the Captain. His voice performed incredible feats of comedy, and his great earthy frame oozed alcoholic amiability'.[5] Like Fitzgerald, Maureen Delany had the ability to 'lift up the house on [her] appearance on stage'.[6] In the eyes of American critic George Jean Nathan, however, Delany's 'winking, snorting, and mugging ... wreck any serious play'.[7] But were the O'Casey plays still serious plays? They had become Dublin character comedies.

In Chicago, the reviewer for the *Herald and Examiner*, compared the Abbey to an American football team: 'all star at the right moment'. The early Abbey style, in which no one moved while a character spoke, and all eyes were on that character like so many spotlights, evolved into a sequence of solo turns, and each turn was an opportunity for individual artistry. In rehearsal, much of the business was left for the actor to devise. The result of setting the actors loose to devise their own by-play struck American spectators as odd. The American custom was to spend a great deal of money on a leading man and leading lady, guarantee spectators lavish set and costumes, and focus on a through-line for the plot, leading to the happy ending. The productions of *Juno and the Paycock* and *The Plough and the Stars* that toured America in the early 1930s lacked these ingredients. They meandered comically towards unhappy endings, with startlingly vivid low-life characters sporting their eccentricities in front of cheap, painted scene-flats.

5

After the return of the company to Dublin from its American tours, Barry Fitzgerald had been restless. Indeed, he had felt that way in his native city since he gave up the London stage in December 1930. At first, he suspected that his Abbey fans were 'off' him: 'people who go away as I did are disapproved of by Dublin people'.[8] The prejudice continued, he thought, even a year later, as notices of the Abbey plays often left him unmentioned, and heaped praise on F.J. McCormick instead. Maybe it was because he was a Protestant and McCormick was not, 'for Dublin is very Catholic now'.[9] It was said of McCormick's wife, Eileen Crowe, when she first appeared for an audition at the Abbey in the early 1920s, 'That girl there would make a very good nun, or a very good actress'. She went on the stage, but carried the air of piety with her, and it did her no harm at all in 1930s Dublin, whereas Barry Fitzgerald's cultural nationalism of the Yeatsian sort was not in vogue; indeed, it had become a kind of embarrassment to the new ruling class.

On 12 August 1935, Fitzgerald reprised his role as Sylvester Heegan in *The Silver Tassie*, a very funny part. But the press slated the play, and Catholic clergy objected to the cross in the second act as a blasphemy. Brinsley MacNamara, a Catholic playwright on the Abbey board, attacked the Abbey's production, and so was forced by fellow-directors to resign. More priests and laymen joined in the brouhaha. Dublin was getting very Catholic indeed. As for Fitzgerald, the audience wanted him only to make them laugh; and they would sometimes laugh even before he had done anything to make them do so. When he took serious roles, critics complained that he was 'hopelessly miscast'; they were a waste of his 'comic genius'; 'Barry Fitzgerald is a clown'.[10]

In interviews Barry Fitzgerald gave to the press during the 1934-35 American tour, one can observe him weighing over in his mind whether to stick it out in Catholic Dublin or jump ship for Hollywood. He was, as already mentioned, a prudent man and no bohemian. It had taken him ten years after going on stage to give up his daytime work as a civil servant and rely solely on the stage for his income. His first experience outside of the Abbey – playing, at O'Casey's request, alongside Charles Laughton in the London production of *The Silver Tassie* (October 1929), and then staying on to do comic turns in a pantomime – had made him more money personally than the

Abbey took in for all its plays during the same period, but it had left him bored and insecure. Work in Dublin Castle at the Department of Unemployment had given him a more than statistical understanding of what joblessness can do to a man.

He had three offers from Hollywood studios, he told a New York interviewer in December 1934, but he was not certain he would ever take one up.[11] Hollywood had enough Irishmen already, in Spencer Tracy and Frank Morgan. Fitzgerald also confessed that he was not sure he would be able to act well without an audience present; the screen test on a silent sound-stage in front of gum-chewing cameramen had left him nonplussed. But then, he reflected, Charles Laughton was a stage actor too, and he was not faring too badly in the pictures. Then there was Ireland to consider. A new Ireland was forming, he explained to the reporter, quoting Shaw to the effect that a man without his nationality is like a man with a broken leg – he can think of nothing else. Now surely Ireland and its playwrights would begin to think of something else, of humanity, and not continue its morbid obsession with Irishness.

A few days later, at the curtain of the Abbey's last New York show, a delegation mounted the stage as the actors took their bows.[12] They presented Barry Fitzgerald with a testimonial. It was signed by Fiorello LaGuardia, Mayor of New York, director Eva LaGallienne, novelist and critic Frank Norris, and all the theatre critics of the New York dailies. It declared Barry Fitzgerald the best comic actor in the English-speaking world. Hollywood talent scouts need scout no longer: here was a prize.

Three months later the company arrived in Los Angeles, and on 17 March 1935, Maureen O'Sullivan, the twenty-four-year-old Roscommon girl, already Tarzan's Jane, hosted a welcome luncheon where the Irish players met celebrities including Victor MacLaglen. Screen tests were set up for Barry Fitzgerald and others.

Speaking to an interviewer a few days later in San Francisco, Fitzgerald said he was surprised not to be more worried about the outcome of those tests, but in fact he did worry.[13] For he began to muse about the one time he had been asked to take a truly stage-Irish part, and that had been in a film.[14] Appearing for work on location forty miles out of Dublin, Fitzgerald was told his job was to play an incorrigible but humorous Irish drunk. This man is caught drinking from the bottle by a priest, who lectures him on the evils of strong drink, extracts a promise of reform, and walks away with the whiskey. The man then peers round the corner, sighs with relief, and draws forth from his long coat a second bottle. Fitzgerald admitted that he was terrified of what members of the Abbey company would say if they ever saw him playing such a part in a film. So he walked off the set.

A day later, giving yet another interview, Fitzgerald continued to seesaw. Sure, nothing might come of that screen test. He wasn't particularly keen for the films anyway. It was cold work on a set without an audience. But there was the money. God knows, he admitted, I want it.[15]

6

And he was going to get it. When the Abbey was in Los Angeles, John Ford was there too, filming Liam O'Flaherty's *The Informer*. Straight away, Ford – an Irish-loving Irish American – hired Denis O'Dea to play a street-singer in the film; Una O'Connor and J.M. Kerrigan, former Abbey players, were already in the cast. Now Ford wanted to make a film with the present company as a whole, and within a year he had financing for *The Plough and the Stars*. He offered the Abbey what it could not refuse: a share of the actors' salaries that exceeded its annual state subsidy. In June 1936, five Abbey stars set sail: F.J. McCormick, Eileen Crowe, Denis O'Dea, Barry Fitzgerald, and his brother Arthur Shields. The film is not good John Ford, and it is worse O'Casey. But some scenes are fascinating to a theatre historian, and the first appearance of Barry Fitzgerald as Fluther Good is one of these.

After an exterior shot of men in uniform, with rifles shouldered, marching down the street, Fluther Good is shown ducking into a pub. He spies three partial glasses of stout on the bar, abandoned by those who rushed out to see the soldiers pass. While the barman looks out the window, Fluther expertly empties the contents of the three glasses into a fourth partly drunk glass, making one brimful pint. He drinks this down with manifest relish, never taking the glass from his lips until it is empty. The barman turns as he hears Fluther leave by the door, and sees four empty glasses on the bar. He shakes his head with disapproval and picks up a blackboard. On the slate already appears the name, 'Fluther Good', with five crosses chalked beside it. The barman chalks four more crosses. Scrounging for free drink, Fluther has been charged for more than he in fact stole.

There is not a word spoken, yet the spectator has a very complete introduction to Fluther Good in his thirty seconds of screen-time. Such a scene would be said by cineastes to be a 'director's touch', because Ford's distinction was the invention of humorous, folksy grace-notes in a serious story. The invention of the business for the scene, however, and the panache with which that business is carried off, is all Barry Fitzgerald. One of the things he had loved about the Abbey was that, unlike the commercial London stage, it allowed actors to improvise. Hollywood directors like Ford did the same. They cast actors that they knew had within them the power to invent parts of the story that the director wished to film.

At the same time, the scene bears an uncanny likeness to that nightmare role that Fitzgerald had refused to play in the English film being shot outside Dublin. It has in common the shambling, work-shy Irishman, the drink, the incorrigible taste for same, and the life that is a joke. It was a stereotype that Barry Fitzgerald would get lots of opportunities to perfect in twenty years of movie-making, whether in Irish, British, Western, or modern-American settings. In 1941 he even did a turn in the African jungle as that staggering, lovable Irishman, with Maureen O'Sullivan and Johnny Weismuller defending *Tarzan's Secret Treasure*. And in 1952, Fitzgerald brought it all back home in *The Quiet Man*.

7

So what does this story reflect? It is a story of a certain style of
acting that was carried to the worlds' millions, one in which
actors – trained by Frank Fay, or in his tradition – learned to
speak words with quiet force, like feathers borne on puffs of
wind, and learned also, after Fay left the company, to invent all
their own stage business. It is a story, on another level, of
globalization, the star system, and the triumph of stereotypes in
media for the masses. It is the story of Protestants in Dublin,
however patriotic, still with a mimetic and parodic relationship
to Catholic culture. It is a story of Protestants who found their
home becoming no home at all in a Free State more like
Franco's Spain than the Republicans' Spain. And of course it is
a story of Ireland becoming a brand name – much loved, and
often consumed in a glass.

¹ *Sunday Times* (Chicago), 12 March 1933, Abbey Theatre scrapbooks
   National Library of Ireland, Mss. POS 8132-8136.
² *Chicago Daily News*, 15 March 1933, Abbey Theatre scrapbooks.
³ In the interview, Fitzgerald says his brother was 13 years old in 1912,
   but this must be a mistake, as Arthur Shields was born in Dublin on
   15 February 1896. Fitzgerald himself was born 10 March 1888 and
   died 14 January 1961.
⁴ Review of New York performance, 29 October 1932, Abbey Theatre
   scrapbooks.
⁵ *Pittsburgh Press*, 15 December 1932, Abbey Theatre scrapbooks.
⁶ Lennox Robinson and Arthur Duff, 27 August 1935; quoted in Robert
   Hogan and Michael J. O'Neill (eds.), *Joseph Holloway's Abbey Theatre,
   Volume Two, 1932-1937* (Dixon, CA: Proscenium Press, 1969), p.46.
⁷ Robert Hogan and Richard Burnham (eds.), *The Years of O'Casey, 1921-
   1926, A Documentary History* (Gerrards Cross, Bucks.: Colin Smythe,
   1992), p.188.
⁸ Barry Fitzgerald to Sean O'Casey, 8 October 1931, in David Krause
   (ed.), *The Letters of Sean O'Casey 1910-41* (New York: Macmillan,
   1975), pp.436-37.
⁹ Barry Fitzgerald to Sean O'Casey (nd), quoted in Sean O'Casey, *Rose
   and Crown* (London: Macmillan, 1952), p.151.

[10] Gabriel Fallon, 'The Genius of Barry Fitzgerald', *Leader* 74:2 (February 1937), pp.40-41.

[11] *New York Evening Journal*, 5 December 1934, p.1, Abbey Theatre scrapbooks.

[12] *New York World Telegram*, 16 December 1934, Abbey Theatre scrapbooks.

[13] *San Francisco Bulletin*, 23 March 1935, Abbey Theatre Scrapbooks.

[14] Since Fitzgerald does not name the English director or title of the stage-Irish film or give a date, it would be useless to speculate on which film it was.

[15] *San Francisco Chronicle*, 24 March 1935, Abbey Theatre scrapbooks.

6 | The Road to God Knows Where: Can Theatre be National?

Chris Morash

'Is it not time that our dramatic art also should be placed on a national basis?'[1]

It was the winter of 1903, and things were rapidly going from bad to worse. Initially, none of the members of the Irish National Theatre Society paid much attention to the distant collapse in the value of Hudson's Bay Company shares, until Annie Horniman wrote to Yeats, on her personalized, daffodil-yellow notepaper, to say that she was no longer in a position to provide financial support for his theatrical ventures, and would not be purchasing a theatre building for the group. Given that hardly anyone in the company actually liked Horniman in the first place, this was less of a blow than the constant worry over the health of John Millington Synge, whose Hodgkin's disease was progressing more rapidly than expected, and would lead to his death in late February. As the bad news mounted, Lady Gregory must have already felt a sense of doubt as she attended the opening night of her first play, *Twenty-Five*, on 14 March 1903. So, when Joseph Holloway stopped her on Molesworth Street immediately after the performance to give his opinion that the play's central premise 'scarcely proved convincing',[2] it is not surprising that she went immediately around the corner to

her rooms in the Nassau Hotel, and wrote that famous note to
Yeats:

> While I shall always continue to do everything in my power to
> help with your work, I feel that the theatre is not really the area
> in which I can be of most service, and so I must withdraw from
> the operations of our little group.

With many of its principal actors already gone, a small notice
appeared in the *United Irishman* a few weeks later informing the
public that the Irish National Theatre Society was no more.

Of course, none of this happened: Horniman's shares
produced a windfall dividend in 1903 with which she bought
the Abbey Theatre building, Synge lived until 1909, and
Gregory (like everyone else) ignored Holloway's dramaturgical
advice. Nonetheless, it can be useful to imagine possible
alternatives to history if we are to overcome what Michael
André Bernstein has called the mental habit of
'backshadowing', 'a kind of retroactive foreshadowing' by
which past events are read in terms of the futures to which they
lead, as if those futures were in some way pre-ordained.[3] While
anyone looking into the early Abbey knows that it was a fragile
little creation in its formative years, and could have easily
collapsed at a number of points, we tend to exclude this
knowledge from our analyses. As early as October 1901, for
instance, Yeats declared in the first issue of *Samhain* that: 'the
Irish people are at that precise stage of their literary history
when imagination, shaped by many stirring events, desires
dramatic expression'.[4] At that point, the Irish Literary Theatre
was still a small group of amateurs who had staged only five
plays, none of which had run for more than a few nights,
reaching a combined audience representing fewer than attended
a week's run at any of the larger theatres.

Today, we read Yeats's words knowing that those few
productions were to evolve into a major theatrical institution
with an international reputation and a central role in subsequent
Irish culture. However, if we imagine for a moment an
alternative future, in which the Irish National Theatre Society
fizzled out in the winter of 1903, then Yeats's claims to have

created a national theatre with his little group of amateur actors in those early years might stand out in a different, harsher, light, marooned by the accidents of history. From such an unfamiliar perspective, the first thing that comes into focus is the astounding audacity of Yeats's pronouncements, whose confidence comes less from a realistic assessment of the actual work of the Irish Literary Theatre up to 1901 (of which Yeats himself would later be critical), than from a conviction that a national theatre was not only possible, but was an inevitable development in a nation's cultural history.

Indeed, for all of his much-discussed Nietzscheanism, Yeats inscribed the Irish Literary Theatre in a teleological narrative whose form is Hegelian, even if not consciously acknowledged as such. 'The spirit's acts are of an essential nature', writes Hegel in the second draft of his *Philosophical History of the World*:

> It makes itself in reality what it already is in itself, and therefore its own deed or creation.... And it is the same with the spirit of a nation; its activity consists in making itself into an actual world which also has an existence in space.[5]

For Yeats (and here he is not alone), the theatre is the paradigmatic manifestation of a national culture, in that it is the art form which most clearly transforms the 'spirit' into 'an actual world which also has an existence in space'. Indeed, the quotation from Wagner with which Yeats headed every edition of one of the early Abbey's magazines, the *Arrow*, puts it succinctly:

> In the Theatre there lies the spiritual seed and kernel of all national poetic and national moral culture. No other branch of Art can ever truly flourish or ever aid in cultivating the people until the Theatre's all-powerful assistance has been completely recognized and guaranteed.

Touring and the National Theatre

'If a dramatic club existed in one of the larger towns near', Yeats speculated in the 1904 edition of *Samhain*,

they could supply us not only with actors, should we need
them, in their own town, but with actors when we went to the
small towns and to the villages.[6]

In imagining a network of small theatres, locally based but
centrally linked and all capable of performing the same
repertoire, Yeats touches here on a possible form for a national
theatre. Indeed, in terms of its ability to create a sense of
solidarity among geographically distant individuals, this
speculative network of linked theatres may remind us of
Benedict Anderson's influential argument regarding the
relationship of print culture to the formation of a national
consciousness. Print, Anderson has argued, 'made it possible
for rapidly growing numbers of people to think about
themselves, and to relate themselves to others, in profoundly
new ways'. Anderson explains this idea by evoking an image of
spatially diffuse masses of individuals reading the morning
newspaper, and thereby participating in:

> a mass ceremony... performed in silent privacy, in the lair of the
> skull. Each communicant is well aware that the ceremony he
> performs is being replicated simultaneously by thousands (or
> millions) of others of whose existence he is confident, yet of
> whose identity he has not the slightest notion.[7]

In other words, print-capitalism – that is, the distribution of
identical copies of a newspaper or book over a wide
geographical area – is one of the features of modern culture
that allows an individual to share a kinship or communion with
thousands or millions of geographically distant and anonymous
others, facilitating the formation of a national consciousness.

However, if we look at theatre as performance, we find that
none of Anderson's arguments apply. A play in performance
takes place in a clearly demarcated space (usually a theatre
building) at a clearly defined time. The audience for any given
performance is limited to those people who are in the same
theatre at the same time. Members of an audience at a play are
not, in Anderson's phrase, an 'imagined community': they are a
real, *albeit* temporary, community whose relationship to one
another is clearly bounded by the temporal and spatial

parameters of the performance as event. Yeats's unrealized suggestion for a linked network of theatres all performing the same repertoire may take us a step nearer to the theatre as newspaper; however, even then there are still fundamental differences between the dynamic Anderson outlines, and the place of theatre in culture.

For Anderson, reading the newspaper is a 'ceremony... incessantly repeated at daily or half-daily intervals throughout the calendar. What more vivid figure for the secular, historically-clocked, imagined community can be envisioned?' The theatrical event is diametrically opposite in form. A particular production of a play is a unique event, existing for a fixed run and then disappearing to be replaced by something else. A revival, as any theatre-goer will attest, is a slight misnomer: there is always a sense in which every revival is a new production. In any case, few would dispute that a substantial part of the aesthetic pleasure (and economic value) of the theatre arises from the performance's status as a unique event. We could even take this further and argue that the performance of a given play is unique from night to night; at the very least, it must be acknowledged that all of the variables that go to make a night at the theatre – actors, audience, events outside the theatre – mean that one performance differs from another far more than one copy of the same newspaper differs from another.

In other words, the experience of watching a play in performance is not formally congruent with the experience of belonging to a *national* community; it is, instead, more like the experience of belonging to a *local* community. Unlike a national community, a local community is made up of individuals who share the same space at the same time, and thus exist in one another's presence. Living in the presence of others entails certain responsibilities, negotiations, and conventions, different in many respects to those required of the individuals who share the imagined community of the nation. In the theatre, these local responsibilities and conventions are clearly understood by audiences, and take the form of the protocols of clapping, interaction with the actors, dress codes, talking during the performance, cat-calling, etc. This is not 'communion ... in silent privacy in the lair of the skull'; it is a participatory act, carried out in the full presence of other members of a living community.

A clear logic emerges from this argument: in the absence of a newspaper-like network of theatres with a shared repertoire, if a theatre wants to make a claim to be national, it must tour. When the early Abbey, for instance, took a production on tour, it took a step closer to replicating the experience of shared national communion that Anderson identifies in the newspaper, in that at least the same event was shared by people spread over a wide geographical area. The audiences in Cork or Galway who watched a play that had been staged in Dublin, it could be argued, were sharing a cultural experience, *albeit* not simultaneously. Such an audience, it could be argued, was transformed from a local community, to become part of a wider national community that is both imagined and real, existing in imaginary communion with other audiences elsewhere in the national space, and simultaneously in real communion with other members of the national audience present in the theatre.

And yet, even with a touring production, there are moments in the history of the early Abbey which suggest that the tension between the local and the national at the heart of the theatrical event continues to pull in two different directions. For instance, when the Abbey brought *Riders to the Sea* to the Cork Opera House on 15 September 1907, the audience included Daniel Corkery who (along with Terence MacSwiney) formed the Cork Dramatic Society the following year. 'A nation's literature is an index to its mind', MacSwiney would later write in an essay entitled 'The Propagandist Playwright'; 'Literature is the Shrine of Freedom, its fortress, its banner, its charter'.[8] The emphasis here – as in Yeats's writing – on drama as *literature* is telling. Literature is part of print culture, and thus can be consumed nationally; when it came to theatre in performance, however, the emphasis switches from the national to the local. So, MacSwiney and Corkery founded the Cork Dramatic Society, as Corkery put it, 'to do for Cork what similar societies have done for Dublin and Belfast'.[9] When they sat in Cork Opera House on that

September evening, even if the content of the play before them on the stage was national in the sense of creating an image of nationality (as MacSwiney would later argue in relation to *Riders to the Sea*),[10] that image existed in tension with the experience of being part of a local audience, which in turn manifested itself as Corkery's determination to create a local theatre. In short, what begins as a *national* tour by a *national* theatre to foster a *national* theatre culture ultimately impels self-described nationalists to found a *local* theatre group.

What happened in Cork was not an isolated instance. In Belfast, Bulmer Hobson – another committed nationalist – was inspired by the early Abbey to found a theatre that would be 'an Ulster branch of the Irish Literary Theatre', the Ulster Literary Theatre.[11] However, from the outset, this tension between the national and the local is already present in the Ulster project, as is clear from the manifesto of the Ulster Literary Theatre, published in the first issue of *Ulad* in 1904:

> We recognize at the outset that our art of the drama will be different from that other Irish art of drama which speaks from the stage of the Irish National Theatre in Dublin, where two men, W.B. Yeats and Douglas Hyde, have set a model in Anglo-Irish and Gaelic plays with a success that is surprising and exhilarating. Dreamer, mystic, symbolist, Gaelic poet and propagandist have all spoken on the *Dublin stage*, and a fairly defined *local school* has been inaugurated [emphasis added].[12]

Note the shift from 'the Irish *National* Theatre', to the description of the 'National Theatre' as 'a fairly defined *local school*', which is then (later on in the passage) further qualified as a '*Leinster* school'. This shift in perspective is useful; from the banks of the Lagan, the Abbey looked not like a national theatre, but just one in a line of local, regional theatres. At the level of repertoire, this same slippage from the national to the local was apparent in Ulster Literary Theatre's choice of plays for its first season in 1902: Yeats's national allegory, *Cathleen ni Houlihan*, followed by James Cousins's Ulster dialect play, *The Racing Lug*.

In fact, if the intention of the early Abbey tours was to create a national theatre culture, its effect was precisely the

opposite: in the case of Corkery and Hobson, it produced a
desire for a *local* theatre. Indeed, we can push these examples
beyond the island of Ireland, for it is well documented that
while the Abbey tour to Glasgow in 1907 inspired Graham
Moffat to found a group that he called 'The Scottish National
Players', it also encouraged another group of Glaswegians to
form 'The Glasgow Repertory Theatre', whose prospectus
described the venture as 'Glasgow's own theatre'[13] – yet another
local theatre generated by a national theatre on tour.

By shifting our focus from the content of plays (whether as
dramatic scripts or as performance) to the experience of
theatre, we come to recognize that the experience of theatre is
fundamentally different from the experience of a shared print
culture, where all members share equally in an *imagined* sense of
community. Hence, the experience of the theatre as
performance always throws the national consciousness into
contrast; a given play may contribute to the creation of a
national consciousness by staging images of national solidarity,
but it can only do so while also bringing into being that which
resists the national, the local. Indeed, it could be argued that
this tension is at the heart of so much of the criticism directed
at the Abbey since it first adopted the title of a 'National
Theatre'; equally, it explains the vitality of the almost 800
amateur theatre companies around the island, most of whom
are deeply rooted in their local communities, as are a growing
number of subsidized professional theatres who conceive of
their mission in terms of presenting plays for a local audience.

Theatre Geography / National History

If theatre in performance creates an event that is by definition
local, even when it is toured, why do we persist in thinking of
the theatre as a national form? It may be that the answer to this
question brings us back to Anderson's equation of print-culture
with national identity; in particular, it may well be the case that
it is not the theatre *per se* that constitutes a national form, but
writing about the theatre which uses print culture to translate
local performances into a national form.

We can make this idea more concrete by turning back to the earliest attempts to construct historical narratives of Irish theatre, and by taking stock of the degree to which their sense of theatrical geography differs from our own. W.R. Chetwood's *General History of the Stage* (1749), Thomas Wilkes' *General View of the Stage* (1759), and Benjamin Victor's *History of the Theatres of London and Dublin From the Year 1730 to the Present* (1761) were written at a time when the spine of the English-speaking theatre world was a London–Dublin axis, along which actors and plays moved freely. For Chetwood or Victor, it mattered only in passing that David Garrick was English by birth and Charles Macklin was Irish. It was more important that these two actors shared the same theatrical world – a world in which Garrick first played Hamlet in Dublin's Smock Alley, while Macklin achieved his greatest success as Shylock in London's Drury Lane. This is not to say that when Garrick played Smock Alley, or Macklin played Drury Lane that either actor was 'on tour', in the sense of taking an entire production on the road. However, the forces that brought Garrick to Dublin and Macklin to London were not dissimilar from those that had carried Dublin-based companies to Cork and Belfast in this same period. Indeed, we can imagine a spectrum here, with the dedicated touring company on one end, and the local company that does not tour on the other; in the middle we have actors, (and other theatre personnel) who inhabit a theatrical geography that defies the fixed boundaries of nations or states; and, in the eighteenth century, this shifting middle ground was very much the mainstream.

It was always going to be problematic, therefore, to make the history of the theatre in Ireland match its actual theatrical geography; nonetheless, a generation or so after Chetwood and Victor, two theatre historians would try to do precisely this. The first volume of Robert Hitchcock's *Historical View of the Irish Stage* and Joseph Cooper Walker's 'Historical Essay on the Irish Stage' both appeared in 1788, in the midst of the debates over nationality and culture that would form the context for the foundation of the United Irishmen in 1791; the second volume of Hitchcock's *Historical View* appeared in 1794, at the same time as the Dublin United Irishmen were being suppressed.

While Hitchcock and Walker would not have considered
themselves to be Irish nationalists in any but the very broadest
sense of the term (although some of Walker's other writings
suggest what might be considered a kind of theoretical
nationalism), they nonetheless shared with the Irish political
thinkers who were their contemporaries the project of defining
the distinctive forms of Irish culture. In this respect, they
differed from their predecessors in their attempts to forge a
correspondence between theatrical geography and the island of
Ireland (even if, in practice, their focus is necessarily on
Dublin). Chetwood's earlier *General History* had traced the
spread of theatre from ancient Greece to Rome and
Elizabethan London, before moving on to a more detailed
history of the shared world of post-Restoration London and
Dublin theatre; by contrast, Hitchcock and Walker began with
the principle that theatrical geography and the geography of the
nation must coincide, and so when their subjects sail off to
London, the historian must wait on the quays (often in vain),
until an actor such as Robert Wilks or Thomas Sheridan or
Spranger Barry returned to Irish soil to rejoin the unfolding
narrative.

Apart from the unsettling mobility of actors, there was
another problem faced by Walker and Hitchcock in their
attempts to write a national theatre history: Irish theatre's
comparative modernity. The earlier generation of writers, with
their less rigid sense of theatrical geography, were not unduly
troubled by the fact that the first theatre building in Ireland
dated from the mid-1630s. Chetwood, for instance, begins his
General History of the Stage with accounts of Greek, Roman and
English Renaissance theatres, eventually reaching Ireland, where
he notes with bemused puzzlement: 'This Kingdom of *Ireland* is
one of the last in *Europe* where establish'd *Theatres* were erected'.
Wilkes, writing a *General History* of the theatre, begins his chapter
on Ireland with a similar observation: 'Yet, tho' there are many
good poems extant in that language [Irish], we have not been able
to find any that are dramatic'.[14] For Chetwood and Wilkes, theatre
was a fluid form that spills over national boundaries; if the tide is
at flood in one part of the world, it is bound to be ebbing

somewhere else. There may not have been much happening theatrically in Dublin in 1601, but in London there was always *Hamlet*. For Walker and Hitchcock, on the other hand, the gaps and absences in Ireland's theatre history, caused by the drift of theatre personnel beyond the island of Ireland, was much more vexing.

The difficulty in claiming the theatre for a national culture in the late-eighteenth and early nineteenth centuries was more than simply theoretical; it was a problem apparent to anyone who actually went to the theatre. As with much of the rest of Europe and North America, the theatre culture of Ireland in this period was increasingly dominated by the economics of touring. The most important Irish theatres of the nineteenth century – the Theatre Royal and Gaiety in Dublin, and the Opera Houses in Cork and Belfast – were all built as touring houses. However, unlike comparable theatres in London or New York, where there was a substantial home audience, economies of scale meant that productions were far more likely to tour into Ireland, rather than the other way around. This tendency increased in the middle decades of the century, but was apparent as early as 1821 when the Theatre Royal opened in Dublin. From the beginning, there were complaints that 'our national theatre' was managed by an Englishman, who presented Irish audiences with a repertoire that mirrored London tastes. 'If a native of India of the Hindoo Cast, were to succeed Mr. Morrison, as the keeper of his Tavern', sniped the *Theatrical Observer* on 7 March 1821,

> he might as well insist on his Guests eating no dishes but such as Hoschenee, Hurrabubbub, Rice, and Cayenne Pepper Soup, because the inhabitants of India prefer those viands to Beef Steaks and Potatoes.[15]

Given the fare on offer in Ireland's largest theatre at the time, it is not surprising that the nationalist Thomas Davis, for instance, wrote essays on just about every conceivable form of cultural production: painting, sculpture, architecture, music, poetry, fiction, historical writing, museum curatorship, publishing – but almost nothing on theatre. Indeed, apart from a series of largely anecdotal articles in the *Dublin University Magazine*, by the manager of the Theatre Royal in Dublin, J.W. Calcraft, and a few other bits and pieces, a national history of Irish theatre is one of the missing books in the library of nineteenth-century Ireland. The one major attempt to write a comprehensive piece of theatre history in nineteenth-century Ireland, W.J. Lawrence's 'Annals of the Old Belfast Stage', is a rambling, anecdotal, but nonetheless fairly inclusive chronicle of the many touring shows (and the relatively few home-produced shows) that played Belfast in the nineteenth century. It is telling, however, that in spite of Lawrence's considerable scholarly reputation, this work remains unpublished in the Linenhall Library to this day, having generated interest from only thirty-five subscribers when it was offered to the public in 1896.[16]

Here then was the dilemma: in a period in which the idea of an Irish 'national' culture was being constructed in terms of a narrative that, if it did not quite stretch back to the dawn of recorded history, was at least traceable to the early medieval period, the comparative modernity of the theatre in Ireland posed the disturbing possibility that the basic narrative of Irish nationality was flawed, that the Irish people had been telling themselves the wrong story. To admit theatre history into the narrative of Irish cultural history was to admit that Irish culture might not have been the pure, ancient lineage that was the touchstone of so much cultural debate in the nineteenth century; to accommodate the theatre, Irish cultural history had to find room for a non-indigenous art form, that had not only *arrived* in Ireland no earlier than the seventeenth century, but was continually *arriving* in the ongoing process of theatrical touring. Finally, when Ireland did produce its own theatre practitioners (as it did in considerable numbers throughout the eighteenth and nineteenth centuries), they showed an alarming tendency to slip off to London or New York in search of better prospects.

In short, without the sustaining narrative of a national theatre history, nineteenth-century Irish theatre was free to revel in its own modernity, and in its own rootlessness. This meant that there were no strong cultural arguments with which to resist the strong economic arguments for international touring. And so, in a mutually reinforcing spiral, in the same years that the *Nation* and its successors were defining the terms of Irish cultural nationalism, Irish audiences were watching an often rich and varied diet of theatre, of which only a small proportion originated in Ireland; and, in the reverse process, Irish theatre practitioners, from Boucicault to Barry Sullivan, were active on stages outside of Ireland. To make matters worse, while the balance of trade overwhelmingly brought theatre into Ireland in the mid-nineteenth century, there were no major Irish theatre companies with the resources to tour within Ireland, where they might – at least in theory – have contributed to the creation of a national theatre culture. Amidst such defiance of national geography, it is little wonder that Edward Martyn would ask in 1901: 'Is it not time that our dramatic art also should be placed on a national basis?'

A National Theatre?

If theatre in performance creates an event that is by definition local, why do we persist in thinking of the theatre as a national form? The answer to this question brings us back to the role of print culture in creating a national theatre culture. Theatre in performance may actively resist many of the features of print that make it so conducive to the creation of a national consciousness, but this does not prevent the theatrical experience from being translated into print. The publication of reviews, play scripts, and the accumulation of these sources in theatre histories re-configures the temporally and spatially specific form of performance into the temporally and spatially diffuse form of print.

When we read a review of a play, read a dramatic script, or read a work of theatre history, we are sharing with those geographically distant and anonymous others that sense of 'communion' of which Anderson speaks, bringing us all together as an imagined community. This was true for the readers of Walker's 'Historical Essay' in 1788; it was true for the readers of Yeats's essays in *Samhain*; and it is true for the reader of this essay today. When the theatrical event enters into print, it can contribute to the formation of a national consciousness, just like any other form of print. By the same token, there is an argument to be made that this means that the experience of theatre can only be truly national at one remove, after it has been mediated through the medium of print. Theatrical touring exists in the liminal space between the national theatre culture created by print, and the local theatre culture created by the moment of performance, and as such a properly historical theorization of the role of touring in Irish theatre is an important undertaking. Of course, a play may contribute to the creation of a national consciousness by staging images of national solidarity; and the print-generated expectations that an audience brings with them into the auditorium may create the illusion that the performance constitutes a national event. However, once the curtain goes up, it brings into being that which resists the national: the local audience. In the end, theatre histories may have worked for more than two centuries to define the spirit of a national theatre; and when a touring production from a 'national theatre' arrives in town, it may seem as if that spirit has been made flesh. However, in the moment of performance, as an audience comes together as a living, local community, that national culture recedes, and we glimpse an alternative, geographically diffuse, history of the Irish stage in which there is no national theatre.

---

[1] Edward Martyn, 'A Plea for a National Theatre in Ireland', *Samhain* 1 (October 1901), p.14.

[2] Joseph Holloway, *Joseph Holloway's Irish Theatre*, ed. Robert Hogan and Michael J. O'Neill (Carbondale, Illinois: Southern Illinois University Press, 1967), p.22.

[3] Michael André Bernstein, *Foregone Conclusions: Against Apocalyptic History* (Berkeley, California: University of California Press, 1994), p.16.

[4] W.B. Yeats, 'Windlestraws', *Samhain* 1 (October 1901), p.4.

[5] G.W.F. Hegel, *Lectures on the Philosophy of World History*, trans. H.B. Nisbet (Cambridge: Cambridge University Press, 1975), p.58.

[6] W.B. Yeats, 'Windlestraws', *Samhain* 4 (December 1904), p.5.

7 Benedict Anderson, *Imagined Communities: Reflections on the Origin and Spread of Nationalism*, revised edn (London: Verso, 1991), pp.35, 36.

8 Terence MacSwiney, *Principles of Freedom* (Dublin: Brian O'Higgins, 1936), p.123.

9 Patrick Maume, *Life that is Exile: Daniel Corkery and the Search for Irish Ireland* (Belfast: Institute of Irish Studies, Queen's University Belfast, 1993), pp.21, 26.

10 MacSwiney, *Principles of Freedom*, p.132.

11 Cited in Sam Hanna Bell, *The Theatre in Ulster* (Dublin: Gill and Macmillan, 1972), p.3.

12 'Editorial Notes', *Ulad: A Literary and Critical Magazine*, Vol. 1, 1 (November 1904), p.1.

13 Donald Campbell, *Playing for Scotland: A History of the Scottish Stage 1715-1965* (Edinburgh: Mercat Press, 1996), pp.92, 94.

14 Thomas Wilkes, *A General View of the Stage* (Dublin: W. Whetstone, 1759), p.305.

15 *Theatrical Observer*, 7 March 1821, p.19.

16 W.J. Lawrence, 'The Annals of the Old Belfast Stage', unpublished; Linenhall Library (1897), pp.iii.

PART TWO:

TOURING IN AND OUT OF IRELAND

7 | Eighteenth-Century Theatrical Touring and Irish Popular Culture

Helen Burke

In 1713, the directors of the Smock Alley theatre rented an old malt house in a yard just off Great Street (now South Main Street) in Cork city, and after they finished their regular season in Dublin that year, they brought their company to that improvised playhouse to perform for the duration of the summer. This was the first extended visit by a Theatre Royal company to an Irish provincial city in the eighteenth century but it was by no means the last. By the 1730s, the Dublin Theatre Royal company was playing in Cork on a regular basis during the summer months and, by the 1760s, it was also taking in Limerick and Waterford on its summer tour, generally timing its visit to coincide with assizes, races, or other major society events in these towns. After Belfast established its own resident company in the 1770s, the Theatre Royal company in that city also began touring, to Derry and sometimes Newry, so that by the end of eighteenth century, there was a well established northern, as well as a southern, summer theatrical touring circuit. Meanwhile, many of the smaller towns that were not on these circuits were receiving regular visits from strolling companies. Often headed by actors from Dublin or London, such itinerant groups began crisscrossing the country in the early eighteenth century so that, by the end of the century, there was scarcely a town of any size in Ireland that was not provided with theatrical entertainment of this kind, at least for some period during the year.

But how were these urban visitors received by the 'native' (that is, Irish Catholic) communities through which they passed, and what impact did their theatre have on Irish popular culture, the culture of the Irish masses? In *The Irish Stage in the County Towns*, William Smith Clark attempts to answer these difficult questions.[1] Since his is the only book-length study of the eighteenth-century Irish provincial theatre, it seems appropriate to rehearse his conclusions. Basically, Clark argues that theatrical touring had a very significant impact on Irish popular culture because it helped disseminate the dramatic arts among a people who had no previous knowledge of them, and he suggests that this new theatrical tradition took hold because all sections of the Irish population were very receptive to the visiting acting companies. 'A sociable, beneficent attitude in a majority of the upper classes, and a remarkable sense of humour in the lower orders', he writes, 'made the eighteenth-century Irish towns an alluring "Ultima Thule" for English as well as native performers' (p.1). Because Clark detects a 'mild, strain of cultural Irishism' in the repertoire of these touring companies (p.290), he also suggests that this activity had some larger nationalist implications. Summing up what he takes to be the cultural and political achievement of the touring companies in the last sentence of his book, Clark writes: '[M]odestly oriented toward an incipient nationalism, the stage activity of this period, founded a strong, country-wide taste for the theatre amongst an instinctively gifted people who had no folk heritage in that art' (p.291).

In this essay, however, I will argue that the touring company was less a vehicle for disseminating a dominant English performance tradition than a site of negotiation between this tradition and a no less vital though subordinate native Irish performance tradition, and I will suggest that the fractured, bicultural productions that came out of this contact zone are better read as evidence of an emergent Irish modernism rather than an emergent Irish nationalism. To recover this alternate history, it is necessary to subject the sources that Clark uses for his comments on reception – primarily players' memoirs – to the same kind of critical scrutiny that we now apply to other early ethnographic and travel writing, seeing them not as transparent accounts of reality but rather as productions of a certain kind of historically-situated spectator who is writing for an equally situated kind of audience.[2] John Bernard's *Retrospections of the Stage* is a case in point.[3] This work by an English comic actor who toured all over Ireland in the early 1780s serves as the direct source for Clark's remarks about Ireland being an alluring 'Ultima Thule' for visiting actors because of the receptive attitude of its people (p.325). But these remarks must be read in the context of their author's larger effort to shape his travel narrative to fit the 'Rambles through Teagueland' genre of travel writing then in vogue in the English literary marketplace – a mode of writing that tended to represent the native Irish as good-natured, though buffoonish, primitives, and the country itself as a rural backwater where the English visitor could experience a welcome release from the pressures of modernity. Bernard also signals that this is his intent when he prefaces the account of his first Irish visit with the following remarks: 'Ireland, dear Ireland, land of whisky and waggery, of palaver and "purtaties," what a charm was in thy name for the exorcism of blue devils! What a prospect in thy sound of a new era in life, a Saturnalian existence of long laughing nights, and strange eventful days' (p.222). The narrator of the 'Teagueland' travel narrative is typically such a detached, urbane spectator – one who adopts this removed 'prospect' perspective towards the Irish scene.[4]

If we look beyond Bernard's own 'palaver', however, and focus instead on the actual events he narrates, we realize that travelling theatre companies did not maintain this kind of distance from the people or their culture, and we also realize that 'dear Ireland' itself was a far more complex place than Bernard's initial remarks suggest. Theatrical tours were first and foremost *travel* events, and like all travelling experiences in unfamiliar territory they exposed those on them to new dangers as well as opportunities, and created the conditions both for negative and positive interactions with local populations. Richard Daly's troupe, the Dublin company that Bernard joined for a Cork-Limerick tour in the summer of 1782, also seemed to have experienced more than its share of the former negative kind of interactions. Some of these unpleasant encounters – the run-ins with inn-keepers, shopkeepers, dishonest maid-servants, and highwaymen[5] – could equally have happened to a traveller in contemporary England but a number of them were also unique to Ireland and pointed to the larger cultural and political tensions that lay just beneath the surface of eighteenth-century Irish life. If the whole company thought it wise to hotfoot it out of 'Butterfelt' [Buttevant], County Cork, for example, after Bob Bowles (Bernard's fellow comedian) stole a skull from a 'mass of human skulls piled up in the form of a cone' in the ancient abbey in that town, it was because they believed they had touched on such a cultural and political nerve (pp.259-60). Earlier on, Bernard and Bowles had been guided around the abbey by Michael O'Galloghan, the abbey's sacristan, and when Bernard told the company what this old man had said about these skulls – that they were:

> the remains of a dreadful battle that had been fought in the neighbourhood many centuries previous, and, that a priest having blessed them, a sacred influence consisted in their safe preservation (p.260)

– the company thought it best to make a hasty exit from the region. Bowles' joke was 'rather too grave', Bernard relates, and they feared 'serious consequences might ensue' (pp.260-61).

Even a problematic incident like this, however, also indicated that the conditions existed in eighteenth-century rural Ireland for a positive interaction between the local population and the visiting theatrical company. Contrary to Bernard's colonialist type of imaginings – and also, it should be noted, contrary to the imaginings of later Irish nationalist writers – the eighteenth-century native Irish people were not frozen in their traumatic past. Instead, as this incident indicates, they existed in a state of 'translation' in Seamus Deane's sense of the word; that is, they were making the adjustments necessary to deal with the social and economic world that was impinging on them in the wake of conquest and expropriation.⁶ Michael O'Galloghan, the old man whom the actors met in the abbey, may have been grounded in the area's conflicted history, for example, but (as he told the players) he also regularly picked up 'some addition to his resources, by showing the "ould ones" to travelers' (p.258), and he obviously had learned sufficient English to be able to communicate with, and even amuse, his customers when he gave them these tours. He was, in effect, part of the new tourism industry that was closely attached to the larger entertainment business in the late eighteenth century – a connection that Bernard underlines when he says (in relation to this old man's stories) that 'the author of the "Arabian Nights Entertainments" never invented more startling impossibilities, nor Jack Palmer in his best days, as "Young Wilding" ever gave deliverance to falsehood more glibly' (p.259). The fact that Bernard and Bowles had decided to stop and explore the abbey and take this tour as they were passing through Buttevant on the return leg of their southern trip also reveals that the theatrical community was at least interested in the local cultures and communities that they encountered on their travels. Even if this particular encounter did not result in a particularly positive exchange, the conditions for such an interaction clearly were there.

A second incident from this southern tour – Bernard's encounter with what he calls 'wild Irish theatricals' (p.240) – also reveals that some other touring theatrical companies were, in fact, engaging in these more positive ways with this community and culture in 'translation', though to see this dynamic at work, we again have to push against the Anglo-centric grain of Bernard's narrative. The encounter with 'wild Irish theatricals' occurred after Bernard and some other members of his company accepted an invitation from the manager of the 'Mallow Theatre' (p.238) to attend a play in his house and, though Bernard does not specifically state this, it seems likely that this manager was the leader of one of those less prestigious troupes of strollers that visited the smaller Irish towns. Whereas Bernard's own troupe included such luminaries of the London stage as John and Stephen Kemble, Lee Digges and Mrs Crouch (then Miss Phillips) (p.283), the Mallow company's principal comedian was a Mr Waker who had lost his job on the Dublin stage after he developed growths on his face, and the actor who played the serious roles was 'a Mr. McShane' whose only claim to being a 'high' tragedian was his six-feet-two height (pp.244-5). Bernard's sense of professional rivalry, as well as his ongoing effort to amuse his urban English reader, lead him to stress what he takes to be the most idiosyncratic features of this Irish theatrical scene. Instead of being brought to a regular playhouse, he relates that he was led by a 'juvenile bog-trotter' (p.240) down puddle-filled, narrow lanes to a barn that had been crudely refurbished as a theatre and, in that location, he explains, the most memorable entertainment was not the comedy or the tragedy but rather the antics of the rural Irish audience in the hayloft turned gallery. Before the play started, Bernard reports, these audience members loudly discussed the health of their animals, jokingly demanded particular tunes from the musicians (a fiddler and a drummer), and then engaged in a 'general dance' which continued with 'wild shrieks and cries' until the fiddler broke a string and was pelted by a shower of potatoes for his pains (pp.241-44).

This supposedly idiosyncratic theatrical scene, however, can also be read as a scene of a negotiation between an English performance tradition and a native-Irish performance tradition – one that, Clark's comments to the contrary, was very much alive in the eighteenth century. As performance studies have pointed out, *all* cultures have some kind of 'theatre' in the sense that all cultures have some kind of storytelling and performing arts, and Gaelic Ireland was no exception to this rule. Pre-Cromwellian Gaelic society, as Alan Fletcher has so persuasively shown, had a range of professional entertainers – jesters, acrobats, satirists, tricksters – who performed at assemblies and at feasts.[7] Even after the downfall of the Irish aristocracy, this tradition also persisted (albeit it in an altered form) at the popular level. Eighteenth-century rural Ireland had its *seanchaí*, its musicians, its singers, its dancers, and even its

local actors – 'strawboys', mummers, and 'borekeen' men –
who performed in dramatic 'games' at weddings, wakes,
Christmas festivities, 'patterns' and fairs.[8] In the Irish
performative tradition, too, as the case of the wake illustrates,
dramatic acting was generally nested within other forms of
amusements such as fiddle-playing, storytelling, singing,
dancing, strength contests; and the 'actors' in one of these
amusements could easily become the audience in another.
Mourners could move seamlessly from listening respectfully to
the keening women in one room, for instance, to acting in a
bawdy and boisterous mock 'Marrying game' in another room.[9]
If the Mallow audience felt that the evening's amusement
should include talking, joking and dancing, and if they thought
that they themselves should provide some of these entertainments, their behaviour could be seen as a carry-over from
this popular performance tradition, and the location itself
would undoubtedly have further encouraged this kind of
cultural transfer. Barns were commonly used as the site for
wake games and dances in eighteenth-century rural Ireland and,
by all accounts, such entertainments were every bit as lively and
interactive as the one Bernard describes. In William Carleton's
description of a Christmas Eve barn dance in pre-Famine
Ireland, for instance, people also called for tunes and joked with
the fiddler and, in both situations, the whole community, young
and old, took part in the dance.[10]

But if the rambunctious dance took place in this particular
barn, it was also because of the Mallow manager's willingness to
accommodate local customs and practices in his playhouse.
(From Bernard's account we can gather that he waited patiently
until the barn dance was over before raising the curtain.) And
the very absence of a commentary on audience behaviour *after*
the curtain was lifted for the play – Bernard says he
remembered nothing of this stage performance other than the
poor quality of the acting – also indicates that the audience was
similarly willing to accommodate the customs and practices of
the urban visitors. As soon as this dance was over, we can
gather, these supposedly 'wild Irish' spectators sat quietly
through the rest of the evening's entertainment – presumably

the standard fare of the contemporary English theatre. There was a show of tolerance on both sides and, even if Bernard failed to see the productive side of this encounter, this readiness to accommodate differences was generating a new kind of cross-cultural performance space.

The memoirs of two other English comedians, John Edwin and Thomas Snagg, also show how the material circumstances of travel and the changing nature of Irish society itself could help generate these new kinds of cross-cultural performance spaces and these new kinds of cross-cultural alliances. The seventeen-year old Edwin was playing at Smock Alley in 1766 when he was invited by one of the veteran actors of the company, Thomas Ryder, to play with the troupe that the latter was leading to Waterford for the summer season. On his way to Waterford and back the perpetually penniless young actor lived very much like an itinerant Irish labourer; he stayed at shebeen houses, frequented taverns, and ate, drank and socialized with the locals. These encounters also introduced him to Irish popular culture and it is evident, even from his self-consciously droll descriptions, that he was an active participant in this culture's practices and rites. When one of his Waterford drinking companions, Patrick O'Keaghehan, was drowned on his way home from a shebeen house in the city, for example, Edwin attended a traditional Irish wake and, there, after a bit of prodding from the assembly, he joined in such customary wake rituals as pipe smoking, drinking and keening, even learning a verse of a song (which he transcribes) from Shelah Mullowney, one of the keening women.[11] Later, as they made their way on foot back to Dublin, Edwin and some of his fellow players also participated in a number of sessions with local singers and musicians and, in the process, new kinds of cross-cultural entertainments were born. One such entertainment, for instance, occurred on a heath where Edwin and three of his strolling companions had decided to amuse themselves by doing the witches' dance from *Macbeth* to the accompaniment of their own singing. This odd, outdoor performance attracted the attention of some 'rustics' including a blind harpist who was 'well skilled in the sweet airs of Carolan' and despite this harpist's lack of knowledge of the English music and dance tradition – Edwin somewhat ungraciously says of him that 'he knew as much about Vestris, and the graces, as a haberdasher does of Hebrew' (p.77) – this cross-cultural collaboration was a resounding success, eliciting positive reviews from all involved. Their 'combination of drolleries occasioned much genuine laughter', Edwin writes, 'and the actors and their audience parted infinitely pleased with each other' (p.79).

The twenty-four year old Thomas Snagg (stage name Thomas Wilks) had similar productive kinds of interactions when he set out on his travels to Ireland some three years later, and his account reveals that the native Irish population's own mobility at this time also helped create the conditions that made possible these more equitable kinds of exchanges. Snagg's first interaction with the Irish people, indeed, was with Irish migrants. On the boat over from Liverpool to Newry, he and a fellow actor helped pay for biscuits and potatoes for the hold passengers who had run out of provisions in the unexpectedly lengthy and stormy crossing, and from his description of these passengers – they were 'men and women ... who had been earning money by harvest work and labour and [who were now] returning to their native home'[12] – it is clear that they were 'spalpeens' or migrant Irish farm labourers. Such migrant workers were becoming an increasing feature of the eighteenth-century Irish and English landscapes. From mid-century on, as Louis Cullen and others have pointed out, a more complex farming system as well as the growth of the manufacturing industry encouraged many in rural Ireland to take to the road and become 'strollers' in search of work and a better life.[13] As migrants and strollers themselves, however, touring players also stood in need of hospitality and, as Snagg's subsequent account shows, they received this hospitality from some of the better-off Irish travellers they met while on this trip. When the two actors landed on the Irish shore, for example, the ship's captain – presumably an Irishman – led them to his mud-walled cabin near Warrenpoint and gave them 'a supper prepared with plenty of wine, spirits and all the hospitality for which the Country is so justly renowned' (p.65). And when they reached the 'New

Inn' at Newry the next day (they were making their way to
Dublin), they were entertained for two successive nights by a
piper who had asked their landlord for 'the honour to play to
the strangers and welcome them to Newry' (p.65). This Irish
musician's ability to negotiate on equal terms with these English
'strangers' also suggests that he was a man who had travelled, if
not between countries, then at least between cultures. Snagg
writes:

> Instead of the miserable poor and blind harpers who often
> accost you in Wales, a polite well-dressed man presented
> himself with freedom and gentility. We became 'jolly
> companions every one' and Mr. Fitzgerald piped most
> admirably (for he was then a good but afterwards a renowned
> player) and sang and drank and enjoyed his joke with the best
> of us, nor indeed was he behind in repartee and good company,
> and we spent the night with hilarity and bacchanalian joy (p.65).

Like his more famous eighteenth-century counterpart, the
harpist Turlough Carolan, this Mr Fitzgerald had clearly
mastered dominant as well as subaltern cultural idioms and, like
Carolan too, these dual-culture skills allowed him to cross easily
between the Gaelic Irish and the English-speaking worlds.[14]

But entertainers with Mr Fitzgerald's dual-culture skills were
also making their way in increasing numbers into theatrical
companies in the second half of the eighteenth century.[15] It is
thus the record of *these* kinds of subjects – the memoirs and
dramatic productions of native touring players and playwrights
– that we must also examine if we are to understand fully the
role of the travelling companies in eighteenth-century Ireland.
In an essay entitled 'Traveling Cultures', the anthropologist
James Clifford argues that the tours and detours of 'ex-centric
natives' – natives who travel away from, or who migrate back
and forth from, their community of origin – are as valuable a
source of knowledge about a particular culture as accounts
based on the observation of settled or 'rooted' natives.[16] He
suggests that if we look more closely at the productions of
those 'traveling "indigenous" culture-makers', we begin to
understand the complexity and the modernity of so-called
primitive cultures: 'Constructed and disputed *historicities*, sites of

displacement, interference, and interaction, come more sharply into view' (p.101). The dramatic productions of 'ex-centric' native Irish players and writers provide a similar window into the modernity of eighteenth-century Irish popular culture. And, as we will see if we look at the performances of the man whom Clark (p.3) describes as 'one of the century's outstanding itinerant comedians' – John O'Keeffe – the touring companies helped bring these 'ex-centric natives' and their unsettling productions into view.

When *Recollections of the Life of John O'Keeffe* was published in 1826, it was criticized by the *Monthly Review* for lacking 'chronological order' and for having the 'appearance of mere fantastic medley'.[17] Similar charges were levelled at the playwright himself. In an earlier biographical essay, for instance, the *Monthly Mirror* suggested that the young O'Keeffe's repeated career shifts proved that 'he had no fixed principles' and was guided only by 'Whim'.[18] If O'Keeffe's life and writings seemed disconnected and disordered, however, then so too was the community into which he was born, and the reasons behind that disorder lay in Ireland's contentious history. O'Keeffe was born in Dublin in 1747 into a Catholic family that was already 'ex-centric' in the sense that it had migrated from the country to the city after losing its land in the Jacobite wars. From O'Keeffe's own account of his childhood, it is clear that his parents had passed on the trauma of this dislocation to his generation. When he was very young, his father and mother (an O'Connor) led him over the lands in Offaly and Wexford that had once belonged to their respective families and, as he also relates, he and his brother Dan would constantly console themselves for their lowly social status by remembering an old family parchment that proved they were entitled to bear the arms of the *Kings of Fermoy*.[19] The education John received was designed to equip him to join the Catholic community's fight to restore such lost glories. He was given a classical education by a Jesuit priest (p.2), and then, according to his daughter, he was sent to Mr West's academy to study 'fortification and drawing' in preparation for 'foreign military service' – that is, for a life abroad with the 'Wild Geese'.[20]

But, as the *Recollections* also reveal, John detoured at an early age from the family plan. He used the skills he had acquired firstly to paint portraits and landscapes for the very elite who had dispossessed families such as his own, and in his late teens he made yet a still more dramatic detour (in all senses of the word) when he decided to go on the stage.[21] If this career decision brought him still further into contact with the English-speaking world, it also, ironically, led him back to the very Irish countryside that his family had left. He began his acting career with Mossop's Smock Alley company in Dublin in 1765-66.[22] But between then and 1781 when he finally emigrated to England, the young O'Keeffe travelled the length and breadth of Ireland, performing with whatever theatrical company would give him work.[23] It seems likely that he was with Thomas Ryder's troupe in Waterford in 1767 (the year after Edwin made that trip), for example, and when Mossop's company went bankrupt in 1769-70, O'Keeffe joined Ryder's company again for a northern tour that lasted the whole winter season.[24] During the 1770s, while he was playing on the Dublin stage, O'Keeffe was also a regular summer visitor to Cork and Limerick as part of the 'commonwealth company' of the Limerick man Tottenham Heaphy, who was to become his father-in-law.[25]

O'Keeffe, then, brought all this 'ex-centric native' experience to bear on the dramatic acts that he began to create for these touring companies and, as we will see, the conditions of touring facilitated the production of his kind of unsettling dramatic act. One of his earliest and most popular attempts at the drama, for example, was 'Tony Lumpkin's Rambles [or Frolicks]',[26] and this one-man act, which he first brought out in Cork in 1773, fore-grounded the perspective of the dislocated and eccentric rural subject when it made Tony Lumpkin the central consciousness. This country trickster character from Goldsmith's comedy was now set down in the middle of the town, and his imaginary travels through the urban landscape became the vehicle for delivering a satirical commentary on city life and contemporary fashions. The advertisement for O'Keeffe's benefit night performance in this role in Cork on 4 October 1780, for example, reads as follows:

After the play, an Histrionic Interlocution,
called, TONY LUMKIN'S Frolicks thro' Cork
By Mr. O'Keeffe,

With a descriptive view of the public Edifices, Streets, Taverns,
Coffee-houses, Red-house-walk, Sunday's well, Etc. Humorous
and Satirical Remarks; Whimsical Adventures, Anecdotes, Etc,
as they may have recently occurred, a Tavern Dinner, Dyke-
house Breakfast, Bet Bouncer full dressed, complete Female
Macaroni for 1780, Tony and Bet in Masks, correct pictures of
a Masquerade and Fashionable Drum, Captain, Quaker,
Dutchman, Patriot, and Lawyer at Cards, a Passage from
England, Tony and Bet at the Play, Etc.[27]

This kind of provincial-based satire – the act implicitly
valorized the provincial over the metropolitan point of view –
would also have had particular appeal for a Cork audience who
were themselves often cast as uncouth provincials in Dublin
and London. And, at a time when the struggle for free trade
and parliamentary independence was at its most intense in
Ireland, the mocking remarks on those women who slavishly
followed London fashions – Tony's tavern-maid girlfriend, Bet
Bouncer, has now become a 'complete Female Macaroni' –
would have had particular appeal for the 'country' or 'patriot'
faction in this audience. An account that appeared in a letter to
a Cork paper during this 1780s tour also suggests that a
Swiftian-inflected satire of imported female fashions was the
main focus of O'Keeffe's act during this time:

When the Tragedy ended, Mr. O'Keeffe made his appearance as
Tony Lumpkin, in which character for near half an hour,
without any auxiliary or stage assistant he amused a very
brilliant audience, with a most laughable interlude on the follies
of Dress. His principal object was the Female World, he
amused with innocence and rallied with respectful delicacy. He
touched pleasingly on the Houses of Recreation in the environs
of this City, and kept the Theatre in an uproar of applause.[28]

At a broader epistemological level, however, this kind of
satirical travelogue act also subverted 'the gaze' that prevailed in
most dominant-culture representations of the native Irishman.
As we have seen, the English spectator in the typical Irish

travelogue at this time tended to see the Irish native and his culture as buffoonish and 'wild', and (as is well known) this perspective was reproduced in the drama throughout the eighteenth century with the figure of the stage Irishman.[29] When the 'ex-centric native' perspective was central, however, as in this Tony Lumpkin act, it was the Anglicized metropolitan subject and his/her customs and manners who appeared ridiculous and freakish – a reverse appropriation that served ultimately to undermine the notion that there was any one privileged way of looking at culture.

By bringing his Irish landscape 'views' on the stage in a more literal sense while on such tours, O'Keeffe similarly undermined the notion that there is any one way of looking at Irish history and, again, the provincial tour would have facilitated the production of this double-sided historical perspective on the stage. On the benefit night mentioned above, for example, the Tony Lumpkin act was followed by a new pantomime entitled 'The Rakes of Mallow; or Harlequin Everywhere', and, according to newspaper advertisements, 'new scenes' were 'Painted from Drawings made on the spot' for this show. These new scenes included 'a view of Mallow Spa; with the Canal, Public Walk, and Country Adjacent, The Ruins of Kilmallock, and Ancient Castle of Buttevant'.[30] The advertisement does not specifically state that O'Keeffe himself did these 'Drawings' but it seems likely that he did since, as his *Recollections* reveal, he was continually painting local 'views' of the countryside at this time both for the purpose of selling these scenes to the local elite and for creating scenery for his localized dramas.[31] In his memoir too, O'Keeffe describes this exact north Cork/- Limerick topography, which he says he saw while on the road (pp.223-28), and he would have recognized its appeal for a Cork and Limerick audience who would have been familiar with that landscape.

But this countryside and its ruins would also have had a special appeal for O'Keeffe himself since north Cork had also been the hereditary home of the O'Keeffes (Fermoy, where the O'Keeffes were once 'Kings', is, like Mallow, on the Blackwater river). And, indeed, when the playwright comments on the ruins and deserted castles in this north Cork/Limerick landscape, an uncharacteristic elegiac note creeps into his memoir, making him sound momentarily like the eighteenth-century Gaelic poet of the Munster dispossessed, Aogán Ó Rathaille. His account of the town of Kilmallock, once the home of the Desmond Geraldines, for example, seems to borrow from the contemporary *aisling* poem; he writes that it appeared to him 'the court of the Queen of Silence', its only inhabitants being 'a few country people, living in the tops and bottoms of these castle-houses like birds and rabbits' (p.227). There is no way of knowing, of course, if the ruin scenes that appeared on the Cork stage conveyed a similar sense of desolation and loss but by appearing in proximity to the orderly Mallow town views – the Spa, the Canal, the Public Walk that all bore testimony to the 'improving' spirit of eighteenth-century Protestant Ireland – they would, at least, have gestured at this other history, creating a double perspective that again dislocated the hegemonic gaze.

In creating these kinds of fragmented landscapes and these disorienting, if comical, stream-of-consciousness dramatic 'interlocutions', however, O'Keeffe and a number of the other 'ex-centric' native actor/writers who worked alongside him during this period also put themselves in the tradition of Irish modernism – a tradition that happened *avant la lettre* in Ireland. As Luke Gibbons notes, Ireland did not have to wait until the twentieth century to experience the shock of modernity; the 'antinomies of colonial rule' produced a similar disorientation and, as he points out, it activated modernism's characteristic language of montage – 'the structuring of identity as the juxtaposition and commingling of opposites' – in a number of earlier Irish literary and dramatic works. Gibbons cites Dion Boucicault's abruptly shifting stage plots and his revolutionary stage craft as an example of this modernism *avant la lettre*.[32] But he could equally have pointed to the rapidly moving, comic dramatic pastiches of John O'Keeffe or Robert Owenson – to mention another famous native performer/dramatist from this period.

Owenson created dramatic acts that were formally similar to O'Keeffe's, while also doing his own, even more daring, riff on the hybridized dramatic tradition that was emerging from the theatrical contact zone. Like O'Keeffe, Owenson used the frame of a 'Tour' to create a humorous entertainment that centred around descriptions of topical events and local landscapes; his benefit performances in Cork in 1779 and 1780, for example, included such acts as 'Larry O'Shaughnessy's Tour Through Dublin with his Return to Cork' and 'The Humours of St. Patrick's Day, or Manus McWhackum's Journey to Cork and His Ramble to Mardyke Field to See the Review'.[33] And, like O'Keeffe too, he frequently used his acts to draw together elements from the native Irish and English traditions in a new, unorthodox mix. One of the most popular musical acts that he wrote and performed on Dublin and provincial stages, for instance, was an original musical 'Prelude' (later subtitled 'The Irish Actor; or the Recruiting Manager'), and while playing this strolling Irish actor role – the part of Phelim Flanagan – on the Cork stage for the first time in 1778, Owenson sang two songs from the Irish tradition: *Pléaráca na Ruarcach* and *Éamonn an Chnoic*.[34]

In singing these Gaelic songs in this role, however, Owenson also gave a specifically native Irish cast to this migrant figure and, by means of his bilingual act, he also introduced a subversive musical counterpart to what we can assume was the stage-Irish speech of Phelim.[35] *Éamonn an Chnoic*, for example, as at least some in the Cork audience would have known, was based on the life of the Tipperary rapparee, Edmund O'Ryan, who turned outlaw when he lost his lands after the seventeenth-century wars.[36] At the most obvious level, this song gives voice to this dispossessed Irishman's grievances through its 'interlocution'. The song begins, for instance, with a young girl asking to know who is outside, banging on her closed door, and in response, Éamonn says:

> Mise Éamonn an Chnoic, atá báite fuar fliuch
> Ó shíor-shiúl sléibhte is gleannta

(I'm Éamonn of the hills, and I'm drowned, cold and wet,
From endlessly walking the mountains and glens)

As someone who has been dislocated and sent 'endlessly
walking', however, Éamonn an Chnoic is also a figure for the
Irish diasporic subject who began his global travelling in the
eighteenth century, and it is the history of these undoubtedly
contemporary kinds of Irish subjects that Owenson would have
also evoked with this song. The near-starving *spalpeens* whom
Snagg met on the Liverpool-Newry boat, for example, were
also 'endlessly walking' in their quest for work and a better life.

The larger significance of the travelling company, then, was
that it helped generate a theatre suitable for a people and a
culture that was in flux and in 'translation'. After centuries of
invasions and plantations, Irish popular culture was itself a
'combination of drolleries' (to use Edwin's term) from different
cultural traditions and pasts. And, with the advent of
modernity, the native Irish subject was increasingly like the 'ex-
centric'/eccentric migratory figures that O'Keeffe, Owenson,
and others brought on to the stage. The travelling theatre,
precisely because it was a theatre in motion – one that was open
to the improvisatory, the local, the topical – provided a space
where those anomalous subjects could speak and where their
anomalous experiences could be shaped into dramatic art.

---

[1] William Smith Clark, *The Irish Stage in the County Towns, 1720-1800*
(Oxford: Clarendon Press, 1965). Subsequent page references are
included in the text.

[2] For an example of this kind of reading in a non-Irish context see Mary
Louise Pratt, *Imperial Eyes: Travel Writing and Transculturation* (London:
Routledge, 1992).

[3] John Bernard, *Retrospections of the Stage*, volume one (London, 1830).
Subsequent references are to this volume and are included in the text.

[4] See Luke Gibbons, 'Topographies of Terror: Killarney and the Politics
of the Sublime', *South Atlantic Quarterly* 95 (1996), p.28.

[5] For example, Bernard and his fellow comedian Bob Bowles were
chased out of a shop in Limerick by an irate shopkeeper; Bowles was
robbed of his clothes by a chamber-maid in Cork; and Bernard and
several of the company were attacked by robbers on the
Cork/Dublin road (Bernard, *Retrospections*, pp.257-58, 263, 269).

[6] Seamus Deane, 'Introduction' in Terry Eagleton, Frederic Jameson and Edward Said (eds.), *Nationalism, Colonialism, and Literature* (Minneapolis: University of Minnesota Press, 1990), p.14.

[7] Alan J. Fletcher, *Drama, Performance, and Polity in Pre-Cromwellian Ireland* (Toronto: University of Toronto Press, 2000), pp.9-60.

[8] See Seán Ó Súilleabháin, *Irish Wake Amusements* (Cork: Mercier Press, 1967); Alan Gailey, *Irish Folk Drama* (Cork: Mercier Press, 1969); Gearóid Ó Crualaoich, 'The "Merry Wake"' in James S. Donnelly and Kerby A. Miller (eds.), *Irish Popular Culture* (Dublin: Irish Academic Press, 1998), pp.173-200; Georges Dennis Zimmermann, *The Irish Storyteller* (Dublin: Four Courts Press, 2001).

[9] See Ó Súilleabháin, *Irish Wake Amusements*, pp.26-55, 96-99; Ó Crualaoich, 'The "Merry Wake"', pp.173-200.

[10] William Carleton, *Traits and Stories of the Irish Peasantry*, volume one (Gerrards Cross: Colin Smythe, 1990; first published 1842-44), pp.339-41.

[11] John Edwin, *The Eccentricities of John Edwin, Comedian*, volume one (Dublin, 1791), pp.64-67. Subsequent page references are also to this volume and are included in the text.

[12] Thomas Snagg, *Recollections of Occurrences*, ed. Harold Hobson (London: Dropmore Press, 1951), p.63. Subsequent page references are included in the text.

[13] Louis Cullen, 'Economic Development, 1750-1800' in T.W. Moody and W.E. Vaughan (eds.), *A New History of Ireland*, volume four (Oxford: Clarendon Press, 1988), pp.168-71. See also Donald MacRaild, *Irish Migrants in Modern Britain, 1750-1922* (New York: St. Martin's Press, 1999), pp.13-41.

[14] See Donal O'Sullivan, *Carolan, the Life, Times and Music of an Irish Harper* (London: Routledge and Kegan Paul, 1958); Frank Llewelyn Harrison, 'Music, Poetry and Polity in the Age of Swift', *Eighteenth-Century Ireland* 1 (1986), pp.37-63.

[15] See my *Riotous Performances: The Struggle for Hegemony in the Irish Theatre, 1712-1784* (Notre Dame, Indiana: University of Notre Dame, 2003), chapters three and seven.

[16] James Clifford, 'Traveling Cultures' in Lawrence Grossberg, Cary Nelson, and Paula A. Treichler (eds.), *Cultural Studies* (New York and London: Routledge, 1992), pp.96-116.

[17] *Monthly Review*, n.s. 3, 1826, pp.344-345.

[18] *Monthly Mirror*, December 1797, p.324.

[19] *Recollections of the Life of John O'Keeffe*, volume one (London, 1826; reprint New York and London: Blom, 1969), pp.7-8. Subsequent references are to this volume and are included in the text.

[20] Adelaide O'Keeffe, *O'Keeffe's Legacy to his Daughter* (London: 1834), p.xxii. O'Keeffe himself says he was sent to West's academy simply because of his own and his parents' 'inclination' for painting (pp.1-2). Such omissions and obfuscations, however, are characteristic of Irish Catholic writing in the era prior to Emancipation.

[21] O'Keeffe's *Recollections*, pp.6, 13, 32, 100, 104, 115, 133, 191-92, 201-2, 205. O'Keeffe repeatedly mentions that he visited various gentry houses in his youth, and though he clearly wishes to suggest that these are purely social visits, all the indications are that he was there in a commercial capacity, either doing portraits and landscapes, or restoring art work.

[22] Robert Hitchcock, *An Historical View of the Irish Stage*, volume two (Dublin, 1788), p.149. O'Keeffe also states that he began his 'dramatic career' with Mossop in 1765 (O'Keefe, *Recollections*, pp.111-12) though with his characteristic evasion about his acting past (see note twenty-four below), he does not specifically state he began as a performer. He does state, however, that he went from Dublin to Sligo in 1765 (pp.149, 164) and this suggests the career of a novice actor. Most beginning actors sought to gain experience by performing in provincial venues.

[23] See *Hibernian Magazine* (April 1782), p.204, where it is reported that O'Keeffe played in Irish provincial venues for about twelve years. In his *Recollections*, O'Keeffe also records that he travelled through various Irish towns at this period of his life (pp.165-293), and though he does not specifically say so, it seems likely that he acted in all these locations. O'Keeffe's daughter later excused her father's 'total omission' of his early career as an 'amateur performer' – an omission that she says 'gave umbrage' to the acting profession – on the grounds that it brought back painful memories of his estranged wife (Adelaide O'Keeffe, *O'Keeffe's Legacy*, pp.xii-xiii). An equally plausible explanation, however, lies in O'Keeffe's life-long desire to cast himself as a gentleman, a desire that conflicted with his dramatic beginnings as a lowly, provincial stroller.

[24] Clark, *The Irish Stage in the County Towns*, pp.149, 228; O'Keeffe, *Recollections*, pp.190-207.

[25] For O'Keeffe's 1772 performances in Cork, see the *Hibernian Chronicle* for September and October 1772; for listings of other performances during the 1770s, see Clark, *The Irish Stage in the County Towns*, pp.103-04, 107-08, 114.

[26] O'Keeffe lists this act among his 'earliest attempts at the drama' (*Recollections*, pp.240-41), and the *Hibernian Magazine* called it his 'chef d'oeuvre in dramatic writing in Ireland' (April 1782), p.204.

27 *Hibernian Chronicle*, 2-5 October 1780.

28 *Hibernian Chronicle*, 24-28 August 1780.

29 While undoubtedly the stage Irishman became a more benign and sentimentalised figure in the later eighteenth century, this shift, as Joseph Th. Leerssen points out, 'took the form of a mere modification of the received type, a reinterpretation of characteristics within the received frame of reference' (*Mere Irish and Fíor-Ghael* [Amsterdam and Philadelphia: John Benjamins Publishing Company, 1986], p.167).

30 *Hibernian Chronicle*, 2-5 October 1780.

31 O'Keeffe, *Recollections*, pp.201-2, 205.

32 Luke Gibbons, *Transformations in Irish Culture* (Notre Dame, Indiana: University of Notre Dame Press, 1996), pp.168, 166-67.

33 *Hibernian Chronicle*, 21-24 August 1780.

34 *Hibernian Chronicle*, October 22-26 1778.

35 Phelim was also surnamed 'OguffnocarrolloCarneyMacfrane' in these Cork performances (see Clark, *The Irish Stage*, p.114), and this ridiculously-sounding name suggests that this character was a typical blundering stage-Irishman.

36 Ray Cashman, 'The Heroic Outlaw in Irish Folklore and Popular Culture', *Folklore* (October 2000), p.5.

8 | Dion Boucicault's 'The Wearing of the Green'

Deirdre McFeely

> O Paddy dear, and did you hear the news that's going round?
> The shamrock is forbid by law to grow on Irish ground;
> St. Patrick's Day no more we'll keep; his colours can't be seen
> For there's a bloody law again the wearing of the green.
> I met with Napper Tandy,[1] and he took me by the hand,
> And he said, 'How's poor old Ireland, and how does she stand?'
> She's the most distressful country that ever yet was seen,
> They are hanging men and women for the wearing of the
> green.[2]

Dion Boucicault (1820-1890) is best remembered for his triptych of successful Irish plays – *The Colleen Bawn* (1860), *Arrah-na-Pogue* (1864) and *The Shaughraun* (1874). Both *The Colleen Bawn* and *The Shaughraun* were written and premiered in New York, where Boucicault lived for a large part of his professional life. Following enormous success in America, Boucicault brought these plays to London, where *The Colleen Bawn* opened in September 1860 and *The Shaughraun* in 1875. Dublin audiences did not have to wait too long to see *The Colleen Bawn*, as Boucicault returned to perform in his native city for the first time in twenty years to open the play at the Theatre Royal on 1 April 1861. Fifteen years later, *The Shaughraun* opened at Dublin's Gaiety Theatre, in December 1876, at the end of an extensive British provincial tour, although without Boucicault in the starring role, a fact much lamented by the Dublin press. At that point in his career, he had withdrawn from acting and had returned to New York following the death of his eldest son, and would not appear in a Dublin production of the play until his final visit to the city in 1881.

Boucicault was resident in London when he wrote *Arrah-na-Pogue* during June, July and August 1864, and the play differs further from the other two in that it is the only one that was rewritten in any way. His frequent assertion that 'plays are not written; they are rewritten', is certainly borne out in *Arrah-na-Pogue*. Although the play was licensed on 26 September for performance at the Theatre Royal in Manchester, Boucicault did not open it there.[3] Since he was resident in London at the time, it could reasonably have been expected that he would choose to open it there, but no. Rather, he revised it slightly and premiered it in Dublin on 7 November at the Theatre Royal on Hawkins Street where it ran for a very successful six weeks, with Boucicault and his wife Agnes Robertson in the leading roles. Further revisions were made before the play opened in London the following March, and it was an amended version of that production which was submitted to the Lord Chamberlain's censor for licensing. It has become a part of Boucicault lore that the song 'The Wearing of the Green' was banned from performances of the play following the Fenian bombing of London's Clerkenwell prison in December 1867. This essay will outline the genesis of *Arrah-na-Pogue*, and in the process will demonstrate that Boucicault's version of 'The Wearing of the Green' was never actually banned.

Dublin – 1864

Boucicault's decision to premiere *Arrah-na-Pogue* in Dublin may have been influenced by the popularity of *The Colleen Bawn* in his native city. When he had brought the play to Dublin in

Sung by M⸳ BOUCICAULT in the Drama
ARRAH NA POGUE.

WEARIN' O' THE GREEN,

Written to an Old Melody

BY

DION BOUCICAULT ESQ.ᴿ

AND

Harmonized

BY

CHARLES HALL.

London.

CHAPPELL & Cᵒ 50, NEW BOND STREET

Illustrations 4 & 5: Sheet music for 'The Wearing of the Green'.
Courtesy of the National Library of Ireland.

Illustration 5: Reverse of 4

1861 he was treated as a conquering hero, and its revival in April 1864 had been greeted with equal rapture. His final night speech to the Theatre Royal audience on that occasion acknowledged the financial success of the run, and expressed a hope to return soon with another Irish play:

> The reception you have given us, and which I will say could not be exceeded in any country outside of Ireland, will be always remembered with pride and gratitude. I was born not a hundred yards from the spot where I now stand, and when a boy I sat night after night in a seat at the corner of the pit and saw Tyrone Power performing on these boards … You are sending us away with our hearts full of joy and our pockets full of money and I hope to be able to return soon with another Colleen Bawn.[4]

Sure enough, Boucicault was back in Dublin with his new Irish play just six months after delivering this speech. On this occasion the playwright and his new play were the toast of Dublin, so much so that the brand new Lord Lieutenant, Lord Wodehouse, chose to make his first public appearance in Dublin at a command performance of the play at the Theatre Royal on 25 November. This carried social significance as in 1864, according to the *Daily Express*, a command night at the theatre was 'an event of such rare importance'.[5]

Arrah-na-Pogue was advertised in Dublin as 'an entirely new and original Irish drama'.[6] The word 'Irish' is predominant in the playbill: 'Irish scenery! Irish homes! Irish hearts!' is printed in large letters to reinforce the national subject matter of the new play.[7] While declaring the play's originality and Irishness, the advertisements also reassure theatregoers that the best of London's theatre professionals were involved in its production. Scenery was by F. Lloyds of the Princess's, one of London's leading scene painters, and music was by Oscar Byrne of Her Majesty's and Drury Lane theatres. Dublin audiences were thrilled that *Arrah-na-Pogue* premiered in their city, and their delight seemed to lie mainly in the fact that *Arrah-na-Pogue* came to Dublin before London. For once, Dublin could have first comment on the work of an international playwright. Even

Illustration 6: Playbill for _Arrah-na-Pogue_ by Dion Boucicault, Dublin, 1864. Courtesy of Trinity College, Dublin.

better still, that playwright was Irish and the subject matter of his play was Ireland. As the _Nation_ declared, '_Arrah-na-Pogue_ did not come before a Dublin audience bearing the stamp of a London audience's approval'. [8] The _Freeman's Journal_ waxed lyrical on the subject, all the while promoting the highly-developed critical faculty of the Dublin audience:

> We believe that Mr Boucicault has acted wisely in seeking first to get the opinion of a Dublin audience expressed on his new drama, and if it meet with approval here, its fame will be fully and enduringly established, for the reason that once a Dublin audience stamps its approbation on a drama, or an actor, or

musician, we have never known an instance where it was not taken as a patent of success.[9]

At the other end of the political spectrum, in a lengthy first-night review in the *Irish Times*, there is anxiety about how Ireland is regarded by other countries, particularly England. The *Irish Times* clearly desires that a 'true picture' of Ireland should be depicted on stage, rather than that of the traditional, blundering stage Irishman. The tone of the piece is very much one of insecurity: it creates an image of a country (or perhaps of an Anglo-Irish minority who would have made up the readership of the *Irish Times* in 1864) that is looking outwards from Ireland for approval, looking for confirmation that they possess a sophisticated national drama, and that they are themselves a sophisticated and cultured race:

> A national drama is, perhaps, the most essential part of a national literature. It not only affords the evidence upon which the verdict of posterity will be based, but it sets a country and its people in their true aspect before those whose opinion is certainly more valuable to them than that of posterity – the inhabitants of other lands. Yet, never was a country better abused by strangers than Ireland by its own dramatists. With the best and most abundant material for a true picture of national life and manners, they contented themselves with the success that is to be obtained by raising a laugh at the expense of their country. It is to their productions and not to the injustice of strangers, that we owe the disparaging estimate of the Celt which, until recently, prevailed in England. A thing of rags and tatters, of blunders and mischief-making, of noise and absurdity – a compound at best of rollicking good nature, impracticable obstinacy and effervescent courage, was the stage Irishman. If Mr Dion Boucicault did no other service, he rectified this ridiculously false impression of Irish character.[10]

The *Nation*, the *Freeman's Journal* and the *Irish Times* all used the Dublin success of *Arrah-na-Pogue* to their own political and social ends, be it to express strong anti-Englishness or to promote the idea of a national drama. While also receiving the new play in an extremely favourable light, the *Daily Express* and the *Dublin Evening Post* put the play's success to a markedly different political end. The *Daily Express* used the spectacle of the command performance of the play to strongly promote the cause of the new Lord Lieutenant by emphasizing the rapturous welcome Lord Wodehouse received. The arrival of the Lord Lieutenant at the theatre was itself a well-staged theatrical event, organized, no doubt, to make a powerful impression on the Dublin public. The extensive entourage was accompanied by an escort of the 11th Hussars, 100 men of the 49th Regiment and the regimental band. If Dublin Castle was trying to impress, events inside the Theatre Royal were equally planned to impress the new Lord Lieutenant, and a high degree of deference was shown by the theatre and also by Boucicault and his company to the Viceroy and the British crown:

> The curtain at the same time being raised, the entire company came forward and sang the National Anthem – a compliment his Excellency evidently appreciated, and which sustained the enthusiasm created by what may be regarded as his Excellency's first appearance in public. His Excellency was dressed in the Windsor uniform, with the ribbon and collar of the Order of St. Patrick. A rich velvet drapery, with the arms and motto of his Excellency emblazoned on a maroon ground, was suspended in front of the seat occupied by the Vice regal party, the Royal Arms on a blue ground, being suspended from above. The entire display was well calculated to impress the Lord Lieutenant favourably with regard to those over whom he has come in a sense to govern.[11]

Like the *Daily Express*, the *Dublin Evening Post* used the success of the command night to promote the cause of Dublin Castle, defending the Vice Regal Court against its critics:

> Those individuals who of late years have been urging the abolition of the Vice Regal Court, and adducing, among many other arguments, the extraordinary one that the Court causes no circulation of money in our city, would have met with a complete refutation in witnessing the brilliant display of fashion exhibited last evening: and on national grounds also we feel proud of the marked respect which was paid Lady Wodehouse on this her first public appearance amongst her countrymen.[12]

It is not without irony that the *Daily Express* and the *Dublin Evening Post* used the command night to promote the cause of

the new Lord Lieutenant, given that the play is set during one
of the most significant times in the history of Irish nationalism:
1798. When writing *Arrah-na-Pogue* and planning to open it in
Dublin, Boucicault may well have anticipated that it would
receive a command performance there. After all, the Earl of
Carlisle, Lord Lieutenant in 1861, had attended the opening
night of *The Colleen Bawn* and returned for a command night
three weeks later. It is even possible that Boucicault, knowing
that a new Lord Lieutenant was to be appointed to Ireland,
wrote the Dublin Castle scene of *Arrah-na-Pogue* with a
command performance of the play in mind.

'The Wearing of the Green'

Given the lyrics of Boucicault's version of 'The Wearing of the
Green', it is easy to accept the claim that 'the song that most
appealed to the Dublin audience was a version of "The Wearing
of the Green", an insurgent song of 1798 ... It took some
effrontery to sing "The Wearing of the Green" from the Dublin
stage'.[13] It is equally easy to accept that *Arrah-na-Pogue* is
'particularly interesting for it originally contained a rebel ballad,
"The Wearing of the Green", to which Dublin Castle objected
when the play arrived in Ireland in 1864'.[14] Boucicault's version
of the ballad is certainly highly subversive and is a powerful
demonstration of patriotism and overt anti-British feeling.
Given the song's tone, it would appear remarkably tolerant of
the Lord Lieutenant to grant the play his endorsement. It would
equally be of note that the Unionist newspapers did not criticize
the song, particularly the *Daily Express* editorial which regularly
condemned the publication of nationalist songs and poetry,
most notably in the *Nation*. Additionally, there is no official
record of any form of complaint or censorship about either the
song or the play.[15]

The reason is that 'The Wearing of the Green', in fact, never
formed part of the original Dublin version of the play and was
never sung in Dublin. While the original prompt copy for the
Dublin production contains in full the first song sung by Shaun,
'Open the Dure Softly', it does not give a title or lyrics for the

song sung by Shaun at his wedding to Arrah.[16] However, the playbill for the Dublin production lists all the music and songs, and includes not 'The Wearing of the Green' but 'Ough gurrum gurrum hoo' [*sic*];[17] the review in the *Freeman's Journal* confirms that this was the song to which Shaun treated his wedding guests in production.[18]

London – 1865

Boucicault used the hospitable environment offered to him by Dublin audiences and press as a provincial trial for *Arrah-na-Pogue* before opening it at the Princess's Theatre in London on 22 March 1865, where it was the hit of the season and ran for 164 nights. However, the substantial changes he made were not based on any criticisms in the Dublin papers but seem to be the result of Boucicault's own dissatisfaction with his work. John Brougham, the actor who played The O'Grady in both the Dublin and London productions, could not understand why Boucicault would want to alter the play after its success in Dublin. When Brougham read the revised London version, however, he was forced to admit that it was a superior play.[19] Some of the changes included the dropping of a character, Grannya, a sub-plot involving her, and a duel scene in the last act. While condensing and tightening the play overall, Boucicault also made some additions, such as Shaun's prison escape scene. One of his most significant revisions was the replacement of 'Ough gurrum gurrum hoo' by 'The Wearing of the Green' as the song sung by Shaun to his wedding guests. Additionally, the revised text expresses a degree of nationalistic sentiment that is absent from the Dublin version. Such revisions to the play after spending three months in Ireland that year suggest the birth of a heightened patriotism in Boucicault.

Dublin version[20]

> **Arrah:** Come, Shaun, for want of a bether we'll take a song from yourself.
>
> **All:** Hurroo! Rise it, Shaun, avich.

Shaun: Ahem! ladies and gentlemin. I've a mighty bad cowld intirely.

Arrah: Ah! go on. If it wasn't for the length of his ears and the cross on his back, ye might take him for a lark.

Shaun: Ah! it is a jackass ye want to make me.

Song – Shaun [no song title or lyrics given]

London version[21]

Shaun: Will, ladies, it's for you to choose the time of it. What shall it be?

Regan: 'The Wearing of the Green'.

All: Hurroo!

Shaun: Whisht, boys, are ye mad? Is it sing that song and the soldiers widin gunshot? Sure there's sudden death in every note of it.

Oiny: Niver fear; we'll put a watch outside and sing it quiet.

Shaun: It is the 'Twistin' of the Rope' ye are axin' for?

Regan: Divil an informer is to the fore – so out wid it.

Shaun: Is it all right outside there?

Oiny: Not a sowl can hear ye, barrin' ourselves.

Shaun: Murdher alive! kape lookin' out.

Song – 'The Wearing of the Green' [full song lyrics given]

There is no doubt that 'The Wearing of the Green' was performed by Boucicault in the role of Shaun from the outset of the London run, as an advertisement lists one of the play's attractions as 'The rebels' song, "The Wearing of the Green"'.[22] Additionally, the opening night review in the *Era* reports that the national sentiment of the song was well received:

> The rebel's song, 'The Wearing of the Green' is admirably rendered by Mr Boucicault and stirs the heart like the sound of a trumpet. The characteristic jig, for which the barn door is brought down as a platform, is full of national spirit.[23]

The performance and warm reception of 'The Wearing of the Green' in London is in piquant contrast to the rendering of the National Anthem by Boucicault and his company for the benefit of the Lord Lieutenant at both the opening and closing of the Dublin command performance.

The London run of *Arrah-na-Pogue* coincided with extraordinary political events. The Fenian movement continued to gather momentum, and the ending of the American Civil War in April 1865 improved the prospects for a rising in Ireland that year. Events came to a head in Dublin in September when the office of the *Irish People* was raided by the authorities. James Stephens, leader of the Fenians, managed to avoid capture until November but many others were arrested on the night of the raid. British warships were stationed off the coast of Ireland to intercept any American vessels that might be carrying volunteers. Habeas corpus was suspended in Ireland, permitting the detention without trial of suspected Fenians, and approximately 150 court martials were held. Two weeks after his capture, Stephens made a daring escape from prison. Against the background of this political activity, Boucicault sang 'The Wearing of the Green' and escaped from prison every night on the London stage without any form of censorship.

Unlike Ireland, England did have a formal system of theatre censorship, and all plays had to be submitted to the Lord Chamberlain's censor for licensing prior to opening. Given the political events of the time and the subversive tone of the lyrics, it is surprising that the song was not removed by the censor, William Bodham Dunne. However, Boucicault deliberately seems to have bypassed the possibility of censorship in two different ways. While *Arrah-na-Pogue* opened on 22 March, it was not submitted to the censor until after it had opened, and was only licensed on 31 March. [24] In a letter to the Lord Chamberlain, Dunne notes, with reference to the 1864 Manchester licence, that *Arrah-na-Pogue*, 'has been playing for several nights and is in all essential respects a new version of a piece already licensed. I have read the present improved manuscript and find it quite unobjectionable'. [25]

However, the hand-written copy of the play submitted to Dunne differed from that already playing on the London stage. It does not contain the words of 'The Wearing of the Green' but merely states in its place, 'A song by Shaun'.[26] Interestingly, all other songs appear in full in the body of the text. The manuscript contains many textual additions and corrections in Boucicault's hand, all of which are perfectly legible. However, in the passage leading up to Shaun's rendition of his wedding song some lines are scored out so as to be illegible. All reference to soldiers, gunshot, death, hanging or informers has been removed. Censorship of the lines can be ruled out because they were not marked with the censor's blue pencil and there is no corresponding entry in the Lord Chamberlain's day book. It would, therefore, seem that Boucicault crossed out the lines himself before submitting the play to the Lord Chamberlain's office.

Lord Chamberlain's version[27]

> **Shaun:** Will, ladies, it's for you choose the time of it. What shall it be?
>
> **Regan:** 'The Wearing of the Green'.
>
> **All:** Hurroo!
>
> [Followed by words which are crossed out and illegible as a result.]
>
> **Shaun:** [Two lines of text which are crossed out and illegible as a result.]
>
> A song by Shaun [no song title or lyrics given]

London – 1867 and 1868

Boucicault revived *Arrah-na-Pogue* at the Princess's from September to November 1867, and its run again coincided with extraordinary political events. A policeman was killed during the rescue of two Fenian leaders in Manchester in September, and the three Irishmen judged responsible, who became known as the 'Manchester Martyrs', were subsequently hanged in November. A revival of *The Colleen Bawn* followed *Arrah-na-*

Pogue at the Princess's, and during its December run the Fenians bombed London's Clerkenwell Prison. In the heightened aftermath of the bombing, in which twelve civilians were killed and many more injured, thousands of special constables were appointed to central London areas such as Newington and Lambeth.

In January 1868 theatrical advertisements in the London newspapers noted that *Arrah-na-Pogue* would shortly return to the stage. This was too much for one Middlesex Magistrate who wrote a letter of complaint to the Lord Chamberlain about the play:

> 14 Norland Place
> Notting Hill
> January 25th 1868
>
> My Lord
>
> I have the honour to draw your attention to advertisements in the daily newspapers of the intended performance of a play, at the Princess's Theatre, entitled *Arrah-na-Pogue*, the scene of which is in Ireland during the Rebellion, and introduces circumstances, and a song called, 'The Wearing of the Green', which I take the liberty of submitting for your consideration as highly improper subjects for dramatic representation at the present time.
>
> I have the honour to be, My Lord
> Your obedient and humble servant
> Francis B. Morley
> Magistrate for Middlesex[28]

The Lord Chamberlain forwarded Morley's letter to the Secretary of State at the Home Office with the recommendation that no action be taken. The entry in the Home Office file for the Lord Chamberlain's letter reads, 'Play *Arrah-na-Pogue*: Lord Chamberlain refused to repress play during Fenian agitation':

> Lord Chamberlain's Office
> St. James' Palace, S.W.
> 30 January 1868
>
> (To the Hon. Adolphus Liddell, Home Office)

Sir,

I am desired by the Lord Chamberlain to forward herewith a copy of a letter from Mr Morley, a Middlesex Magistrate, questioning the propriety of allowing a piece called *Arrah-na-Pogue* to be performed at the Princess's Theatre.

I am to add that the play in question was licensed in 1865, and that in submitting Mr Morley's letter for the consideration of the Secretary of State the Lord Chamberlain wishes me to express his opinion that the power given to him of repressing licensed pieces by the 6 & 7 Victoria Cap would not be judiciously exercised in the present instance.

I have the honour to be, Sir, your obedient servant. Spencer Ponsonby[29]

The Home Office concurred with the Lord Chamberlain: *Arrah-na-Pogue* subsequently reopened at the Princess's on 10 February and ran until 7 March. When considering why the Lord Chamberlain made this recommendation, it must be noted that there is no evidence to suggest that either the song or the play was being used or received in a political manner. While the newspapers and periodicals, including the satirical *Punch* and *The Tomahawk*, were full of comment on the Fenians, no reference was made to *Arrah-na-Pogue*. Despite the recent Clerkenwell atrocity and the resulting tension in London, theatre audiences were clearly not reading any political intent in *Arrah-na-Pogue*. Additionally, Boucicault's success had always lent him great influence in the London theatrical scene: in 1865 his opinion had been sought by the Lord Chamberlain on the proposed new bill to amend the law relating to theatres. The Lord Chamberlain would have known that Boucicault was adept at using controversy to his own advantage, and that he would have undoubtedly turned any attempt at censorship of his work into self-promotion.

Boucicault's most recent biographer, Richard Fawkes, points out that in later years both Boucicault and his wife were to recall the 1867 London revival of *Arrah-na-Pogue* as if it had been the first London production. Boucicault even claimed that the opening night coincided with the Clerkenwell bombing. It seems likely that when reminiscing, Boucicault changed the date of the London premiere and possibly even fabricated a story about the song being banned. As Boucicault became more patriotic and nationalistic in his later years, as reflected in *The Story of Ireland* published in 1881, it no doubt suited him to be able to link his Irish plays to important events in Ireland's history. Such myths, and many more, are reflected in Townsend Walsh's biography of Boucicault, published in 1915:

> When Boucicault first sang the song ['The Wearing of the Green'] in London on the opening night of *Arrah-na-Pogue*, there was a storm of protest. The blowing up of Clerkenwell prison by the Fenians was an event of recent occurrence. Against the advice of his manager and friends, who implored him not to sing it, he persisted. Then came an edict from the cabinet ministers of Queen Victoria prohibiting the song in Great Britain; and for years, although it thrilled the heart of every Irishman, it was never heard in the British Dominions.[30]

The first significant piece of modern Boucicault criticism, David Krause's essay which formed the introduction to *The Dolmen Boucicault* (1964), drew heavily on Walsh's biography and the banning of 'The Wearing of the Green' became further established as fact. Later critics concur, some of whom refer directly back to Krause.[31] While Fawkes corrects the date of the opening night of *Arrah-na-Pogue*, he does not offer any evidence to support the claim (which he reiterates) that 'The Wearing of the Green' was banned throughout the British Empire.

Dublin – 1868

Boucicault returned to Dublin to open the revised version of *Arrah-na-Pogue* at the Theatre Royal on 2 November 1868. Although the play was presented to the Dublin public as a 'New and Original Drama', newspaper reportage of the event was muted. The political and social atmosphere in Dublin was very different to what it had been four years previously. Elections were forthcoming and riots were widespread in both England and Ireland. The Duke and Duchess of Abercorn had replaced Lord and Lady Wodehouse at Dublin Castle, and they were not undertaking many public social activities at that time. There would be no command night for this production of the play. In contrast to 1864, when its columns were filled with letters about the theatre, the *Irish Times* did not publish any correspondence, theatrical or otherwise, in the run up to the election. It was practically devoid of theatre reviews and only carried a short notice about *Arrah-na-Pogue* following its opening. The paper reported extensively on the demand for an amnesty for political prisoners, a major issue of the time. In the run up to the general election, there was a popular assumption in Ireland that Gladstone, once in office, would as a matter of course free the Fenian prisoners. The Dublin run of *Arrah-na-Pogue* coincided with the first anniversary of the execution of the Manchester Martyrs, and the *Irish Times* reported on events taking place in both England and Ireland to commemorate the occasion.

In contrast to the muted tones of the *Irish Times*, and the *Freeman's Journal*, the *Daily Express* was effusive in its several 1868 reviews of *Arrah-na-Pogue*. In a long review of the opening night, it praises the music, thereby suggesting that 'The Wearing of the Green' was omitted from the performance.[32] At a time of heightened nationalist tension, it is remarkable that the *Daily Express* used its review of *Arrah-na-Pogue* to promote the political rulers of the day and their 'beneficent régime', while also denying the national aspect of the play:

> It would, indeed, be a matter for wonder if a work so full of touching idylls of love and heroism, of racy and grotesque humour, and thrilling historical associations, failed to excite the approbation and delight of a people so keenly sensitive to the beauties and traditions of their native land. The dark days of political oppression which it illustrates have long passed away, but the virtues of bravery and devotion which they evoked continue to flourish under a more beneficent régime, and the deeply human interest which runs through the whole work, owes its power to neither traditional sentiment nor national prejudice, but to the common sympathies of mankind.[33]

As suggested by the tone of the *Daily Express* review, Boucicault did not sing 'The Wearing of the Green' during this Dublin run. According to Fawkes, 'when Boucicault returned to

Dublin with the play he was asked to drop the song on grounds of expediency'.[34] A letter from Boucicault published in the *Freeman's Journal* two days after the closing of *Arrah-na-Pogue* shows that the playwright, for once, had indeed exercised self-censorship:

> Mr Dion Boucicault
>
> To the Editor of the *Freeman*
>
> Sir – When *Arrah-na-Pogue* was produced in London the following song was sung by Shaun the Post. I have been frequently urged to sing it during my late engagement at the Theatre Royal, but, in view of the political excitement agitating the country at this moment, I declined to do so. The last four lines of the first verse belong to an old Dublin street ballad. These stirring lines inspired me to complete a national song to be called 'The Wearing of the Green'
>
> [First two verses of song are reproduced in full.]
>
> These words, sung nightly at the Princess's Theatre, in London, and in the great cities throughout England and Scotland, have been greeted by all classes with unmistakeable sympathy, the applause being as deep as it was fervent. For the moment, at least, those multitudes were Irishmen. Every little helps.
>
> Yours faithfully, Dion Boucicault.[35]

The letter was also published in the *Nation* on 5 December. While Boucicault may have been proclaiming his self-restraint, he actually succeeded in having the lyrics of his song reproduced in two popular newspapers. However, the play had by then already closed, so Boucicault was not running any risk of attracting the attention of the authorities: seditious music was a subject that was occupying Dublin Castle at that time. It would seem that pressure was brought to bear upon Boucicault to omit the song, most likely by the management of the Theatre Royal who would have been anticipating a full house for the run of the play. Despite his nationalist protestations, Boucicault was first and foremost a theatrical entrepreneur who would have been loath to sacrifice profit to political principle.

Conclusion

Although often overshadowed by *The Colleen Bawn* and *The Shaughraun*, *Arrah-na-Pogue* is, in many ways, the most remarkable of the three plays. It is notable for the instability of its script, both as text and in production, and the seemingly contradictory aspects of its reception in Dublin and in London. The play's premiere was an event resonant with significant cultural implications for Dublin audiences, and the subsequent press commentary demonstrates the manner in which opposing political factions turned the play to their own advantage. Boucicault deftly operated in the different theatrical and political environments of the two cities. He deliberately bypassed the possibility of formal censorship at the hands of the Lord Chamberlain's censor while actually producing a much more politically inflammatory version of the play on the London stage to the apparent delight of the English critics. In contrast to its Dublin reception, London audiences received the play as yet another successful play from a playwright with whose work they were very familiar. There was no necessity for cultural or political appropriation of such a work in the diverse theatrical world of London. When political anxiety about Fenian activity did eventually prompt formal complaint about the seditious nature of the play, the complaint was dismissed by the authorities. Yet in the theatrical environment of Dublin, which was officially free of censorship, Boucicault chose to withdraw 'The Wearing of the Green'. That he felt compelled to do so demonstrates the potential power of the song in Dublin at a time of great political unrest. It would appear that in Ireland in the 1860s, when attempts by the Fenians to overthrow British rule were unsuccessful, music operated as a forceful voice in the call for political change and as an important tool in the promotion of a nationalist ideal. The ready acceptance by critics of the song's official censorship, in the late afterlife of the play, further demonstrates its subversive power.

I wish to acknowledge funding received from the Irish Research Council for the Humanities and Social Sciences as a Government of Ireland Research Scholar.

1 Napper Tandy (1740-1803), United Irishman.

2 *Arrah-na-Pogue* in David Krause (ed.), *The Dolmen Boucicault* (Dublin: Dolmen Press, 1964), Act 1, pp.133-4.

3 Register of Lord Chamberlain Plays, 1852-1865, British Library Add. MS. 53703.

4 *Freeman's Journal*, 25 April 1864, p.3.

5 *Daily Express*, 26 November 1864, p.3.

6 *Freeman's Journal*, 31 October 1864, p.1.

7 Playbill for *Arrah-na-Pogue*, 10 November 1864, Trinity College Dublin Library.

8 *Nation*, 12 November 1864, p.183.

9 *Freeman's Journal*, 7 November 1864, p.3.

10 *Irish Times*, 8 November 1864, p.3.

11 *Daily Express*, 26 November 1864, p.3.

12 *Dublin Evening Post*, 26 November 1864. Cutting in file on the Earl of Kimberley 1864/5/6 in Larcom Manuscripts, National Library of Ireland MS 7507.

13 John McCormick, *Dion Boucicault* (Cambridge and Alexandria, VA: Chadwyck-Healey, 1987), pp.39-40.

14 Christopher Morash, *A History of Irish Theatre 1601-2000* (Cambridge: Cambridge University Press, 2002), pp.91-92.

15 Chief Crown Solicitors Papers 1859-1869, National Archives of Ireland. The issue of seditious music first appears in the Fenian Files compiled by Dublin Castle in March 1866 (National Archives of Ireland, Fenian Files 6314R (Carton 10)). The Larcom Manuscripts (National Library of Ireland) contain an article from the *Daily Express* of 25 September 1865 about a woman being arrested for singing a seditious ballad (1865 Fenian Supplement (Letters), MS 7688).

16 *Arrah-na-Pogue*, Theatre Royal, Dublin, 1864 promptbook, Harvard Theatre Collection TS 3055.45, pp.8, 22.

17 Playbill for *Arrah-na-Pogue*, 10 November 1864, Trinity College Dublin Library.

18 *Freeman's Journal*, 8 November 1864, p.3.

19 Richard Fawkes, *Dion Boucicault, A Biography* (London: Quartet Books, 1979), p.157.

[20] *Arrah-na-Pogue*, Theatre Royal, Dublin, 1864 promptbook, Harvard Theatre Collection TS 3055.45, p.22.

[21] *Arrah-na-Pogue* in Krause (ed.), *The Dolmen Boucicault*, Act 1, p.133. This is a reproduction of the London publisher French's acting edition, which claims to be as originally played at the Princess's in 1865.

[22] *The Times*, 20 March 1865, p.8.

[23] *Era*, 26 March 1865, p.11.

[24] Register of Lord Chamberlain Plays Volume II, 1852-1865, British Library Add. MS. 53,703(a).

[25] Letter from William Bodham Dunne to the Lord Chamberlain, 31 March 1865, British National Archives LC1/153.

[26] *Arrah-na-Pogue*, The Lord Chamberlain's Plays, British Library Add. 53041 A.

[27] Ibid.

[28] Letter from Francis Morley to the Lord Chamberlain, 25 January 1868, British National Archives, LC1/200.

[29] Letter from the Lord Chamberlain to the Secretary of State at the Home Office, 30 January 1868, British National Archives, LC1/202.

[30] Townsend Walsh, *The Career of Dion Boucicault* (New York: The Dunlap Society, 1915), p.52.

[31] See for example, Morash, *History of Irish Theatre*; Elizabeth Butler Cullingford, *Ireland's Others: Ethnicity and Gender in Irish Literature and Popular Culture* (Cork: Cork University Press, 2001); Stephen Watt, *Joyce, O'Casey, and the Irish Popular Theater* (Syracuse: Syracuse University Press, 1991); McCormick, *Dion Boucicault*; Richard A. Cave, 'The Presentation of English and Irish Characters in Boucicault's Irish Melodrama' in Wolfgang Zach and Heinz Kosok (eds.), *Literary Interrelations: Ireland, England and the World, Volume 3: National Images and Stereotypes* (Tübingen: Narr, 1987); James M. Nelson, 'From Rory and Paddy to Boucicault's Myles, Shaun and Conn: The Irishman on the London Stage, 1830-1860', *Éire/Ireland 133* (Autumn 1978); Robert Hogan, *Dion Boucicault* (New York: Twayne, 1969); Séan McMahon, 'The Wearing of the Green: The Irish Plays of Dion Boucicault', *Éire/Ireland 2* (Summer 1967), David Krause 'The Theatre of Dion Boucicault', in *The Dolmen Boucicault* (Dublin: Dolmen Press, 1964).

[32] *Daily Express*, 3 November 1868, p.2.

[33] Ibid. 9 November 1868, p.3.

[34] Fawkes, *Dion Boucicault*, p.158.

[35] *Freeman's Journal*, 30 November 1868, p.3.

9 | The Gate – Home and Away

Richard Pine

The Dublin Gate Theatre, under the management of Hilton Edwards and Micheál mac Liammóir, worked outside the Irish Free State/Republic of Ireland, on twenty-two occasions between 1935 and 1967.[1] Nine of these were excursions into Northern Ireland, two of them at the invitation of CEMA, the Council for the Encouragement of Music and the Arts, which was the forerunner of the Arts Council. Of the remainder, two were to London (1935, 1947), five were to Egypt, the Balkans and Malta, one was to Glasgow (1947), one to Canada and New York (1948), one to Elsinore in Denmark (1952), one to Switzerland, Luxembourg, Belgium and Holland (1962), and two were to New York in 1966 and 1967 with productions of plays by Brian Friel.

This essay examines the pre-Second World War tours to London, Egypt and the Balkans, focusing in the first case on the plays presented before the split between Lord Longford (the Gate's principal sponsor from 1930 to 1936) and the Edwards-mac Liammóir partnership, in the second on the cause of the split, and in the third on the relevance of the Gate's presence in the Balkans on the eve of the War.

In 1935, seven years after the establishment of the Gate Theatre by Edwards and mac Liammóir, and five years after it had moved to its premises in a converted eighteenth-century concert hall in the Rotunda complex, the theatre received an invitation to play at the Westminster Theatre, London.[2] The Westminster was itself a new venue, and was also a conversion of an eighteenth-century building, in this case the Charlotte Chapel in Palace Street which functioned first, in 1924, as a cinema and, from 1931, as a theatre.[3] Its impresario, Anmer Hall, had the same artistic policy as Edwards and mac Liammóir, and as Peter Godfrey's pioneering Gate Theatre in London (which had been the chief inspiration for the Dublin venture): the presentation of new and experimental work.[4]

For Edwards and mac Liammóir, the challenge was to present their work outside the confines of the Irish theatrical context, both for the experience of playing abroad and to test their work on foreign audiences. Mac Liammóir records that they had investigated the possibilities of Paris, without success, but that Edwards had urged:

> Look at our position. Both of us turning out rep which no one ought to stay at for more than three years unless he's a born hack. Are you or I born hacks? Fourth raters? Useful fillers in? Perhaps we are. One loses perspective in this country of charades.[5]

Hall had become aware of *Yahoo*, a work on the life of Jonathan Swift by Lord Longford. *Yahoo*, in Longford's words, was 'a tribute to the man I regard as the father of modern Irish nationalism'.[6] It was Longford's generosity which had kept the company buoyant, in financial terms, for the previous five years. Longford had been hesitant about accepting the invitation to the Gate to play in London until May 1935 when *Yahoo*, with a Gate actress, Betty Chancellor, in the role of Stella, was enthusiastically received at another experimental venue, Terence Gray's Cambridge Festival Theatre.[7] It was decided that *Yahoo* would be accompanied by *Hamlet*, in which mac Liammóir was rapidly forging a reputation as a great interpreter of the title role, and a work by Denis Johnston (who was later to marry Betty Chancellor). Johnston hoped that this would be his new play, *A Bride for the Unicorn*, but, apparently at mac Liammóir's insistence, his first play, the notorious *The Old*

Lady Says 'No!', was chosen instead, allegedly because it gave mac Liammóir a better chance to star in the role of the Speaker/Emmet. Edwards who, in my opinion, was the superior actor, played the role of Swift in *Yahoo*.[8] The play was billed as 'a Fantastic Commentary on Jonathan Swift by the Earl of Longford', *The Old Lady Says 'No!'* as 'a satiric review of everything Irish by Denis Johnston, author of *The Moon in the Yellow River*' (which had been produced in Birmingham, Malvern and London), and *Hamlet* needed no introduction except for the name of mac Liammóir in the title role. Eight performances were given of each play.

Illustration 7: **Micheál mac Liammóir in *The Old Lady Says 'No!'***

Mac Liammóir recorded that the partners had had misgivings about presenting Irish plays which were 'too obscure. Too local', even though they were 'vital and new and different'.[9] He went on to say that it was

> necessary to give copious programme notes to explain what in Ireland needed no explanation, that Robert Emmet was the leader of the Rebellion of 1803, that Sarah Curran was his

betrothed … that Grattan … was the leader of the Irish
Parliament of the late eighteenth century.[10]

We should note the anxiety, which is just as evident today, in
presenting Irish plays outside Ireland – especially in the light of
a story that a New York prize-giving recently announced a play
by Brian Friel as *Dancing at Lasagne*. Among drama critics it is
almost a commonplace that a play which is intimately derived
from, and related to, Irish preoccupations and history, may
have a universal appeal, but it continues to be a given that
special pleading is required to make that universality apparent
to a non-Irish audience. This is in sharp and ironic contrast to
the expectation that 'Irish' plays travel easily to audiences
experienced in other cultures and other histories.

Perhaps to the directors' surprise, *Yahoo* and *The Old Lady*
sold out and were very well received. But we can well
understand the anxiety of the company in presenting, during a
period of uneasy relationships between the British and Irish
governments, plays emphasizing the political and cultural
differences between the two countries, the differences that had
been the bedrock of cultural mobilization by figures such as
Douglas Hyde and W.B. Yeats since the 1880s.

Hamlet, however, became a nightmare for mac Liammóir,
who recorded in his somewhat fanciful autobiography –
ironically, in respect of this production, entitled *All for Hecuba* –
that his best performance had been in Sofia (in 1939) and

> my worst was in the Westminster Theatre … when I was
> obsessed by terror of the only effective weapon the English
> have against the Irish, that bantering, indulgent smile as of a
> kindly doctor for a fractious child.[11]

Nevertheless he also recorded that when he came to the
lines 'conjures the wand'ring stars/ And makes them stand like
wonder-wounded hearers' and paused before 'This is I, Hamlet,
the Dane', a voice in the audience called 'Good boy, splendid
chap, exactly where Irving paused'.[12] But, acknowledging that he
was bringing coals to Newcastle, mac Liammóir continued, 'I
knew that *Hamlet* was a failure and felt ashamed … throughout
the run I think I did not give one performance of distinction'.

However, at least one London critic applauded the performance, since Sydney Carroll wrote in the *Daily Telegraph* that mac Liammóir

> has ... all the fitness, and suitability for the part. His voice is sonorous, musical and yet natural. He does not boom, rant or rave. He uses a Heaven-sent organ with a justness, a precision, a harmony that to me are beyond praise. He is good to look at, youthful, handsome, well made, always picturesque, he never poses or prances. Above everything else he is original and vital.[13]

We see here a reversal of the process by which, in the eighteenth century, Cathal Maclochlainn, the young lad from Inishowen, transformed himself into Charles Macklin, one of the giants of the English stage, and a definitive interpreter of the role of Shylock. The major irony was that, as the little Londoner, Alfred Willmore, the future mac Liammóir had been a juvenile star in London, playing opposite such figures as Herbert Beerbohm Tree, and was now posing as an Irishman and yearning – unsuccessfully on this occasion – to become one of the greatest Hamlets of his day. It was a role which earned him the reputation of a matinée idol, and he continued to play Hamlet up to the company's appearance in Elsinore in 1952, when he was fifty-two years old. His complete lack of Irish blood, and the fact that he was English through and through, was unknown to all but his immediate family and his lifelong partner, until well after his death.[14]

At the time of the excursion to London, Edwards had been anxious to bring a tour to Egypt, which several English companies had undertaken with appreciable financial benefits. Pretending that he had received an invitation to do so (whereas in fact he had offered the tour to the Egyptian agents) Edwards tried, unsuccessfully, to persuade Longford to agree. The board of the Gate was evenly split, and an uneasy compromise was reached whereby Edwards and mac Liammóir would take all of the company who could afford to travel at their own expense (which in fact amounted to all but three of the Gate company). One of those who could not travel was the young Edward Ball, from the Dublin suburb of Booterstown, whose mother refused to pay for his ticket. In reprisal, Ball chopped up his mother with an axe and threw her remains into the sea at the bottom of Corbawn Lane in Shankill, a village in south County Dublin. The body was never discovered, but Ball was found 'guilty but insane' and incarcerated in the Central Criminal Lunatic Asylum. On release many years later he took up work in an insurance company in London.[15]

By agreement with Longford, the Egyptian party was billed as the Dublin Gate Theatre. This was the first of three visits to Egypt in consecutive years, and was the cause of a diplomatic rift between Edwards-mac Liammóir and what became the new company of Longford Productions. During the Egyptian season (the plays performed are listed in the appendix) it was learned that Longford, on foot of the success of the previous year's visit, had taken a company back to London, also billed as the company of the Dublin Gate Theatre. After a successful 'return' to the Westminster Theatre with his own *Armlet of Jade* and Eugene O'Neill's *Ah, Wilderness!*, the company transferred to the Ambassador's, adding Johnston's *A Bride for the Unicorn* to the bill.[16] Frantic communications travelled between Cairo, Dublin and London, but it was impossible to resolve the situation until Edwards and mac Liammóir returned. It was then agreed that the two companies would share the theatre premises on a six-monthly basis, and this in turn gave rise to substantial touring by both companies – Edwards and mac Liammóir spending considerable time in the major centres of Cork and Belfast (in addition to their foreign tours) while Longford Productions earned a nationwide reputation touring the smaller towns of Ireland, in the tradition of the fit-up companies of the nineteenth and early twentieth centuries. The Longford company gave a start to the careers of several later prominent actors, including Milo O'Shea and Harold Pinter, Iris Lawler and Aidan Grennell (who became husband and wife) and RTÉ's first television newsreader, Charles Mitchel. Many productions were designed by Kay Casson, wife of actor Christopher Casson.

In 1939, perhaps in emulation of a handsomely produced volume chronicling the achievements of the Gate prior to the time of the 'split', Longford Productions published a relatively modest brochure which stated, somewhat disingenuously, that in 1936 the Dublin Gate Theatre Company Ltd

> gave up all active work in theatrical production, and ceased to maintain a Company of actors. Early in 1936 Messrs. Edwards and MacLiammoir [*sic*] departed on a tour of their own to Egypt with many of the old Company.[17]

Two further Egyptian seasons followed for Edwards-mac Liammóir in 1937 and 1938. During this period the partners had holidayed in Greece where they had met Walter Bridges-Adams, the representative of the recently established British Council, who engaged the Gate to appear in Athens after its third Egyptian tour in 1938. The French-language *Messager d'Athènes* referred to the visit as 'une brillante manifestation d'amitié Anglo-Grecque'.[18]

Perhaps on foot of this 'manifestation', Bridges-Adams visited Dublin in October/November 1938, while the company was performing *Mourning Becomes Electra*, to discuss whether the Gate company could credibly be regarded as ambassadors for British drama in a tour of the Balkan states. The British Council was rapidly becoming a central part of Britain's diplomatic efforts to retain the allegiance of the smaller central-European states as war became an inevitability. In March 1939, the House of Commons was told that the Balkan states had sought increased activity by the Council at all levels:

> Britain may well look to the British Council as being the means of nullifying false propaganda and restoring in due course the ancient prestige of this country among the nations of the world.[19]

Having experienced border controls between the Free State and the North of Ireland during the company's first tour to Belfast in March 1939, Hilton Edwards announced that 'remote and impenetrable as the Balkans appear from Dublin, it is easier to get into Bulgaria than across the frontier of the six counties at the top of our own map', and mac Liammóir added that, 'weather and war permitting, we shall make a European tour'.[20] In December 1939, the British Prime Minister informed the

House of Commons that the Gate's initial engagement in Athens had cost the British Council £719.9.6d, and that the cost of the Balkan tour had been £7,056.1.8d.[21]

The six months before war officially began in September 1939 saw the gradual dismantling of Czechoslovakia: Germany annexed the Sudetenland, Slovakia was ceded to Hungary, and Hungary occupied Ruthenia in March 1939. There was a very real sense of impending disaster in April, when the company set out for Ljubljana, capital of Slovenia. It was therefore in exceptional circumstances that they embarked on this 'European tour', which was in fact the most extensive undertaken by the Gate until its 1962 tour with *Othello* to thirteen cities in Luxembourg, Switzerland, Belgium and Holland.

The repertoire for the tour was 'British' in the catholic sense of representing works mainly by English playwrights – pre-eminently Shakespeare, with *Macbeth* and *Hamlet* (which are thought to have received their first English-language productions in Belgrade on this occasion) as well as *The Comedy of Errors* – but also including Shaw and Wilde, and the thrillers *The Unguarded Hour* (1936) by Ladislas Fodor and *Night Must Fall* by Welshman Emlyn Williams (which had been in the Gate repertory since 1937, a year after its first production). *Night Must Fall* had been included expressly at the wish of the British Council to represent contemporary British drama, and would become a regular feature in the Gate repertoire.[22] Emily Brontë's *Wuthering Heights* was presented in a dramatization by Ria Mooney and Donald Stauffer – Mooney was later to become the *de facto* artistic director of the Abbey – and the tour also included *And So To Bed*, a light-hearted view of Samuel Pepys written in 1927 by the Belfast-born James B. Fagan.[23]

Slovenia, Croatia and Serbia had only ten years previously been unified as the 'Kingdom of Yugoslavia' in an uneasy alliance of Slovenes, Croats and Serbs – to say nothing of Montenegrins, Macedonians and Herzegovinians. In 1939, the cities visited by the Gate were the historic capitals of some of Europe's smallest and most vulnerable states, which recent history has demonstrated to be capable of both federation, internecine war and newly asserted independence: Ljubljana, capital of Slovenia; Zagreb, capital of Croatia; Belgrade, capital of Serbia; followed by the Macedonian/Greek city of Thessaloniki (Salonica, which itself had only become a part of modern Greece after the Anatolian débâcle of 1922), and the capitals of Bulgaria (Sofia) and Romania (Bucharest).

Irish newspapers questioned the propriety of an Irish company undertaking 'British propaganda', and in Britain the *Daily Express* inveighed against the British Council's policy.[24] The players were ostensibly representing 'Britain', and were expected not to flaunt their Irishness. Several newspapers referred to the company as 'English' – chiefly, one supposes, due to the anglophone nature of their repertoire – but one, *La Parole Bulgare* (the French-language weekly of Bulgaria) – carried an open letter from Pierre Ouvaliev addressed 'Aux Acteurs Britanniques', in the course of which they were informed that, whatever about Belgrade, Sofia, far from being ignorant of English-language drama, had witnessed three different interpretations of *Hamlet* in recent years and 'ce public a vu, compris et aimé Oskar Wilde', but acknowledged that this would be the first time that *British* actors would be presenting the works of their compatriots.[25] Since the company was openly billed as 'Dublin Gate Theatre' it can of course be understood that the term 'British' was being interpreted in its geographical sense, but the cultural assumption is embedded in the letter.

Almost twenty-five years later, in an unpublished paper on 'Nationalism in the Theatre Today' delivered during the Dublin Theatre Festival, Hilton Edwards unwittingly defeated the British Council's purposes when he said that while

> There may be works so universal that they overleap boundaries, most plays bear the unmistakeable stamp of their origins and rarely can writers, actors or directors see their innately national qualities sufficiently to obliterate this sigil. When, for instance, has an Irish play been satisfactorily presented – even in English – by non-Irish actors, or an English play by Irish actors?[26]

Certainly the fact of emanating from Dublin was not hidden from view, and, according to *All for Hecuba*, in Belgrade, mac

Liammóir found himself before a large group of journalists who asked about the difference between English and Irish acting styles. His reply reminds us of recent exchanges of opinion about whether or not there is, or ever has been, an 'Abbey style' of acting:

> A manner must grow out of the life of a nation … It would be of no avail that the Irish actor should hunt for a style as one hunts for a taxi or a fox; it must grow out of his innermost self, out of his soul through the pores of his skin. The fountainhead is the nation, and language is important but not almighty. American acting is the proof of that … Why am I hoping that Ireland may discover a new and separate style? … If Irish acting never finds more distinctive things to say than the platitudes of an outworn English school clothed in the homespun of a brogue, our movement has been so much waste of time, and we would do much better to look for jobs in London or New York which indeed is where the best of us have finally gone … because nothing has happened in Ireland that is definite enough to give us a standard … In the Irish theatre we live in a shapeless chaos, and whether we are doing well or ill is understood only by a handful of people. The Celtic Twilight in fact is not poetic invention, it is a most ominous and destructive reality, and the only work our generation can do is to keep the little candles we have lighted from blowing out in the wind.[27]

Given that the Second World War, like the first, was concerned with determining the rights and destinies of small nations (many of which, like Ireland, had struggled to promulgate their cultural as well as political identities in the previous fifty years), mac Liammóir's reflection on the strengths and perils of nationalism, voiced in Belgrade in 1939, merits attention today.

In conclusion, mac Liammóir also recorded that after the company's last performance on tour, in Bucharest, he found himself extemporizing a curtain speech, which, again, brings home to us today the precarious and ambivalent role of the arts in a sectarian or war-torn context:

> I heard myself, in the midst of much conventional gratitude, launching into a discussion of the peace and brotherhood of the

arts. Who, I enquired, that knew his Shakespeare and his
Goethe, could wish to make war upon the people of either?
What man on whom the muses had ever bestowed the meanest
glance could give his mind whole-heartedly to the blind fury
demanded by war, could work himself into that state of passion
in which the aims of this or that political leader meant more to
him than the possession and the interchange of permanent
things? Could not the arts of all countries, when the futile storm
should break, become the images to be kept always before the
mind's eye, so that sanity should be preserved, the slenderest
bridge still arching rainbow-like over the rivers of hell? ... In all
the countries of Europe there was one imperishable link, one
common heritage; it was the only tangible thing we knew, the
only outward sign of grace. [28]

Index

Gate Theatre productions outside the Irish Free State/Republic of Ireland 1935-67

1935: London (Westminster Theatre)

Yahoo (Earl of Longford)
Hamlet (Shakespeare)
The Old Lady Says 'No!' (Johnston)

1936: Cairo (Opera House) and Alexandria (Alhambra Theatre)

Berkeley Square (Balderston and Squire)
Romeo and Juliet (Shakespeare)
Hamlet
The Taming of the Shrew (Shakespeare) [new to the Gate repertoire]
Payment Deferred (Jeffrey Dell) [new to the Gate repertoire][29]
Heartbreak House (Shaw)
The Provok'd Wife (Vanbrugh)
Apollo in Mourne (Richard Rowley), for broadcast on Egyptian Radio

1937: Cairo and Alexandria; Malta

Othello (Shakespeare)
Twelfth Night (Shakespeare)
The School for Scandal (Sheridan)
Death Takes a Holiday (Alberto Cassella)
Portrait in Marble (Hazel Ellis)
Close Quarters (W.O. Somin)
Carmilla (Le Fanu/Longford)
The Importance of Being Earnest (Wilde)
Laburnum Grove (J.B. Priestley)

1938: Belfast (Grand Opera House)

Macbeth (Shakespeare)
Hamlet
Night Must Fall (Emlyn Williams)
The Old Lady Says 'No!'
The Provok'd Wife
Victoria Regina (Lawrence Housman)

1938: Alexandria; Malta; Athens

Othello
Twelfth Night
Macbeth
Hamlet
Laburnum Grove
Portrait in Marble
Victoria Regina
The Provok'd Wife
Night Must Fall [at Port Said]

1939 (spring): Belfast

Wuthering Heights (Brontë/Ria Mooney and Donald Stauffer)
And So To Bed (James B. Fagan)
Night Must Fall

1939 (spring): Ljubljana [Slovenia]

Wuthering Heights
The Unguarded Hour (Ladislas Fodor)
And So to Bed

1939: Zagreb [Croatia]

Hamlet
Don Juan in Hell (Shaw)
The Importance of Being Earnest
Night Must Fall

1939: Belgrade [Serbia]

Macbeth
Hamlet [first English-language productions in Belgrade]

1939: Thessalonika [Greece]

Macbeth
The Comedy of Errors (Shakespeare)
Don Juan in Hell
Hamlet

1939: Sofia [Bulgaria]

The Comedy of Seriousness [The Importance of Being Earnest]
Macbeth
Hamlet
Night Must Fall

1939: Bucharest [Romania]

Night Must Fall
Macbeth
The Comedy of Errors
Don Juan in Hell
Bunbury [The Importance of Being Earnest][30]
Hamlet

1940: Belfast

Where Stars Walk (mac Liammóir)
Marrowbone Lane (Robert Collis)
Night Must Fall
A Hundred Years Old (Quintero brothers)
Gaslight (Patrick Hamilton)

1943: Larne, Ballymena, Omagh and Armagh

Arms and the Man (Shaw)
Gaslight
The Importance of Being Earnest
Ghosts (Ibsen)
Blithe Spirit (Coward)

1945: Northern Ireland tour at the invitation of CEMA: Bangor, Ballymena, Ballymoney, Portstewart, Derry, Omagh, Newry, Armagh, Portadown

Where Stars Walk
Othello
A Hundred Years Old

1947: Belfast

The Old Lady Says 'No!'
Portrait of Miriam (mac Liammóir)
Where Stars Walk

1947: Glasgow (Citizens' Theatre) and London (Embassy Theatre, Swiss Cottage)

The Old Lady Says 'No!'
Where Stars Walk
John Bull's Other Island (Shaw)

1948: Canada and New York: Ottawa (Grand Theatre), Montreal (His Majesty's Theatre), Toronto (Royal Alexandria Theatre), London [Ontario], Bradford

[Ontario]; New York (Mansfield Theatre) [six-week season]

John Bull's Other Island
The Old Lady Says 'No!
Where Stars Walk
Portrait of Miriam

1948: Belfast [in association with CEMA]

Ill Met by Moonlight (mac Liammóir)
The Drunkard (W.H. Smith)

1952: Elsinore [Denmark]

Hamlet [31]

1954: Belfast

Tolka Row (Maura Laverty)
Saint Joan (Shaw)

1955: Belfast

A Slipper for the Moon (mac Liammóir)
Not for Children (Elmer Rice)
Liffey Lane (Laverty)
Tolka Row

1956: Cairo and Alexandria; Malta

The Merchant of Venice (Shakespeare) [new to Gate repertoire]
Oedipus Rex (Aeschylus/Yeats)
The Man of Destiny (Shaw)
The Picture of Dorian Gray (Wilde/mac Liammóir)
The Lark (Anouilh)
The Seagull (Chekhov)
Ring Round the Moon (Anouilh)

1962: Tour of *Othello*
Switzerland (Geneva, Lausanne and Basel), Luxembourg, Belgium (Antwerp and Brussels), Holland (Utrecht,

Eindhoven, Rotterdam, Nijmwegen, Heerlen, Deventer, Hague)

1966: New York (Helen Hayes Theatre)
Philadelphia, Here I Come! (Friel)

1967: New York (Vivian Beaumont Theatre)
Lovers (Friel)

---

[1] See Appendix: factual information is derived from Richard Pine (ed.), *All for Hecuba: the Dublin Gate Theatre 1928-1978* (Dublin: Gate Theatre, 1978), Richard Pine, *The Dublin Gate Theatre 1928-1978* (Cambridge: Chadwyck-Healy, 1984), and Christopher Fitz-Simon, *The Boys: A biography of Micheál mac Liammóir and Hilton Edwards* (London: Nick Hern Books, 1994). The surname 'mac Liammóir' was a translation into Irish from the original 'Willmore', and appeared with lower-case 'mac' at its author's insistence.

[2] The Dublin Gate Theatre Studio was originally housed in the Peacock Theatre, the experimental stage of the Abbey (National) Theatre. The premises in the Rotunda, to which the Gate moved after renovation and adaptation by architect Michael Scott, were part of a complex originally erected in the eighteenth century for the purpose of fundraising to support the adjacent Rotunda maternity hospital.

[3] The Westminster Theatre continued to function, with further modifications in 1966 and 1972, until it was destroyed by fire in 2002.

[4] Anmer Hall (the name of an Elizabethan stately home) was the stage name of C.P. Horne, a member of a notable firm of clothiers: I am indebted to Richard Cave for this information. For a brief account of the influence of Peter Godfrey on Edwards and mac Liammóir, see Micheál mac Liammóir, *All for Hecuba: an Irish theatrical autobiography* (London: Methuen, 1946) pp.51-3, 58.

[5] Ibid., p.217.

[6] Quoted in Pine, *The Dublin Gate Theatre*, p.56.

[7] See Richard Cave, *Terence Gray and the Cambridge Festival Theatre* (Cambridge: Chadwyck-Healy, 1980).

[8] Due to the fact that he directed almost all productions, Edwards acted far less frequently than mac Liammóir but he excelled in roles such as Cyrano de Bergerac, Captain Shotover in Shaw's *Heartbreak House* and, in 1969, in a *tour de force* in the title role of Conor Cruise O'Brien's *King Herod Explains*.

[9] Mac Liammóir, *All for Hecuba*, p.217.

[10]Ibid., p.220. Today it would probably be equally necessary to explain these 'nuances' to an *Irish* audience.

[11] Ibid., p.165.

[12] Ibid., p.221.

[13] *Daily Telegraph*, 20 June 1935.

[14] See Fitz-Simon, *The Boys*.

[15] The incident was dramatised in 1994 as 'The Car in Corbawn Lane' (directed by Paul Cusack) as part of RTÉ Television's *Thou Shalt Not Kill* series on Irish murders.

[16] The Longford Company returned to the Westminster Theatre again in 1937.

[17]*Longford Productions: Dublin Gate Theatre Souvenir 1939*, p.10. The brochure listed Sligo, Galway, Tralee, Limerick, Clonmel, Waterford, Kilkenny, Thurles, Cork, Belfast and Dundalk as the venues for its 1936 Irish tour, to which it added Mullingar, Birr, Athlone, Longford, Cavan, Castlepollard, Tullamore, Drogheda, Carlow and Nenagh the following year. See also Bulmer Hobson (ed.), *The Dublin Gate Theatre* (Dublin: Gate Theatre, 1934).

[18] *Le Messager d'Athènes*, 6 April 1938.

[19] Hansard, Fifth series, vol. 344, col. 1955, 7 March 1939.

[20] Quoted in Fitz-Simon, *The Boys*, p.109.

[21] Hansard, vol. 355, cols. 1310-11, 14 December 1939. These sums would approximate to €18,000 and €175,000 respectively at current values.

[22] Fitz-Simon, *The Boys*, p.118.

[23] First performed on 9 November 1927, written, directed and produced by Fagan (1873-1933).

[24] Fitz-Simon, *The Boys*, pp.111, 123.

[25] *La Parole Bulgare*, 30 April 1939.

[26] H. Edwards, 'Nationalism in the Theatre Today', 1963, four-page typescript, collection of Northwestern University.

[27] Mac Liammóir, *All for Hecuba*, pp.349-50.

[28] Ibid., p.360; cf. Fintan O'Toole's article on the cultures of Europe, 'Have we finished drawing our borders in blood?', *Irish Times*, 27 April 2004, supplement 'The New Europe'.

[29] First performed 30 September 1931.

[30] *Bunbury* is a frequently used title for *The Importance of Being Earnest* in German-language countries.

[31] The Danish town of Elsinore invited, each year, a foreign theatre company to stage *Hamlet*.

10 | Marina Carr in the US: Perception, Conflict and Culture in Irish Theatre Abroad

Melissa Sihra

Now, more than ever before, there is a fascination with what it means to be Irish. This can be traced in no small way to the immense popularity of Irish theatre world-wide. From the founding of the Irish Literary Theatre in 1899 by poet W.B. Yeats and playwright Augusta Gregory, Irish drama has been consumed with producing and interrogating notions of 'Irishness'. This tendency towards the self-referential has not diminished and it is important to consider the ways in which staging Ireland today invokes both explicit, and at times more subtle, ideological, often contentious issues of representation which are fundamental to how the culture is processed. Each production and re-production of an Irish play, whether in Ireland or abroad, explores and performs the key question 'What is 'Ireland?', enabling, as Colin Graham observes, 'Ireland [to] become a plenitude of images, replicating itself for continual consumption'.[1] This essay will consider the reception of a number of recent productions of the plays of contemporary Irish dramatist Marina Carr in the United States. One such production, the Gate Theatre/Druid presentation of Carr's 2000 drama *On Raftery's Hill,* was directed by Garry

Hynes and toured to the Island: Arts from Ireland Festival in
Washington in May 2000. The other productions that will be
discussed are American rather than Irish touring shows;
however, these too involve the broader representational politics
of culture and performance.

Diverse responses to key Irish plays open up a way of
exploring the complex politics of performing 'Ireland'. A
comment made by a patron in an audience-survey questionnaire
at one of Marina Carr's plays in Pittsburgh in 2001 brings
together the central issues regarding the often divided and
resistant responses to Carr's work in the United States, and gets
to the heart of considering Irishness on the stage. The
comment reads as follows:

> Very positively disgusting. The Irish may drink and swear and
> fight but surely not as they were portrayed in the play (if that's
> what you call it). My kind of Irish are not interested in such
> *trash*.[2]

The play in question is *Portia Coughlan,* which was produced
by the Pittsburgh Irish and Classical Theatre Company in
March 2001. While this patron's response is extreme, it
importantly identifies an essential ontological investment in a
'kind of Irishness' that Carr's work ostensibly desecrates. The
equation of the content of the play with the underlined word
'trash' is revealing, identifying the work with waste-matter and
connoting undesirability and excess. In *Powers of Horror: An
Essay on Abjection,* Julia Kristeva discusses the nature of
repulsion aroused by residues, or what she calls 'the remainder',
highlighting their potential:

> Remainders are residues of something but especially of
> someone. They pollute on account of incompleteness … The
> remainder is a strongly ambivalent notion … defilement as well
> as re-birth, abjection as much as high purity.

Kristeva argues that the remainder is:

> a challenge to our mono-theistic and mono-logical universes
> [where] such a mode of thinking apparently needs the ambi-
> valence of remainder if it is not to become enclosed within *One*
> single-level symbolics.[3]

The positive disgust felt by this patron, and their association of the drama with rubbish or waste-matter, points to the containable, monological, or '*One* single-level symbolics' of Irish culture that Carr's representation seemingly exceeds and challenges.

The crucial part of this quotation is the subjective notion of Irishness that is implied in 'my kind of Irish'. If the politics of identity and authenticity are predicated upon the dynamic of exclusion, it would seem that there is a specific kind of Irishness to which *Portia Coughlan* does not relate. The second part of the quotation 'The Irish may drink and swear and fight but surely not as they were portrayed in the play (if that's what you call it)', would lead one to believe that there are 'acceptable' levels and types of fighting, swearing and drinking that *do* occur in Ireland and which, again, this play exceeds in, or deviates from, in terms of an innate Irish moral sensibility. The final notion, of calling into question whether this is a 'real' play at all, reveals an implicit association of 'permissible' representation with a privileged romantic and idealistic sensibility.

Such conflict occurs when a playwright's artistic vision confronts the spectator's sense of cultural identity and 'authenticity', and alienates or removes the spectator from their subjective comfort-zone, as occurred with J.M. Synge's *The Playboy of the Western World* in both Ireland and America in the last century. Carr's mature plays may be described as heightened realism, but realism nonetheless. Her characters inhabit spaces that are neither anachronistic nor atavistic, but which depict a deterioration of certainty in contemporary Irish society. Each one of Carr's plays explicitly reveals the rupture or increasing void created by the diminished authorities of church, family and state in Ireland. While Carr's theatre may privilege the remote, the rural, the local and the mythic, her vision is fundamentally recalcitrant to ahistorical bucolic and romantic representations of 'Irishness', most specifically in terms of landscape/place, language, the family, patriarchy and the Irish woman and/or mother figure. Evidently, it is this cultural and representational renegotiation that precipitates and exacerbates an identifiable diasporic trauma amongst certain Irish-American audiences. In her recent examination of Irish society, *Kicking and Screaming: Dragging Ireland into the 21st Century,* Ivana Bacik refers to Thomas Cahill's 1995 'emerald-tinted' US best-seller *How the Irish Saved Civilisation: The Untold Story of Ireland's Heroic Role from the Fall of Rome to the Rise of Medieval Europe.*[4] Bacik goes on to say that the study:

> leaves a cloying feeling, similar to that evoked by misty-eyed reminiscences of 'the oul' sod' by those who have never lived in this country. We know it is stretching the green fabric of patriotism beyond its elastic point. Yet this account of the unique Irish civilising influence holds sway with a large section of the Irish-American diaspora, in whose eyes we often see ourselves reflected from abroad. We may well be cynical about their romantic notions, but his highly skewed take on Irish history retains its influence and even thrives in some places, which means it is an image we must contend with.[5]

The response to the Pittsburgh *Portia Coughlan* is revealing. In a post-show discussion with the company's artistic director, Andrew Paul, a few notable issues came to light. He noted that:

> audiences [had] some difficulty with the structure of the play, and with the relentless intensity of the performance. Several patrons commented on their inability to connect or empathize with the characters.[6]

During the performances that I attended, as I have noted elsewhere, audience members laughed uncomfortably at swear words and, in particular, at the image of Portia and Gabriel making love in the womb.[7] While positively received by the critics, the reviews tended to cast the writing in a 'rather gloomy, grim, light'.[8] Chief critic of the *Pittsburgh Post-Gazette,* Christopher Rawson, whose notice was headed 'Portia is Drenched in Grim Truths', commented: 'Carr reminds me of Beckett – a great desolation is painfully and poetically probed without hope of deep change'.[9] It seems that the word 'grim' is a death-knell to shows in the United States and Paul believes that the tone of the critical response was a 'deterrent to the relatively conservative Pittsburgh casual arts consumer'. He continues that, 'Comedies and titles with instant name-recognition always perform better at the box-office'.[10] He saw the humour inherent in the writing emerge as the run progressed, until later audience members described the play as 'hilarious'. In considering the reception of *Portia Coughlan*, it seems that the lyrical quality of the writing, the women's roles and the ebullient moments of humour are what most resonated with the audience, while the structure, with Portia's death revealed in the middle, and the seeming lack of possibility for change or transformation (and in the case of this production, the fact that there was no interval), the subject-matter of incestuous relations and the abundance of alcohol and cursing, are what prevented audiences from relating fully to the work.[11]

In terms of the reception of Carr's plays in the United States, I note a tension between what critics and audiences have praised as being, on the one hand, Carr's theatrical writing skill with, on the other, the content of the plots, which have often alienated, and in some cases revolted audience members who have displayed difficulty in reconciling the lyrical elements of the plays with the uncompromising nature of the story-lines. Paul elaborates:

> It took me several years to develop the company to the degree that I could take risks with this type of *raw* drama. I think the play will challenge Pittsburgh audiences, and that is a good thing.[12]

Paul, who had seen *On Raftery's Hill* in Washington the previous year, noted how 'Its disturbing tone clearly unsettled the audience'. He went on to say:

> I think Carr's voice is unique, and will take more time to establish itself among American theatre-goers. Her vision of Ireland is certainly not one the Irish-Americans want to see and embrace. We seem to prefer Frank McCourt.[13]

Frank McCourt's narrative of an abject and abysmal Irish childhood in *Angela's Ashes* is mediated through the lens of history, offering a relatively distant past that, in order to remain visceral and emotive yet uncontroversial, must *remain* in the past. McCourt's trauma is expressed in the language of the past tense, transmitting the experience through the temporal screen of memory. He begins:

It was, of course, a miserable childhood ... Out on the Atlantic
Ocean great sheets of rain gathered to drift slowly up the River
Shannon and settle forever in Limerick.[14]

Carr's plays, on the other hand, are alarming in their *immediacy*,
an immediacy that seems to defile the diasporic investment in
nostos and any comforting notion of a genuine, absolute and
essential site of authentic origins. As Deirdre Mulrooney notes
in a review of *On Raftery's Hill*: '[it is] a scenario which is much
more terrifying [than the faraway fantasy land of *By the Bog of
Cats...*] because it is within the reach of reality'. [15] The
fetishization of a notional 'land of heart's desire' implied in the
utterance 'my kind of Irish' reveals the traumatic chasm
between an imagined, yet ostensibly knowable, sacred version
or vision of homeland or mother-land and Carr's depictions of
an Ireland in various present states of distress, crises and
transition.

The demographic of the Pittsburgh Irish and Classical
Theatre Company is important, and the fact that it is the '*Irish
and Classical Theatre Company*' immediately associates the
company with a specific cultural group, with a large proportion
of Irish-Americans funding and subscribing to the company.
The dominant characteristics of the patrons are as follows: they
are an average of fifty-three years old with incomes in excess of
$75,000. They are married and educated to post-graduate level.[16]
This is not irrelevant social minutiae, but reveals to a large
extent the target consumers of Irish theatre in the United
States. A fairly elite and, to quote Andrew Paul, 'conservative'
demographic can thus be identified. Key responses to *Portia
Coughlan* in the questionnaire include:

Mysterious, perverted psychological screw-up.

Very dysfunctional, difficult to watch or empathize with
characters.

Did not like the play.

More light material please – mysteries, musical comedy,
inspirational.

Time sequence difficult, old lady impossible, Ugh.

No excuse for no intermission when performance over 75 minutes long – we are too old.

Very well done but so depressing.[17]

Similarly emotive and vociferous responses resounded during the run of *On Raftery's Hill* at the Island: Arts from Ireland Festival at Washington's John F. Kennedy Center for the Performing Arts, which ran from 13-28 May 2000. Here, popular figures of Irish culture paraded one after the other: the President of Ireland, Mary McAleese, spoke about Ireland in the shadow of J.F.K. as Bill Whelan's *Riverdance* joined with the music of Mary Black, Sharon Shannon, Liam Ó Maonlaí and the poetry of Seamus Heaney, against a backdrop of moody romantic images by Paul Henry, Sir William Orpen and Walter Osborne. The theatre programme of the festival was billed as follows:

From Oscar Wilde to Samuel Beckett, Irish playwrights have delivered compelling characters, exciting drama and unforgettable dialogue ... theatre lovers make your plans now before the shows sell out.[18]

Carr's play, billed alongside Donal O'Kelly's *Catalpa* and Stewart Parker's *Pentecost*, was framed thus:

Ireland's 1998 Playwright of the Year Marina Carr has created [a] potent and visceral work with indelible characters of surreal eccentricities. This American première is one you will remember for years to come.[19]

Whatever about the play being visceral and potent, reactions certainly were, as people walked out in disbelief at the image of contemporary Ireland with which they were being confronted. The production was greeted with shocked silence, making it certainly an American premiere that would be remembered 'for years to come'. While invitations to readings by writers such as Frank McCourt and Jennifer Johnston offered an opportunity to 'experience the passion, pathos and profound humanity of Irish literature' *On Raftery's Hill* was seen as an atrocity upon the Ireland of the imagination.[20] Juxtaposing this reception with a positive local Irish review of the play, it is illuminating to see the ways in which one culture deems a work progressive and another, regressive. For the *Offaly Press*, Declan Meade wrote:

> It is brave of Carr to take on the theme of child sexual abuse at a time when Ireland, like so many other countries, is just beginning to come to terms with its prevalence. And she is braver still in her decision to steer away from any neat resolution.[21]

Inscribed within Carr's theatrical representation is a refusal to romanticize contemporary social realities. In her plays, domestic violence, cycles of sexual abuse, incest and death pervade most of the relationships on stage. For Carr, the notion of loss and 'the family [are] central to the drama'.[22] Carr says: 'All of my characters tend to be outsiders'.[23] However, while Carr's plays challenge accepted and acceptable notions of 'Irishness', certain aspects of her work are extremely popular in the US. It may be said that Carr's reputation is soaring in America, especially in universities and theatre cities such as San Francisco, Chicago, Boston and New York. Why then, is there such a dichotomy in terms of the reception of Carr's plays, when they are all equally violent and traumatic? It is due to the fact, as Mulrooney points out, that:

> [*On Raftery's Hill*] courageously tackles the tough and unappealing rural Irish variety [of characters and place] as opposed to the more palatable Greek version, head on and unflinchingly.[24]

Questions of form, as well as content, are intrinsic to how the work is mediated and received. The unanimously positive reception of Carr's 1998 drama *By the Bog of Cats...*, which has enjoyed multiple sell-out productions in the United States, indicates that an immensely different kind of cultural response is operating, due to the mediating factor of the Classical origins of this play, as distinct from the contemporary context of *Portia* and *On Raftery's Hill*.

The Chicago Irish Repertory Theatre produced the American premiere of *By the Bog of Cats...* in 2001. This high-profile company is not simply producing theatre, but promoting and selling access to an authentic sense of Irishness. A browse at the company website, www.irishrep.com, will reveal invitations to 'get involved', to attend functions with key Irish-American Chicagoans and Irish playwrights, actors and practitioners, and be a part of a community. [25] San José Repertory Theatre Company, which also produced the show in 2001 with Holly Hunter in the lead role, achieves similar levels of cultural association and context: San José is officially twinned with Dublin. This kind of cultural doubling, or mirroring, lends another level of authenticity to the project which is effectively commodified for consumption, again offering 'face-time' to major sponsors with playwrights such as Marina Carr at exclusive gala dinners and corporate receptions. Furthermore, Carr's plays are desirable because most of them have premiered at the Abbey, Peacock or Gate Theatres in Dublin. Such positioning and artistic association is attractive to international practitioners and audiences. The Abbey Theatre, especially, has instant name-recognition in the United States, which offers further levels of cultural and artistic authenticity to the marketing project abroad in offering a product that is perceived as the very best of contemporary Irish theatre.

Audience and critic receptions of *By the Bog of Cats...* were unanimously positive. In the *Chicago Sun-Times*, a critic wrote: 'Shakespeare was a master at orchestrating ... volatile moods. The young Irish dramatist Marina Carr clearly shares his gift'.[26] West Coast critics commented repeatedly on the desirability of the role of Hester: 'It is a role that every great actress would love to obtain', noted Richard Connema.[27] Similarly, with the other productions of *By the Bog of Cats...* the scale of the narrative was praised:

> Carr has emerged quietly as one of Ireland's finest on the strength of her ability to draw characters and situations on an operatic scale.[28]

It would appear then that *By the Bog of Cats...*, which is loosely based on Euripides' *Medea*, seems to be a less controversial depiction of contemporary Ireland than *On Raftery's Hill* or *Portia Coughlan*, due to the mythic distance which is afforded it. A contemporary version of *Medea* culturally

contextualizes, and in a sense, validates, the narrative content of
infanticide, on-stage suicide, attempted rape and incest
contained in *By the Bog of Cats*.... While many audience
members left at the interval, or indeed walked out, of *On
Raftery's Hill* when it played in Washington, the same action of
attempted rape, which occurred in both US stagings of *By the
Bog of Cats*... (with Xavier physically forcing himself upon an
incapacitated Hester in Act Three, graphically simulating an act
of sexual violation), did not cause the same audience reaction.
This raises the question as to whether on-stage violence and
violation is more palatable when filtered through a
transhistorical, Euripidean lens, than off-stage, 'un-Classically'
mediated suicide, in the case of *Portia Coughlan*. While *By the Bog
of Cats*... is considered 'fearless', 'sweepingly theatrical' and
'courageous', *Portia* is viewed as grim, unrelenting, hopeless and
despairing.

Carr's heightened and excessive theatrical explorations of
violence, death, loss and abjection are something for which she
has been continually criticized and yet her representation of
these immense themes is what has confirmed her central
position in contemporary Irish theatre. Riana O'Dwyer
comments that Garry Hynes,

> who has been centrally involved in the development of scripts
> by women both in the Druid Theatre in Galway and during her
> tenure as the Artistic Director in the Abbey Theatre, has
> identified some limitations in the scripts that she has read.

Back in 1995, Hynes significantly complained: 'I just sometimes
long for a woman to write, please, on a broader, more public,
more epic scale'.[29]   In terms of Carr's uncompromising and, at
times, brutal dramaturgic confrontations, Frank McGuinness
observes: 'Seeing the development of Marina Carr — that has
been, I think, the development of a major new voice, a fearless
voice, a woman who will take on enormous challenges'.[30]

'Diaspora' has its roots in the Greek *diaspeirein*, meaning
disperse, and the Irish theatrical diaspora continues to disperse,
and perpetuate or regenerate various conceptions of Irishness.
As Bacik observes:

There are many Irelands, just as there are many facets of Irish
identity, and to attempt to describe a collective form of
'Irishness' represents an exercise in gross generalization.[31]

If theatre does not ask difficult questions and interrogate our
assumptions, it is redundant. Carr's plays are difficult, but
crucial in their vocalization of the immense recent changes in
attitude in Irish society. Lyn Gardner says of the recent Olivier
Award nominated production of *By the Bog of Cats...* in London's
Wyndham Theatre:

What marks out Carr's work is her knowing compassion for the
damaged, the distraught, for those who howl and rage as they
rush towards their inevitable doom.[32]

It is crucial that theatrical representations of Ireland are not
ossified by stable and paralysing preconceptions of culture,
context and expression. The artist's vision must be allowed
expression, even if it is considered by some to be a 'mysterious,
perverted psychological screw-up'. Carr says:

There is a place for the moral high ground, but it is not in art.
You have to let the characters have their say. Plays are written
with the imagination, not with the head.[33]

The traumatic chasmic gaps of authority in the late twentieth
century are reflected and expressed in Marina Carr's plays, and
this immediacy and renegotiation of what Irishness is will
continue to provoke a complex and necessary set of responses,
as both Irish and American audiences attempt to reconcile past
perceptions with present realities and future possibilities.

---

[1] Colin Graham, *Deconstructing Ireland: Identity, Theory, Culture*, (Edinburgh:
Edinburgh University Press, 2001) p.2.

[2] Melissa Sihra, 'Reflections Across Water: New Stages of Performing
Carr', in Anna McMullan and Cathy Leeney (eds.), *The Theatre of
Marina Carr: ...before rules was made* (Dublin: Carysfort Press, 2003),
p.102.

[3] Julia Kristeva, *The Powers of Horror: An Essay on Abjection* (New York:
Columbia University Press, 1986), p.76.

[4] Ivana Bacik, *Kicking and Screaming: Dragging Ireland into the 21st Century*
(Dublin: O'Brien Press, 2004), p.13.

5 Ibid., p.14.

6 Unpublished e-mail correspondence between Andrew Paul and Melissa Sihra, 10 April 2001.

7 McMullan and Leeney (eds.), *Theatre of Marina Carr*, p.102.

8 Unpublished Pittsburgh Irish and Classical Theatre audience survey, March-April 2001.

9 *Pittsburgh Post-Gazette*, 28 March 2001, p.12.

10 Unpublished e-mail correspondence between Andrew Paul and Melissa Sihra, 22 January 2001.

11 Ibid..

12 Ibid..

13 Ibid..

14 Frank McCourt, *Angela's Ashes: A Memoir of a Childhood* (London: Flamingo, 1997), p.1.

15 Deirdre Mulrooney, 'Marina Carr Climbs Up Raftery's Hill', www.deir.ie/OnRaftery'sHill.html, site accessed 1 March 2004.

16 Unpublished PICT audience survey, March 2001.

17 Ibid..

18 http://kennedy-center.org/irishfestival. Site accessed 7 March 2004.

19 Ibid..

20 Ibid..

21 http://offaly.local.ie/content/50488.shtml/literature/books. Site accessed 1 March 2004.

22 Melissa Sihra, unpublished interview with Marina Carr, 8 February 1999.

23 Ibid.

24 Mulrooney, 'Marina Carr Climbs Up Raftery's Hill'.

25 www.irishrep.com. Site accessed 18 February 2004.

26 *Chicago Sun-Times*, 5 June 2001, p.36.

27 Regional News & Reviews: San Francisco, http://talkinbroadwaycom/regional/sanfran/s139.html. Site accessed 27 September 2001.

28 *San Francisco Weekly*, 26 September 2001, p.18.

29 Riana O'Dwyer, 'The Imagination of Women's Reality: Christina Reid and Marina Carr' in Eamon Jordan (ed.) *Theatre Stuff: Critical Essays on Contemporary Irish Theatre* (Dublin: Carysfort Press, 2000), p.239. O'Dwyer cites Garry Hynes, in Harris (Moderator): 'Is Ireland a Matriarchy or not? The Experience of Women as Theatre Artists', Discussion Document for ACIS-CAIS, Belfast Conference, 1995.

30 Frank McGuinness in conversation with Joseph Long, in Lilian Chambers, Ger Fitzgibbon and Eamonn Jordan (eds) *Theatre Talk:*

Voices of Irish Theatre Practitioners (Dublin: Carysfort Press, 2001), p.307.

[31] Bacik, *Kicking and Screaming*, p.18.

[32] Lyn Gardner, 'Death Becomes Her', *Guardian*, 29 November 2004, p.16.

[33] Gardner, 'Death Becomes Her'.

11 | Druid Theatre's *Leenane Trilogy* on Tour: 1996-2001

Patrick Lonergan

The international success of *The Leenane Trilogy* helped to make Druid Theatre one of Ireland's most celebrated companies – but it also helped to make Martin McDonagh one of Ireland's most controversial dramatists. I want to consider how Druid's five-year tour of McDonagh's plays managed to generate these apparently contradictory responses, suggesting that Druid's impact on McDonagh's career has been undeservedly neglected. By doing so, I want to offer an analysis of the impact of Irish theatre on tour on Irish theatre criticism.[1]

1

Druid's tours of *The Leenane Trilogy* lasted from 1996 to 2001. A co-production with London's Royal Court Theatre, *The Trilogy* played in thirty-one venues in Ireland, north and south, and was also produced in England, Australia, the United States, and Canada. Its production history offers an excellent example of the many different ways in which it is possible to speak of Irish theatre on tour: I want therefore to give an overview of that history before proceeding to a consideration of the productions themselves.

The Beauty Queen of Leenane premiered in Galway on 1 February 1996. It was chosen by Druid's artistic director Garry

Hynes to mark two special occasions: the twenty-first birthday
of Druid, and the opening of a municipal theatre in Galway.
The production then toured to Longford, Kilkenny, and
Limerick, before transferring to the Royal Court Theatre
Upstairs in May 1996. *Beauty Queen* arrived in London at a time
when new writing was becoming increasingly popular, especially
at the Royal Court. Under the artistic directorship of Stephen
Daldry, the Court premiered new writers such as Sarah Kane
and Mark Ravenhill, and helped to raise the international profile
of other important dramatists, many of them Irish.[2] Following
its London premiere, *The Beauty Queen* went on one of Druid's
famous 'unusual rural tours',[3] playing in Skibbereen, Portmagee,
Lisdoonvarna, each of the three Aran Islands, Arrain Mor,
Rathlin Island, and Erris Island. Druid also visited larger venues
in Tralee, Enniskillen, and Derry, before concluding in Leenane
in County Galway, itself. A week later, *Beauty Queen* transferred
to the West End. By this time, McDonagh had won a number
of awards for the play, and was developing a reputation for bad
behaviour after a highly publicized drunken argument with the
actor Sean Connery.

In June 1997, A Skull in Connemara and The Lonesome
West premiered, again in Galway, joining Beauty Queen to
become The Leenane Trilogy. McDonagh's reputation for
loutish out-spokenness was by this time well established, as he
may himself have been acknowledging when he gave the most
loutish and outspoken character in his Trilogy – Máirtín in A
Skull in Connemara – the Irish version of his own name. After
its West End run, The Trilogy ran for a week in Cork, and
played for ten days at the 1997 Dublin Theatre Festival, where
the production was named 'Reuters Play of the Year' (by a
three-person jury that included Marina Carr) in a festival that
also featured new work from Robert Lepage and Thomas
Kilroy.

McDonagh's international profile grew throughout 1998: *The
Trilogy* appeared at the Sydney Festival, and *Beauty Queen* opened
in New York, where it later won four Tony Awards. *The
Lonesome West* opened with its original cast on Broadway in 1999
and, although it was less popular than *Beauty Queen*, it was

nominated for four Tony Awards. In the same year, Garry Hynes directed local casts in Australian and Canadian productions of *The Beauty Queen.*

The Irish media had kept its readers apprised of McDonagh's success, both nationally and internationally, with the result that Dublin theatregoers expressed frustration that his plays were not more frequently produced in Dublin. These complaints appeared even before *The Trilogy* premiered there, with letters to the *Irish Times* complaining that Druid was neglecting Dublin audiences. Druid company manager Louise Donlon replied to these complaints by stating that Druid's 'first commitment is to its audiences in Galway and its touring venues in Ireland'. [4] The plays were performed at the 1997 Dublin Theatre Festival some months later, but did not receive a sustained run in the Irish capital until 2000, when *The Beauty Queen* played at the Gaiety, a large commercial theatre. In 2001, *The Lonesome West* appeared at the same venue. The final Druid production of McDonagh's Leenane plays was a two-week run of *The Lonesome West* in Galway in October 2001.

This five-year tour involved a variety of venues and audiences, and achieved many objectives. The premiere of *Beauty Queen* in Galway was an act of localized, civic celebration. *The Trilogy's* tours in Ireland – including visits to some of the most isolated parts of the island – are an excellent example of the capacity of subsidized theatre to operate as a force for cultural inclusion. As a co-production with the Royal Court, *The Trilogy* formalized a partnership between Irish and English theatre that has since been a feature of the work of such writers as Conor McPherson, Sebastian Barry, and Stella Feehily. *The Trilogy* can also be seen as an example of event-driven theatre, which made it ideal for the Sydney Festival and the Dublin Theatre Festival. The 1999 productions of *Beauty Queen* in Sydney and Toronto – with local casts directed by Garry Hynes – offer an interesting way of thinking about Irish theatre on tour: the Druid aesthetic remained in place, but audiences received the plays as local productions. And on Broadway and in Dublin, the plays appeared in commercial, rather than subsidized, venues.

This variety is important when one considers how debate about McDonagh's work had become increasingly contentious while the plays were on tour – so that, by the time *Beauty Queen* reached the Gaiety in 2000, McDonagh's work was considered objectionable in two ways. First, it was argued that he was parading images of degraded Irish stereotypes before middle-class, urban audiences, portraying rural Ireland as a 'benighted dystopia' in a way that allowed those audiences to evade their responsibilities to the genuinely marginalized members of Irish society.[5] A second accusation was that McDonagh's 'depiction of the Irish is particularly problematic when it's exported, because … It feeds the whole *Angela's Ashes* view of Ireland. When it travels, it's taken at face value'.[6] These debates rarely included consideration of the role of Druid in the reception of McDonagh, with analyses often proceeding directly from McDonagh's scripts to inferences about audience response. Writing about a 2002 production of *The Lonesome West* in Avignon, Ian Kilroy could remark that 'Druid's role in the rise of McDonagh seems to have been air-brushed away'.[7]

Illustration 8: **Garry Hynes in rehearsal. Courtesy of Druid Theatre Company, photo by Ivan Kincyl.**

Although this claim was slightly hyperbolic, it does have some validity, since many of the criticisms directed against McDonagh persist because Druid's influence on his career has yet to receive substantial attention. To illustrate this, Druid's influence on the reception of McDonagh's work must be considered.

Illustration 9: **Martin McDonagh in rehearsal. Courtesy of Druid Theatre Company, photo by Ivan Kincyl.**

2

Garry Hynes – both at Druid and the Abbey Theatre – has had an important impact on the development of contemporary Irish playwriting, by commissioning and directing some of the most significant plays of recent years, including Murphy's *Bailegangaire* (1985) and Carr's *Portia Coughlan* (1996). [8] Questions about McDonagh's work should thus include a consideration of Hynes's influence on his writing. Contrary to Richard Eyre's assertion that McDonagh had 'sprung from the womb a fully-fledged playwright'[9], Hynes did not just discover McDonagh but, as Michael Ross states, she developed him too – working with him to cut scenes and lines from his original scripts, which developed through many drafts. For example, *The Lonesome West* originally involved only three characters, the two brothers and a

female character from England; it was only in later drafts that
the female character became Girleen, while Fr Welsh was
added. [10] Similarly, questions about the impact of Synge on
McDonagh might start with Hynes, whose reputation is
founded on her productions of *The Playboy of the Western World*
(1975, 1977, 1982, 1985, 2004-5). McDonagh had not read
Synge before he wrote the *Leenane* plays; but he had done so
before they premiered, as shown when he told an interviewer in
April 1997 that 'the darkness of [*The Playboy*] amazed me. I
thought it would be one of those classics that you read in order
to have read, rather than to enjoy, but it was great'. [11]

McDonagh is frequently described as a provocative
playwright, but Druid also has a history of challenging its
audiences' assumptions, ideals, and pieties. For example, Hynes
explains that she chose *Beauty Queen* to mark the opening of the
Town Hall Theatre from a desire to surprise her audience. The
opening night audience, she said, would arrive at the theatre,
'expecting a particular kind of play' – presumably a work similar
to Druid's signature pieces such as *The Playboy* and *Bailegangaire*.
'For the first few moments', said Hynes, 'the audience will feel
"oh lovely, this is a Druid play, we know where we are". And
then'. [12]

The style of performance employed by Druid is particularly
important in this regard. As Fintan O'Toole observes,
McDonagh's plays are an ideal vehicle for Druid's acting style,
which is famous for exploding 'naturalism from within, starting
with the apparently familiar and making it very strange'. [13]
Hynes's style of direction during *The Trilogy* therefore presented
the absurd naturalistically. When she directed *The Lonesome West*,
she stated that actors and director

> have to absolutely believe that Valene will not allow his brother
> to eat a packet of his Tayto [potato crisps]. If you think of that
> as a joke, and take that attitude to it in rehearsal, then the play
> doesn't exist. [14]

This presentation of the strange as if it were familiar is evident
throughout the *Trilogy*. Each play in *The Trilogy* represents one
of the major institutions in Irish life – *Beauty Queen* deals with

the family, *Skull* with the law, and *The Lonesome West* with the church – at a time when the place of those authorities in Ireland were being severely undermined by revelations about political corruption, and institutional and familial abuse. *The Leenane Trilogy* therefore confronts many uncomfortable Irish truths, and is troubling precisely because of its resemblance to, but divergence from, the apparently familiar.

This meant that the plays were received in a variety of ways by audiences throughout Ireland. An excellent example of this is the contrasting responses of audiences in Leenane and the Aran Islands – two places that McDonagh himself presents as interchangeable – to the *Beauty Queen*. During the first scene of the play, Mag and Maureen debate the merits of the Irish language. Irish, says Mag, 'sounds like nonsense to me. Why can't they just speak English like everybody? ... Where would Irish get you going for a job in England? Nowhere'.[15] Uinsionn Mac Dubhghaill explains that Mag's statement exposes a 'deeply-felt conviction, held in many Gaeltacht communities, that Irish is of no value'. This feeling, he suggests, is 'not often articulated openly in public, for fear of jeopardizing the community's chances of getting any grants that might be going'. The performance of this line on the Aran Islands meant that someone 'on stage [is] saying what many privately feel, and the audience [in Inis Mór] is loving it'.[16] However, when the play was performed in Leenane, the audience was silent during the same scene, because, Mac Dubhghaill proposes, Mag's opinion came as 'an unwelcome reminder in an area where the decision to abandon Irish as a community language is still uncomfortably close'.

There are numerous other examples of this kind of diversity. In her review of the Belfast production of *A Skull in Connemara*, Joyce McMillan points out that 'some of the audience at the Lyric clearly found the tone objectionable, and one or two walked out'.[17] She notes that the audience responded interestingly to McDonagh's reference to an IRA bombing. When Thomas states that 'I would *like* there to be bodies flying about everywhere, but there never is', Mick suggests that he should '[g]o up ahead North so. You'll be well away. Hang about a bookies or somewhere'. [18] Understandably, this line generated different responses in Belfast, Armagh, Sligo, Tralee, and Dublin. The important point however is that Druid's tours of *The Trilogy* allowed audiences throughout Ireland to explore distinctively local preoccupations.

As with Joyce, Synge, Murphy, and many other important Irish artists, Garry Hynes's imagination might be said to be dominated by the image of the mirror – the cracked looking glass – that presents the audience with a skewed version of itself. This has been a literal feature of her versions of *The Playboy of the Western World* and her inaugural Abbey production, *The Plough and the Stars* (1991), and features in her versions of plays such as Stoppard's *Real Inspector Hound* (1980) or Mark O'Rowe's *Crestfall* (Gate Theatre, 2003). It also operates metaphorically throughout her work. *The Leenane Trilogy* may be considered in the context of this tradition, since it involves audience members in the theatrical event by drawing their attention to the artificiality of the action. It is also a central, if neglected, feature of Martin McDonagh's writing, which in its entirety explores the divergence between representation and reality. McDonagh's ability to exploit, and draw attention to, his audiences' willingness to receive information passively has dominated his six produced plays, explicitly so in *The Pillowman* (2003). This explains Fintan O'Toole's suggestion that if Martin McDonagh had not existed, Garry Hynes would have invented him. [19] McDonagh and Hynes are driven by similar preoccupations; the disproportionate emphasis on McDonagh's input into their joint success therefore seems inappropriate.

The most important impact of Druid on McDonagh is the theatre's touring policy. Before *The Leenane Trilogy* premiered, Druid had (according to Garry Hynes) visited seventy-one different venues in Ireland and abroad, including London, Sydney, and New York. Hynes explains that by the time they premiered *The Beauty Queen*, touring was 'not just something we do after we do everything else', but was in fact central 'not just to the strategic policy of the company but to the artistic policy as well'.[20]

When Druid took *The Trilogy* abroad, the company already had a well-developed reputation. It first toured internationally in 1980, bringing four plays to the Edinburgh Festival.[21] Visits to London with *The Playboy of the Western World*, *Bailegangaire*, and *Conversations on a Homecoming* followed, and there were also tours to Sydney and New York. This meant that the arrival of Druid at the Royal Court in 1996 marked the *return* of a company whose style was familiar to many London critics. To an extent, this was also the case in Sydney, where the company has a 'huge following' after tours of *The Playboy of the Western World* and *At the Black Pig's Dyke*.[22] Put simply, *The Leenane Trilogy* would probably not have appeared in London, New York, and Australia if Druid had not already developed relationships with producers and audiences in those places. The assertion that McDonagh's work was received at 'face value' by international audiences thus overlooks the fact that Druid toured McDonagh with a reputation behind them, and put a great deal of energy into maintaining the integrity of that reputation. The company ensured that the premiere of the play in each of the major Anglophone theatrical centres was directed by Garry Hynes, illustrating its commitment to determining the reception of McDonagh's work. The evidence available in Ireland suggests that these efforts were for the most part successful, and that perhaps more can be learnt about the plays by considering their reception in terms of the local issues – social, cultural, or political – in each location on the tour.

3

Although Druid presented almost identical versions of the plays in London, Sydney and New York, there were substantial differences in the responses of audiences in each place.

The reception of McDonagh in London may, for example, be considered in terms of the role of celebrity in British culture. The importance of celebrity to the British theatre intensified considerably during the 1990s: increasing numbers of Hollywood stars appeared in the West End, and writers who had become well-known in other media, such as Irvine Welsh,

Ben Elton and, notoriously, Jeffrey Archer, had plays produced on the strength of their reputations. Writers also achieved success by writing *about* celebrities. Terry Johnson's *Cleo, Camping, Emmanuelle and Dick* (1998), which presented Barbara Windsor, Sid James and Kenneth Williams, was very successful. Similarly, *The Play Wot I Wrote* (2001) by Sean Foley and Hamish McColl is not only about Morecambe and Wise, but also starred a different celebrity on each night of its performance, featuring guest appearances from Ralph Fiennes, Kylie Minogue, David Beckham, and numerous others during its London run.

This fascination with celebrity has influenced the media's relationship with many playwrights, notably Martin McDonagh and Sarah Kane. McDonagh, in the words of Fintan O'Toole, became famous not for his writing, but for 'telling Sean Connery to fuck off'. [23] Similarly, only three years after her début, Sarah Kane was forced to produce *Cleansed* under the pseudonym 'Marie Kelvedon', which was, according to David Grieg:

> partly a private joke and partly a serious attempt to allow her work to escape, briefly, from the shadow of being [written by] 'Sarah Kane, the controversial author of *Blasted*'. [24]

Another important feature of McDonagh's reception in England is the way in which he exposed anxieties about Ireland's role in British society in the 1990s. At the start of that decade, Anglo-Irish relations were dominated by the Troubles; by the turn of the century they were dominated by the influx of Irish investment capital into British commercial property. McDonagh's work plays provocatively with the confusion generated by this transformation. His plays are accused of presenting the stereotypical Irish male as an inexplicably violent rural caveman, feeding into stereotypes associated with the Irish during the IRA's bombing campaign in England. Yet McDonagh's public persona plays against a new Irish stereotype: the cosmopolitan *nouveau riche* Anglo-Irishman. Particularly in the case of *The Beauty Queen*, *The Trilogy* highlights the existence of anti-Irish prejudice in Britain. McDonagh states that many aspects of Mag's description of her time in London

came from stories my mum told me – she worked in similar
jobs when she first came over from Ireland. And, like the play,
she had to have a black woman explain what those abusive
words meant.[25]

It appears then that McDonagh's consideration of the role of
the Irish in Britain confused many, especially when they realized
that the playwright did not conform to received images of
Irishness.

The plays reached Australia at a time when that country was
undergoing a growth in cultural self-confidence. Like Ireland,
Australia was becoming more aware of itself as occupying a role
on the global stage, and culture was an important element of its
attempt to come to terms with this development. Hence, media
coverage, both of the original 1998 Druid production and the
1999 touring Sydney Theatre Company production directed by
Garry Hynes, focussed more on what the plays might be saying
to Australia, than on what they might be saying about Ireland.
The Irish origin and setting of the plays was certainly
considered: when the question of authenticity arose, it was
treated as if the reader would understand that the plays are self-
evidently inauthentic. One report on the visit of the touring
production to Canberra encapsulates this well, telling readers
that 'of course it's not an Ireland that exists any longer', and
that 'one might argue that *The Beauty Queen of Leenane* is actually
a post-modern play written about the stage Irish more than the
real people'.[26] Considerably more attention was paid to
McDonagh's use of Australian soap opera. Indeed, in the 1999
tour of Beauty Queen, the lead role was given to Maggie
Kirkpatrick, one of the stars of *Prisoner, Cell Block H*, implying
that Australian producers wanted to highlight this aspect of the
play. So while Irish critics worried about Australians taking
McDonagh literally, in Australia, his plays appear to have
become part of that country's debate about how its own
cultural exports play out for overseas audiences.

Similarly, in New York, both *The Beauty Queen* and *The
Lonesome West* were received in the context of American
preoccupations. Whereas in Britain, McDonagh was presented

as the 'bad boy' of British theatre, American journalists
celebrated him as an example of the American 'rags to riches'
narrative. A major news report broadcast on NBC focused on
his overnight success, concluding with the message that
'McDonagh's take is five percent of the box office. So, with a
good five-week run, he could leave America with $100,000 in
his pocket' (the play, it should be noted, ran for almost a year).[27]
Similarly, *Beauty Queen* was seen as one of a number of foreign
imports needed to shake Broadway out of a perceived lethargy.
'Sometimes you don't even know what you've been craving
until the real thing comes along', wrote Ben Brantley in the *New
York Times*, who thought that watching *The Beauty Queen* was
'like sitting down to a square meal after a long diet of salads and
hors d'oeuvres'. [28] This might be some kind of subliminal
evocation of the impact of the Irish Famine on American life,
but Brantley's explicit statement is that the function of the play
is not to represent Ireland, but to transform American drama.
The Lonesome West was also received in terms of American
society: because it opened soon after 1999 high-school
shootings in Colorado, it became part of the debate about the
relationships between violence and art in America, with Garry
Hynes being called upon for her opinion on American gun-
control in pre-publicity for the show.[29]

   There is little evidence that audiences took either of the
Druid productions on Broadway at 'face value'. Maeliosa
Stafford, who played Coleman in *The Lonesome West* on
Broadway, stated that 'New York audiences "get" everything,
they are with us, they understand Martin's dark humor.'[30] Dawn
Bradfield, who played Girleen in the same production, agreed,
stating that she was surprised most by the conservatism of
American audiences: 'there was a huge reaction to the bad
language and to taking the piss out of the priest'.[31]

   So, just as Irish people's engagement with an American film
in *The Cripple of Inishmaan* prompts the observation that, 'Ireland
mustn't be such a bad place so if sharks want to come to
Ireland', the performances of McDonagh's play in Britain,
America and Australia were used to initiate discussions about
localized concerns.[32] The evidence available in Ireland – while

no substitute for actual attendance at the plays – suggests that although some audiences do take the plays as literal representations of Irish life, it is possible to consider McDonagh's international reception from many perspectives.

In 1999, the rights were released to *The Leenane Trilogy*, after which some versions of the plays were produced independently of Druid, and in ways that might be troubling for an Irish audience. For example, when Bernard Bloch directed and translated *The Lonesome West* as *L'Ouest Solitaire* at the 2002 Avignon Festival, he stated that

> the directorial approach will be to look at the fratricidal combat of the Connor brothers as a conflict reminiscent of the Northern conflict between Protestants and Catholics'.[33]

Similarly, one of the earliest regional US productions of *The Beauty Queen* took place in 1999 in Virginia, where the director declared outright that the play is 'a true representation of Ireland, particularly in the north.[34]

This suggestion that the senseless violence portrayed onstage might serve as a direct analogy for political violence in Northern Ireland might worry some Irish audiences. But it is worth observing that many theatre companies superficially invoke military conflicts in productions of everything from Sophocles to Shakespeare as a way of creating the appearance of relevance and depth, frequently where none exists.

There are, however, many examples of positive treatments of the plays. In November 1998, a *Los Angeles Times* critic, reviewing an American production of *The Cripple of Inishmaan* at the Geffen playhouse, stated that McDonagh's negative representation of the Irish arose from his being a Londoner. This gave rise to a well-informed debate in the letters page of that newspaper about the Irish elements of the play.[35] In the same year, the Court Theatre of Christchurch, New Zealand, also produced *Inishmaan*, accompanying their production with a programme that included background information about McDonagh, the Aran Islands, Robert Flaherty [director of *Man of Aran*], and many other aspects of the play. It also produced an educational resource kit for students, which included an interesting 'before and after' exercise. Student audiences were asked before the show to write down three stereotypes commonly associated with the Irish; they then had to consult their list when the play had finished, and discuss how McDonagh had undermined their preconceptions. Drawing attention to the difference between the world that 'we live in' and the 'world [that] is imagined by others', the booklet asked its audience to consider how the play might apply to New Zealand.[36]

The diversity of these responses is important: the same play means different things, to different people, at different times. To suggest therefore that people abroad took the plays at 'face value' is a disservice to the sophistication of audiences and theatre practitioners throughout the world. It also ignores the efforts made by Druid to ensure that the plays were received appropriately, and it ignores the success of those efforts. How then can the persistence of the view that McDonagh's reception abroad is objectionable be explained?

4

Irish awareness of the international reception of McDonagh is derived from reports appearing in the news, rather than the arts, sections of Irish and British newspapers. The opening of *The Beauty Queen* on Broadway prompted the *Sunday Times* to declare that Druid's achievement proved that it was 'hip to be Hibernian'.[37] The *Irish Times* also emphasized the value of the play, not by discussing its subject matter but by printing comments in praise of Druid from Mick Lally and Jennifer Aniston. This, of course, was an interesting blend of *Glenroe* and *Friends* that resonates with McDonagh's own mix of tradition and postmodernity.[38] And a month later, that newspaper also ran an article about how Druid's achievement showed that is was 'hip to be Irish'.[39] A similar process was under way in the British media, where the success of McDonagh's play was mentioned in articles with headlines such as 'Broadway bows to Brits'.[40] Throughout the subsequent coverage in both countries' media of the play's success at the

1998 Tony Awards, there was genuine pleasure at Garry Hynes's achievement in becoming the first woman to win a Tony Award for best director. Yet these reports never involved substantial discussion of the theatrical elements of Druid's work, or the relationship of that work to contemporary Irish and British society. Instead the plays' success was invoked in ways that can only be called nationalistic. This is unfortunate, since the work of Druid can in no way be considered consistent with the notion that it might be hip to be Hibernian, or that Britannia might be cool.

One consequence of this is that our understanding of McDonagh's work has been conditioned by journalism that was written by people who in some cases had no knowledge of theatre, leading to reporting that is often inaccurate, superficial, and sensationalistic. *Time* magazine reported that the performance in London's West End of *The Leenane Trilogy* and *The Cripple of Inishmaan* made McDonagh 'the only writer this season, apart from Shakespeare, to have four plays running concurrently in London'.[41] This report transformed quickly into the wild assertion that McDonagh was the first playwright *since* Shakespeare to have four plays running in London.[42] In his early interviews, McDonagh stated that he had not seen many plays, but talked intelligently about Joe Orton and Synge, and explained that his use of an Irish idiom was an attempt to escape the influence of Pinter and Mamet.[43] Such references dropped out of later interviews, in which McDonagh was portrayed as 'an upcoming enigmatic pop-star', an iconoclast, out to puncture the complacent self-regard of London's theatre elite.[44] Confronted with a mass of contradictory and self-evidently absurd information, some commentators began to think that the writer himself might be a fraud.[45]

A second consequence of this focus on the international reception of McDonagh is that Druid's rural and provincial tours of the plays have been ignored. Serious touring in rural Ireland has long been central to Druid, and its Irish tours are a significant aspect of *The Leenane Trilogy's* production history. Of the thirty-one Irish venues where the plays were produced, only six could be described as urban: the remaining twenty-five included provincial and rural locations throughout Ireland, north and south. Druid's Irish tours were not separate from the international performances. A week before *The Beauty Queen* transferred to the West End, it played in Leenane itself. Two months before *The Lonesome West* opened on Broadway, Druid cast Pat Shortt and Jon Kenny of the comedy-duo D'Unbelievables in the same play, and brought them on an eleven-venue Irish tour.

This complicates the suggestion that McDonagh is writing for the urban middle class. It may well be true that urban audiences throughout Ireland reacted complacently to his plays, but it is troubling and ironic that those audiences' reactions have been considered sufficient to define the reception of the plays for Ireland in its entirety. The omission of rural and provincial Ireland from discourse about the plays means that our understanding of McDonagh's reception in Ireland is incomplete and imbalanced. That omission fails to take account of the fact that Druid's touring policy asserts the *value* of provincial and rural Ireland. Druid made this assertion by bringing the plays to provincial and rural venues; and by bypassing the capital, directly representing Ireland on the international stage. Druid's tours of *The Trilogy* should therefore be seen as part of the company's history of challenging Dublin's claim to be a cultural centre that could define Galway as peripheral.

5

Why has the role of Druid Theatre in Martin McDonagh's career been 'airbrushed' away? In part, this erasure occurs because criticism of McDonagh's work operates within a globalized framework, in which information that is accessible across national boundaries will, understandably, tend to be favoured over subjective accounts of individual performances. Hence, there has been a tendency within discussions of McDonagh to proceed directly from textual evidence to inference about audience response, with journalism used as a surrogate for actual attendance at performances. While there is much value in such an approach, three problems arise from it.

First, theatre fundamentally involves the subjective experience of individual performances: audiences do not receive a text that can be reduced to essential categories of meaning but experience performances within contexts that generate a nexus of meanings. Martin McDonagh's texts are closed objects, which may be subjected to literary analysis, but Druid's five-year tour of *The Trilogy* was an evolving process that generated a variety of responses. As is particularly notable in the contrast between audience reactions to *Beauty Queen* in Leenane and the Aran Islands, those responses are often not just various but divergent. The issue that arises here is that in establishing the relationship of an Irish play to Irish society, performances are more relevant than play texts. Druid's tours of Ireland disrupt the notion that it is possible to speak of an homogenous 'Irish' response to McDonagh, revealing instead that there are a multiplicity of responses, all of them equally valuable.

The second problem that arises is how Irish critics might understand the global reception of McDonagh's work. Critical responses to McDonagh appear to be grounded in the assumption that the viability of Irish culture should be determined by an analysis of its performance overseas. Irish critics often worry about what the plays might mean for audiences on Broadway, while ignoring the meaning of the plays for audiences in Leenane itself. Brian Friel may have been correct when he suggested that Irish drama exists to be overheard abroad; but it is also the case that Irish audiences and critics are now displaying the self-consciousness of people who believe that others are listening to them. Irish criticism is thus in danger of engaging with other cultures only insofar as they confirm our sense of who we think we are, while also over-looking evidence within our own borders.

A third problem is the issue of methodology. How may a theatre criticism that styles itself as national (as Irish criticism currently does) meaningfully address the work of writers such as McDonagh, whose reputation and reception are strongly predetermined by both global and local factors? Furthermore,

how can such a criticism address the fact that much of the
material used in studying such writers – journalism, marketing,
programme notes – now operates within an internationalized
media that sometimes involves the diffusion of inaccurate
information? It has been shown above that much of what we
think we know about McDonagh has been derived from news
stories that involve the promotion of celebrity or nationalism,
rather than accuracy. This essay has attempted to come to terms
with this situation, by showing how textual analysis, the use of
secondary sources, and the material evidence derived from
attendance at productions and archival material may be
combined. What arises from this discussion is not a homogenous interpretation of McDonagh's work, but rather an
exploration of the variety of subjective, localized responses
generated by his writings and their production. The variation
between understandings of McDonagh's script and the various
productions of *The Trilogy* reveals the need to move beyond
existing categories of criticism. By analysing these productions
in their social context, I sought to provide a model for what
such a criticism might entail: textual analysis, attendance at
performances, archival work, reception analysis, social con-
textualization, and discussion with practitioners. This implies
that globalization is not simply transforming the manner in
which Irish theatre is organized – by making international
touring easier, for example – but that it also affects the manner
in which theatre must be received and studied.

This gives rise to two suggestions. The first is that Irish
criticism must engage with international responses to Irish
work. The second arises from the fact that, although there is
evidence that many productions of Martin McDonagh rely
upon and reinforce internationalized stereotypes about Irishness, there is also evidence that many productions are using
those stereotypes creatively, both in Ireland and elsewhere. Just
as Irish critics should condemn stereotypical representations of
Irishness on the global stage, we must also be alert to the
danger of essentializing the responses of non-Irish audiences.

An awareness of the relationship between Druid and
McDonagh is therefore essential. Such an awareness offers a

better understanding of McDonagh's writing, complicating the criticisms most frequently directed against him. Additionally, such an awareness makes it difficult to accept uncritically the many assumptions that persist about McDonagh's career, and his place in Irish theatre. The relationship between Druid Theatre and McDonagh thus reveals the benefits of looking both outwards *and* inwards, bringing local knowledge into a global conversation about an important Irish dramatist.

Appendix

First Productions

Martin McDonagh, *The Beauty Queen of Leenane*.
Directed by Garry Hynes, Town Hall Theatre, Galway, 1 February 1996.
Martin McDonagh, *A Skull in Connemara*.
Directed by Garry Hynes, Town Hall Theatre, Galway, 3 June 1997.
Martin McDonagh, *The Lonesome West*.
Directed by Garry Hynes, Town Hall Theatre, Galway, 10 June 1997.

---

[1] I wish to acknowledge the assistance of the Irish Research Council for the Humanities and Social Sciences, which provided funding in support of the work from which this paper derives.

[2] Interestingly, more attention has been given to the Royal Court than to Druid in considerations of McDonagh's career to date: see Aleks Sierz, *In-Yer-Face Theatre* (London: Faber and Faber, 2001), and Dominic Dromgoole, *The Full Room* (London: Methuen, 2000).

[3] This phrase has been used throughout Druid's history to describe its pioneering tours of rural Ireland, especially during its first twenty years of operation. cf. Jerome Hynes (ed), *Druid: The First Ten Years* (Galway: Druid Performing Arts and the Galway Arts Festival, 1985).

[4] Louise Donlon, 'Waiting for Druid', *Irish Times*, 16 May 1997, p.13.

[5] Victor Merriman, 'Settling for More: Excess and Success in Contemporary Irish Drama' in Dermot Bolger (ed.), *Druids, Dudes and Beauty Queens: The Changing Face of Irish Theatre* (Dublin: New Island, 2001), pp.55-71

[6] Karen Fricker, 'Ireland sees power of "Beauty"', *Variety*, 21-27 August 2000, p.27.

[7] Ian Kilroy, 'Artscape', *Irish Times*, 6 July 2002, Weekend section, p.5.

[8] Hynes was artistic director at the Abbey from 1991-1993, and worked with Druid from 1975-1990, and from 1994 to the present.

[9] Jack Bradley, 'Making Playwrights', in the programme for *The Cripple of Inishmaan* (London: Royal National Theatre, 1996).

[10] Michael Ross, 'Hynes Means Business', *Sunday Times*, 18 May 2003, Culture section, p.10.

[11] Fintan O'Toole, 'Nowhere Man', *Irish Times*, 26 April 1997, Weekend section, p.1.

[12] Paddy Woodworth, 'Druid – Celebrating in the Present Tense', *Irish Times*, 24 January 1996, p.10.

[13] Fintan O'Toole, 'Murderous Laughter', *Irish Times*, 24 June 1997, p.12.

[14] Michael Ross, 'Bad Boy Back on the Block', *Sunday Times*, 12 July 1998.

[15] Martin McDonagh, *Plays 1* (London: Methuen, 1999), pp.4-5.

[16] Uinsionn Mac Dubhghaill, 'Drama Sails to Seven Islands', *Irish Times*, 27 November 1996, p.12

[17] Joyce McMillan, 'The Life and Soul', *Herald* (Glasgow), 28 November 1997, p.21.

[18] McDonagh, *Plays 1*, p.89.

[19] O'Toole, 'Murderous Laughter', p.12.

[20] Mac Dubhghaill, 'Drama sails', p.12

[21] These were Hynes's own plays, *Island Protected by a Bridge of Glass* and *The Pursuit of Pleasure*, and *Bar and Ger* and *A Galway Girl* by Geraldine Aron. See Jerome Hynes, *Druid – The First Ten Years*, pp.25-27.

[22] Victoria White, 'First Bite at the Big Apple', *Irish Times*, 18 September 1997, p.12.

[23] Fintan O'Toole, 'Martin McDonagh is Famous…' *Guardian*, 2 December 1996, p.11.

[24] David Grieg, 'Introduction' to Sarah Kane, *Complete Plays* (London: Methuen, 2001), p.xiii.

[25] Liz Hoggard, 'Playboy of the West End World', *Independent*, 15 June 2002, pp.10-13.

[26] Jeremy Eccles 'Freak Redefines Beauty', *Canberra Times*, 12 August 2000, Section A, p.12.

[27] NBC News Transcripts, 'Playwright Martin McDonagh Takes Broadway By Storm', Today Show, 16 April 1998.

[28] Ben Brantley, 'A Gasp for Breath Inside an Airless Life', *New York Times*, 27 February 1998, Section E, Part 1, p.1.

[29] Philip Hopkin, 'The Queen of Broadway is Back!', *Irish Voice*, 4 May 1999, p.17.

[30] Diana Barth, 'Maeliosa's Malevolent Turn', *Irish Voice*, 11 May 1999, p.26.

[31] Michael Ross, 'Dawn Bradfield is Rising Once Again As The Star of Jane Eyre', *Sunday Times*, 23 November 2003, Culture section, p.16.

[32] Martin McDonagh, *The Cripple of Inishmaan* (London, Methuen, 1997), p.55.

[33] Quoted by Kilroy, 'Artscape', p.5.

[34] Sue Van Hecke, 'Irish Actors Lend Authenticity, Insight To "Lonesome West"', *Virginian-Pilot*, 20 January 2000, p.W6.

[35] LA Times, 'Theatergoers Come To The Defense Of "Cripple Of Inishmaan"', *Los Angeles Times*, 7 November 1998, Calendar, Part F, p.4.

[36] Court Theatre website: http://www.courttheatre.org.nz/handlers/getfile.cfm/4,14,63,37, html, accessed 1 September 2003.

[37] Michael Ross, Mick Heaney, Gerry McCarthy, Marian Lovett, and Brian Boyd, 'Be Here Now', *Sunday Times*, 10 May 1998. p.2.

[38] Helena Mulkerns, 'Broadway Toasts McDonagh's Play', *Irish Times*, 25 April 1998, p 3.

[39] 'It's Hip to be Irish', *Irish Times*, 20 June 1998, Weekend section, p.1.

[40] Matt Wolf, 'Broadway bows to Brits', *Guardian*, 27 May 1998, p.14.

[41] Mimi Kramer, 'Three for the Show', *Time*, 4 August 1997, p.71.

[42] Those who made the claim include: Diana Barth, 'Man of Aran', *Irish America*, 28 February 1998, p.55; Sean O'Hagan, 'The Wild West', *Guardian*, 24 March 2001, Weekend section, p.24. At various times, both Noel Coward and Dion Boucicault had five plays running simultaneously in London, while W. Somerset Maugham had four. Undoubtedly, many other examples exist.

[43] O'Toole, "Nowhere Man".

[44] Karen Vandevelde, 'The Gothic Soap of Martin McDonagh' in Eamonn Jordan (ed.), *Theatre Stuff: Critical Essays in Contemporary Irish Theatre* (Dublin: Carysfort Press, 2000), p.292.

[45] See, for one example, Mary Luckhurst, 'Martin McDonagh's Lieutenant of Inishmore: Selling (-Out) to the English', *Contemporary Theatre Review*, Volume 14, Number 4 (November 2004), pp.34-41.

Notes on Contributors

Helen M. Burke is an Associate Professor of English at Florida State University. She is the author of *Riotous Performances: The Struggle for Hegemony in the Irish Theater, 1712-1784* (University of Notre Dame Press, 2003), and she has also published articles on eighteenth-century British literature and drama.

Richard Cave is Professor of Drama at Royal Holloway College, London. He is an authority on Renaissance and modern drama, particularly the plays of Yeats and his contemporaries. His books include *Ben Jonson* (1991) and editions of Yeats's and Wilde's plays.

Adrian Frazier is Director of the MA in Drama & Theatre Studies, and the MA in Writing, at the National University of Ireland Galway. He is author of a number of books, including *Behind the Scenes: Yeats, Horniman, and the Struggle for the Abbey Theatre* (1990) and *George Moore, 1852-1933* (2000). He is currently writing a book about Abbey actors who went to Hollywood in the 1930s.

Nicholas Grene is Professor of English Literature at Trinity College, Dublin. He has written extensively both on Renaissance and on modern Irish drama; his most recent books are *The Politics of Irish Drama* (Cambridge University Press, 1999) and *Shakespeare's Serial History Plays* (Cambridge University Press, 2002).

John P. Harrington is the Dean of the School of Humanities and Social Sciences at Rensselaer, a technological university in upstate New York. He is the author of *The English Traveller in Ireland*, *The Irish Beckett*, and *The Irish Play on the New York Stage*, and the editor of *Modern Irish Drama* in the W. W. Norton Critical Editions series.

Seamus Heaney is Ireland's leading poet, the winner of numerous awards including the Nobel Prize for Literature (1995); his most recent volume of poetry is *Electric Light* (2001). He was one of the Directors of the Field Day Theatre Company, which produced *The Cure at Troy* (1990), his adaptation of Sophocles' *Philoctetes*. In 2004 his version of *Antigone* was produced by the Abbey Theatre and published by Faber.

Peter Kuch is a Senior Lecturer in the School of English and Convenor of Irish Studies at the University of New South Wales, Australia. He is the Australian representative on the organizing committee of the Irish Theatrical Diaspora project, has published widely on modern Irish and Australian literature, including *Yeats and Æ: 'The Antagonism that Unites Dear Friends'* (1986). He has also convened several conferences, and runs the annual Irish Film Festival in Sydney and Melbourne.

Patrick Lonergan teaches at the Department of English, National University of Ireland, Galway. He is Book Reviews editor of *irish theatre magazine* and reviews theatre in the west of Ireland for the *Irish Times*. He has published articles on many Irish dramatists, including Sean O'Casey, Martin McDonagh, Billy Roche, and Marie Jones.

Deirdre McFeely is currently completing a Ph.D. at Trinity College Dublin on the politics of Dion Boucicault's Irish plays.

Chris Morash is Director of Media Studies, at the National University of Ireland, Maynooth. He is author of *A History of Irish Theatre 1601-2000* (Cambridge University Press, 2002), *Writing the Irish Famine* (Oxford University Press, 1995), and numerous articles on Irish culture. He also writes theatre reviews for the *Times Literary Supplement*.

Richard Pine is Academic Director of the Durrell School of Corfu, and a former secretary of the Irish Writers' Union. In 1978 he organized the Golden Jubilee exhibition of the Dublin Gate Theatre, and has published definitive studies of Brian Friel (1990/1999) and Lawrence Durrell (1994/2005), in addition to *The Thief of Reason: Oscar Wilde and Modern Ireland* (1995) and the official history of the Royal Irish Academy of Music, of which he is a governor and an honorary fellow. From 1974 to 1999 he worked in Radio Telefís Éireann, and continues to broadcast frequently.

Melissa Sihra is Lecturer in Drama at Queen's University Belfast. She is a professional dramaturg and is currently writing a monograph on the theatre of Marina Carr. She is co-editor of *Contemporary Irish Theatre*, forthcoming with Colin Smythe & Oxford University Press.

Anthony Roche is Senior Lecturer in the School of English at University College Dublin. He is the author of *Contemporary Irish Drama* (1994) and numerous articles on Irish theatre. He is currently preparing *The Cambridge Companion To Brian Friel*.

Index

Abbey Theatre (Dublin), *passim*
Aberdeen, 12
Adelaide, 33, 81f., 88, 137
Adelaide Advertiser, 82, 88
Age (Melbourne), xvi, 70, 81, 83, 88
Aldwych Theatre (London), 20, 30f.
Allgood, Molly, 55, 60, 76, 83, 92
Allgood, Sara, 19, 29, 55, 63, 73, 91f.
Allied Domecq, 26
Allied Irish Bank, 46
American National Theatre and Academy, 39
Ancient Order of Hibernians, 1
Anderson, Benedict, 104ff., 108, 113, 115
Aniston, Jennifer, 206
Aran Islands, xiii, 16, 194, 199, 205, 209
Archer, Jeffrey, 202
Armagh, 33, 200
Arrain Mor, 194
Arrow (Dublin), 103
Arts Council (Northern Ireland), 161

Asche, Oscar, 78
Athens (Greece), 167f.
Athlone, 58, 177
Atlantic Ocean, xv, 38, 135, 184
Australia, xiv, xvi, xviii, 9, 69-88, 91, 193, 201, 203f., 216
Avignon Festival, 205

Bacik, Ivana, 182, 188ff.
  Kicking and Screaming, 182, 189, 191
Bailey, W.F., 72, 74, 87
Balkans, 161, 167
Ball, Edward, 165
Baltimore, Maryland, 89
Barnes, Ben, 48
Barnes, Clive, 47, 50
Barrault, Jean-Louis, 21
Barry, Sebastian, 195
Barry, Spranger, x, 89-99, 110, 113
Beckett, Samuel, 37, 47, 182, 185, 216
Beckham, David, 202
Behan, Brendan, 22, 32
  Richard's Cork Leg, 22
Belasco, David, 42

Belfast, xii, 75, 106-115, 119, 166ff., 190, 199, 217
Belgrade, 168ff.
Beltaine, 17
Benjamin, Walter, xv, xix
    The Work of Art in the Age of Mechanical Reproduction, xv
Bentley, Eric, 45, 47, 50
Bergman, Ingmar, 21, 33
Bernard, John, 82, 84, 121-25, 135, 205
    Retrospections of the Stage, 121, 135
Bernstein, Michael André, 102, 114
Bijou Theatre (Melbourne), 81
Birmingham (England), 163
Blackpool, 73
Blythe, Ernest, 21, 45
Boston, 36, 49, 65, 186
Boucicault, Dion, x, xii, xvii, 16, 21, 31, 113, 133, 139-59, 213, 216
    Arrah-na-Pogue, x, xii, xvii, 139-59
    Colleen Bawn, The, 139f., 147, 151, 157
    Shaughraun, The, 21, 31, 139, 157
    Story of Ireland, The, 154
Boucicault, Dion ('Dot), 78, 81, 87
Bowles, Bob, 122f., 135
Boyd, Ernest, 43, 213
Boyle, William, 12, 29, 83, 89
    Building Fund, The, 12, 83
Boyne, Battle of the, 59
Bradfield, Dawn, 204, 213
Brantley, Ben, 204, 212
Bridges-Adams, Walter, 167
Britain, xiv, 15, 18, 28, 37, 136, 154, 167, 169, 202ff.
British Council, 167-69

Broadway, 48, 90, 194f., 204, 206, 208f., 212f.
Brontë, Emily, 168
    Wuthering Heights, 168
Brook, Peter, 47
Brooklyn Academy of Music, 46
Brougham, John, 148
Bucharest, 169f.
Bulgaria, 167, 169
Bulletin, 77, 83-88, 99
Bunraku National Theatre (Japan), 21
Burke, Helen, xi, 119, 215
Burnham, Richard, 75, 86f., 98
Butt, Alfred, 73
Buttevant [County Cork], 122f., 132
Byrne, Oscar, 143
Byzantium, 20

Cahill, Thomas, 182
    How the Irish Saved Civilisation, 182
Calcraft, J.W., 112
Cambridge, 12, 86, 114, 158, 162, 215, 217
Cambridge Festival Theatre, 162
Canada, xiv, 76, 78, 87, 161, 193
Canberra, 203, 212
Cardiff, 12, 29
Carleton, William, 3, 125, 136
Carolan, Turlough, 126, 128, 136
Carr, Marina, viii, xvii, 27f., 34, 179-90, 194, 197, 217
    By the Bog of Cats, 184, 186f., 189
    On Raftery's Hill, 179, 183-87
    Portia Coughlan, xviii, 27f., 34, 180-84, 187, 197
Casson, Christopher, 166
Casson, Kay, 166
Castledawson, 1

Cave, Richard, xiv, 9, 34, 159, 176, 215
Celtic Tenors, 37
Chambers Dictionary, 66
Chaplin, Charles, 78
  The Kid, 78
Chekhov, Anton, 34, 40
Chetwood, W.R., 109f.
  General History of the Stage, 109f
Chicago, 36, 42, 49, 89-93, 98, 186f., 190
Chicago Daily News, 91, 98
Civic Repertory, 39
Clare, 52, 62
Clark, William Smith, 120f., 124, 129, 135, 137f.
Clifford, James, 128, 136
Coliseum (London), 19, 71f.
Colum, Padraic, 53
Columbia University, 38, 49, 189
Comédie Française, 20
Connema, Richard, 187
Connery, Sean, 194, 202
Cook, George Cram ('Jig'), 42
Coole Park, 55
Cork, xi, xii, xviii, 3, 32, 106f., 109, 111, 119, 122, 130-38, 159, 166, 194
Cork Dramatic Society, 106
Cork Opera House, 106
Corkery, Daniel, 106, 108, 115
Costa Rican National Theatre, 39
Court Theatre (Christchurch, NZ), 62, 205, 213
Court Theatre (Galway), 62, 205, 213

Cousins, James, 107
  The Racing Lug, 107
Creagh, 1

Crowe, Eileen, 31, 94, 96
Cullen, Louis, 88, 127, 136
Curran, Sarah, 163
Czechoslovakia, 21, 168

Daily Express (London), 33, 143, 145, 146f., 155, 158f., 169
Daly, Richard, 122
Dark Rosaleen, 43
Darley, Arthur, 16
Daubeny, Peter, 20f. 30-32
de Filippo, Eduardo, 20
Deane, Seamus, 122, 136
Delany, Maureen, 83
Department of Foreign Affairs (Ireland), 26
Derry, xiii, 1, 3, 119, 194
  City, xviii, 33f., 37, 46ff., 83, 131
  County, 1, 120, 122, 135, 137, 166, 194
Desmond, Nora, 83, 133
Deuteronomy, 10
Digges, Dudley, 90
Digges, Lee, 124
Dillingham, Charles, 76
Doctor O'Toole, 84
Donlon, Louise, 195, 211
Drama League of America, 39
Druid Theatre (Galway), x, 188, 193, 196f., 208, 211
Drury Lane (London), 109, 143
Dublin Drama League, 43
Dublin Evening Post (Dublin), 145f., 158
Dublin Theatre Festival, 22, 47, 169, 194f.
Dublin University Magazine, 112
Dundalk, 54
Dunne, William Bodham, 150f., 159

Easter Rising, 74, 77, 91

Edinburgh, 12, 33, 66, 115, 189, 201
Edwards, Hilton, 161-69,
Edwin, John, 126, 130, 135f.
Egypt, 34, 161, 165ff.
Elliot, Gertrude, 78
Elsinore, xvi, 3, 161, 165
Elton, Ben, 202
Emmet, Robert, 2, 33, 163
England, vii, x, xiv, xviii, 9, 11, 13f., 19ff., 26, 32, 34, 42, 52, 55, 60, 70, 73, 75, 77, 122, 130f., 145, 150, 154, 156, 159, 193, 198f., 202
Enniskillen, 194
Era (London), 149, 159
Erris Island, 194
Ervine, St John, 74, 92
Euripides, 187
    Medea, 187
Evening Sun (New York), 37, 49
Everyman Theatre (Cork), 3

Fagan, James Bernard,
    And so to Bed, 173
Farquhar, George
    The Recruiting Officer, 69
Fawkes, Richard, 153ff., 158f.
Fay, Frank, 63f., 98
Fay, W.G., xv, 29, 67
Feehily, Stella, 195
Fenians, 150, 152ff., 157
Fettes, Christopher, 19
Field Day Theatre Company, 3, 216
Fiennes, Ralph, 202
Fitzmaurice, George, 22
Flaherty, Robert, 96, 205
Fletcher, Alan, 124, 136
Fodor, Ladislas, 168
    The Unguarded Hour, 168
Foley, Sean and McColl, *Hamish*, 202

The Play Wot I Wrote, 202
Ford, John, x, 96f.
    Plough and the Stars, The, 96
    Quiet Man, The, x,
Frazier, Adrian, ix, xvi, 89, 215
Friel, Brian, 3f., 24, 32ff., 48, 50, 161, 164, 209, 217
    Aristocrats, 48
    Dancing at Lughnasa, 23, 27
    Freedom of the City, The, 32
    Making History, 4
    Translations, 3f.
Friends, 206

Gaiety Theatre (Dublin), 139
Gallipoli, 71, 87
Galway, xiii, 51, 56, 58-64, 89, 106, 188, 193ff., 208, 211f., 215f.
Galway Pilot and Galway Vindicator (Galway), 62
Garrick, David, 109
Gate Theatre (Dublin), 161, 166-79, 187, 200, 217
Gate Theatre (London), 162, George III, King, 69
Gibbons, Luke, 133, 135, 138
Gladstone, William Ewart, 155
Glasgow, 12, 108, 161, 212
Glasgow Repertory Theatre, 108
Glaspell, Susan, 42, 43, 50
    Trifles, 43
Glenroe, 206
Globe Theatre, 45
Godfrey, Peter, 162
Gorki, Maxim, 20
Gort, 16, 29
Gowen, Peter, 26
Graham, Colin, 179, 189
Granville Barker, Harley, 39
Grattan, Henry, 164
Gray, Terence, 162
Greek Arts Theatre, 20

Green Room, 79, 84, 87f.
Gregory, Augusta Lady, xi, xiii,
    17, 29f., 39f., 49, 51-66, 70-
    75, 83, 87, 89, 91f., 101
    Hyacinth Halvey, 12, 58, 60, 62
    Our Irish Theatre, 49, 65ff.
    Spreading the News, 12, 28, 57,
    58, 60, 64
    Gaol Gate, The, xiii, 56f., 59,
    60-65
    Rising of the Moon, The, 44, 61f.
    White Cockade, The, 58f.
    Workhouse Ward, The, 58, 83
Grene, Nicholas, xi, 215
Grennell, Aidan, 166
Grieg, David, 202, 212
Griffiths, D.W., 78
Grotowski, Jerzy, 47
Gussow, Mel, 46, 50

Hall, Anmer, 162, 176
Hamilton, James, Duke of
    Abercorn, 154
Hampstead Theatre Club, 26
Harrington, John, vii, xv, 35,
    216
Hattiesburg, Mississippi, 44
Hawk's Well Theatre (Sligo), 3
Hayes, J.J., 43, 45, 50
Heaney, Seamus, xii, 1, 185, 216
    'Station Island', 4
Heaphy, Tottenham, 130
Hearts of Erin, 42
Hegel, G.W.F., 103, 114
    *Philosophical History of the
    World*, 103
Henry Street Settlement, 36, 39,
    49
Henry, Paul, 185
Herald and Examiner (Chicago),
    93
Hickey, Tom, 45, 47
Hicks, Seymour, 78

Hillhead, 1f.
Hitchcock, Alfred, 91, 109f, 137
Hobson, Bulmer, 107
Hobson, Harold, 20, 31, 136
Hogan, Robert, 66, 75, 86, 87,
    98, 114, 159
Holloway, Joseph, 63, 66, 98,
    101f., 114, 215
Holt, Thelma, 26
Hull (England), 12
Hungary, 168
Hunt, Hugh, 21f.
Hunter, Holly, 187
Hyde, Douglas, 107, 164

Ibsen, Henrik, 58
    Hedda Gabler, 21
Iceland, 21
Iden Payne, Ben, 42
Inis Mór, 199
Invisible Man, The 90f.
Ireland, *passim*
Irish Echo, 48, 50
Irish Free State, 19, 43, 161
Irish Literary Society (London),
    12
Irish Literary Theatre, 35, 39,
    102f., 107, 179
Irish National Theatre Society,
    12, 19, 38, 54, 90, 101f.
Irish People (Dublin), 150
Irish Players of America, 42
Irish Theatre Company, xiii
Irish Theatre, Inc., 43
Irish Theatrical Diaspora Project, xiv
Irish Times (Dublin), 145, 155,
    158, 195, 206, 211ff., 216

James, Henry, 38
James, Sid, 202
Johnson, Terry, 202
    *Cleo, Camping, Emmanuelle and
    Dick*, 202

Johnston, Denis, 162, 166, 185
  A Bride for the Unicorn, 162, 166
  Moon in the Yellow River, 163
  Old Lady Says 'No!', The, x, 163
Johnston, Jennifer, 185
Jones, Henry Arthur, 38f., 43, 49f.
Jones, Marie, 216
Joyce, James, 3, 37, 159, 199f., 212

Kane, Sarah, 194, 202, 212
Kane, Whitford, 42, 50
Kavanagh, Patrick, 1
  Great Hunger, The, 1
Kavanagh, Peter, 45
Kelly, P.J., 90
Kemble, John, 124
Kemble, Stephen, 124
Keneally, Thomas
  Great Shame, The, 9, 28
Kenny, Jon, 208
Kent, Jonathan, 19
Kerrigan, J.M., 73, 92, 96
Kerry, 52
  (West), 16
Kilroy, Ian, 196, 212
Kilroy, Thomas, 3, 32, 48, 56, 65f., 194
  Madam McAdam's Travelling Theatre, 4
  Talbot's Box, 22
Koun, Karolos, 20
Krause, David, 98, 154, 158f.
Kristeva, Julia, 180, 189
  Essay on Abjection, 180, 189
Kuch, Peter, vii, xvi, 69, 87, 216

La Gallienne, Eva, 39
La Parole Bulgare (Sofia), 169
LaGuardia, Fiorello, 95

Lally, Mick, 206
Lane, Hugh, 71
Larne, 42, 174
Laughton, Charles, 94f.
Lawler, Iris, 166
Lawrence, W.J., 112, 115, 136
Leeds, 12
Lepage, Robert, 194
Lewisohn, Ludwig, 42, 50
Lexington Opera House, 42
Limerick, 119, 122, 130, 132ff., 177, 184, 194
Lincoln Centre Festival, 48
Linenhall Library (Belfast), 112, 115
Lisdoonvarna, 194
Little Dutch Girl, The, 79
Liverpool, 12, 127, 135
London, xii, xiv, xv, xvi, 12, 19, 21, 27-38, 50, 52, 56, 65f., 69, 71, 74, 76, 88, 90, 91-94, 97f., 109-112, 115, 119, 124, 131, 135-44, 148-66, 189f., 193f., 200-202, 207, 211-215
Lonergan, Patrick, xviii, 193, 216
Longford Productions, 166f.
Lord Chamberlain's Office, 152
Los Angeles, 95f., 205, 213
Lusitania, 71, 87
Luxembourg, 161, 168
Lyric Theatre (Belfast), 19
Lyric Theatre Studio (Hammersmith), 19

Mac Anna, Tomás, 23, 33
Mac Dubhghaill, Uinsionn, 199, 212
mac Liammóir, Micheál, x, xvi, 20, 31f., 161-76
  All for Hecuba, 164, 169
  Armlet of Jade, 166
MacIntyre, Tom, 45, 47

The Great Hunger, 1, 45f., 50
Macklin, Charles, 109, 165
MacLaglen, Victor, 95
MacNamara, Brinsley, 94
MacSwiney, Terence, 106, 115
Maid of the Mountains, 79
Malta, 161
Malvern, 163
Mamet, David, 207
Manchester, 12, 42, 140, 150f.,
    155
Manners, J. Hartley, 73f.
    Peg O' My Heart, 73
Martyn, Edward, 39, 113, 114
Mason, Patrick, 23
Matthews, Brander, 38
Maxwell, Rene, 79
Mayne, Rutherford
    The Drone, 42
    Red Turf, 42
Mc Cormack, W.J., 55, 65
McCormick, F.J., 94, 96
McCourt, Frank, 37, 183, 185,
    190
McCourt, Malachy, 37
McDonagh, Martin, x, xviii, 193-
    216
    A Skull in Connemara, 194,
    199, 211
    Beauty Queen of Leenane, 193-
    96, 198-211
    Cripple of Inishmaan, The, 204f.,
    207, 212f.
    Leenane Trilogy, viii, 193f.,
    199ff., 205, 207
    Lonesome West, The, 194-99,
    203ff., 208, 211
    Pillowman, The, 200
McFeely, Deirdre, ix, xii, xvii,
    139, 216
McGuinness, Frank, 24, 26ff.,
    33, 188, 190
    Mary and Lizzie, 26

*Observe the Sons of Ulster
    Marching Towards the Somme*, x,
    24f.
McKenna, Siobhán, 19
McMaster, Anew, xii, 1
McMillan, Joyce, 199, 212
McPherson, Conor, 195
Meade, Declan, 186
Melba, 78
Melbourne, xvi, 69f., 74f., 78,
    81ff., 88, 216
Memorial Theatre (Stratford), 19
Messager d'Athènes (Athens), 167
Metropolitan Club (New York),
    37
Minogue, Kylie, 202
Mitchel, Charles, 166
Moffat, Graham, 88, 108
    Bunty Pulls the Strings, 81, 87
Molière, J-B. P. de
    Le Médecin malgré lui, 64
Moncrieff, Gladys, 79
Mooney, Ria, 168
Morash, Chris, v, vi, xi, xiii, 69,
    86, 101, 158, 159, 217
Morgan, Frank, 95
Morgan, J.P., 37
Morgan, Sydney, 81
Morley, Francis B., 152f., 159
Morrison, Conall, 47, 111
Moscow Art Theatre, 20
Mosman, 73
Mossbawn, 4
Mossop, Henry, 130, 137
Mullingar, 58
Mulrooney, Deirdre, 184, 186,
    190
Murphy, Tom, 66, 197, 200
    Bailegangaire, 197f., 201
    Conversations on a Homecoming,
    201
My Lady's Dress, 78

Nacodoches, Texas, 44
Nathan, George Jean, 44f., 47, 50, 93
Nation (Dublin), 113, 144f., 147, 156, 158
Nation (New York), 40, 50
NBC, 204, 212
Neighborhood Playhouse (New York), 36
New Haven, 36, 49f.
New Testament
  Epistle of James, 10
New York, xii, xv, xvii, xix, 33, 36-50, 57, 67, 76, 89, 93, 95, 98f., 111f., 136, 139, 159, 161, 164, 170, 186, 189, 194, 200-204, 212, 216
New York Times (New York), 37, 39, 43f., 46, 49f., 204, 212
New Zealand, 73, 205
Newcastle (England), 12, 47, 164
Newry, 119, 127, 135
Nic Shiubhlaigh, Máire, 55
Norris, Frank, 95
Northern Ireland, 28, 48, 161, 205

Ó Rathaille, Aogán, 133
O'Casey, Sean
  Juno and the Paycock, 20, 31, 74, 89, 91ff.
  Plough and the Stars, The, 20, 31, 46, 52, 92f, 96, 200
O'Kelly, Donal
  Catalpa, 185
O'Neill, Eugene, 41
  Ah, Wilderness!, 166
  Mourning Becomes Electra, 167
O'Neill, James, 41
O'Neill, Maire – see Allgood, Molly, 55, 60, 63, 76, 83, 92

O'Rowe, Mark
  Crestfall, 200
Offaly, 129, 186
Oklahoma!, 37
Old Testament
  Deuteronomy, 10
Old Vic (London), 22
Olivier Award, 189
Olympia Theatre (Dublin), 22
Opera House (Belfast), xii, 111
Opera House (Cork), xii, 106, 111
Orpen, William, 185
Orton, Joe, 207
Osborne, Walter, 185
Owenson, Robert, 133ff.
Oxford, ix, 12, 28, 49, 66, 67, 87, 135f.
Oxford English Dictionary, 9, 28

Pakenham, Edward, Lord Longford, 161f.
  Yahoo, 162, 164
Palace Theatre (Sydney), 77, 84
Paris, 33, 162
Parker, Stewart, 4, 185
  Pentecost, 4, 185
Paul, Andrew, 182, 184, 190

Paulin, Tom, 4
  The Riot Act, 4
Peacock Theatre, Dublin, 23, 27
Pearson, Noel, 22f., 32
Pethica, James, 57, 66
Phillip, Arthur, Captain, 69
Pickford, Mary, 78
Pine, Richard, x, xvi, 161, 217
Pinter, Harold, 166, 207
Pittsburgh, xvii, 44, 89, 98, 180, 182ff., 190
Pittsburgh Irish and Classical Theatre Company, 180, 184

Pittsburgh Post-Gazette
(Pittsburgh), 182, 190
Pius XI, Pope, 90
Playbill, 37
Pocatello, Idaho, 44
Poel, William, 19
Polini, Emilie, 78
Polish Contemporary Theatre
(Łódź), 20
Pollyanna, 78
Ponsonby, Spencer, 153
Portmagee, 194
Provincetown Players, 42
Punch (London), 153

Queensland, 85
Quinn, John, 40, 49
Quinn, Maire, 90

Rathlin Island, 194
Rawson, Christopher, 182
Rea, Stephen, 3
Rebellion (1803), 152, 163
Repertoire Company, 42
Restoration, 10, 110
Robinson, Lennox, 35, 44, 75,
77, 82, 87, 89, 92, 98
White-headed Boy, The, 75-85
Roche, Anthony, xi, xii, 51, 217.
Rogoff, Gordon, 47, 50
Romania, 169
Roosevelt, Theodore, 40, 49
Roscommon, 95
Rothenberg, David, 46
Royal Court Theatre (London),
22, 27, 32, 193, 194
Royal Dramatic Theatre
(Sweden), 21
Royal Irish Academy (Dublin),
ix, xiv
Royal National Theatre
(London), 23, 33, 37, 40, 212

Royal Shakespeare Company
(London), x, 24ff., 30, 33, 48
Ryder, Thomas, 126, 130

Saddlemyer, Ann, 28f., 62, 65ff.,
73, 87
Samhain (Dublin), 17, 102f., 114
San Francisco, 95, 99, 186, 190
Scotland, 55, 60, 115, 156
Scottish National Players, 108
Serbia, 168
Shakespeare, William, 19, 26, 33,
48, 168, 187, 205, 207, 216
Comedy of Errors, 168, 173
Hamlet, xvi, 3, 4, 109, 111,
162, 164f., 168f.
Macbeth, 126, 168
Measure for Measure, 19
Othello, 168, 172, 174f.
Shaw, George Bernard, 42, 56,
82, 95, 168
Sheik, The, 78
Sheridan, Thomas, 110
Shields, Arthur, 81, 83, 92, 96,
98
Shortt, Pat, 208
Sihra, Melissa, xvii, 179, 189f.,
217
Sinclair, Arthur, 73f., 76, 92
Skibbereen, 194
Sligo, 3, 137, 200
Slovenia, 168
Smock Alley (Theatre Royal,
Dublin), xif., 119, 130
Snagg, Thomas, 126f., 135f.
Snowblind, 78
Sofia, 164, 169
Sophocles, 205, 216
South Africa, 85
South Australia, 82
Soviet Union, 21
Sparks, The, xii, 1-4
St Patrick's Day, 46

Stage and Society, 70, 77, 87
Stark, Pauline, 78
Starkie, Walter, 89
Stauffer, Donald, 168
Stephens, James, 150
Stoppard, Tom, 38, 42, 200
    Real Inspector Hound, 200
Sullivan, Barry, 113
Sunday Times (Chicago), 31, 90,
    91, 98, 206, 212f.
Swift, Carolyn, 21
Switzerland, 161, 168, 175
Sydney, xvi, xviii, 69f., 75-88,
    165, 194f., 200f., 203, 216
Sydney Festival, 194f.
Sydney Morning Herald, 70, 76, 79,
    87
Sydney Theatre Company, 203
Synge, J.M., xvii, 12, 22, 29, 51-
    67, 79, 80-84, 88, 90, 92,
    101f., 181, 198, 200, 207
    In the Shadow of the Glen, 12,
    83
    *Playboy of the Western, The
    World*, xiii, xvii, 10, 36, 44, 49,
    52, 80, 88, 181, 198, 200f.
    Riders to the Sea, 12, 16, 28, 44,
    58, 62, 106
    Well of the Saints, The, 22

Tait, J. and N., 72f., 75, 77
Taylor, Laurette (Cooney), 73
Teatro Stabile (Rome), 21
Théâtre de France, 21
Theatre Magazine, 76, 80, 87f.
Theatre of Ireland, 35, 37, 39,
    43, 54f.
Theatre on the Balustrade
    (Czechoslovakia), 21
Theatre Record, 24, 26, 33f.
Theatre Royal (Adelaide), 82
Theatre Royal (Belfast),119
Theatre Royal (Dublin), 81

Theatre Royal (Hawkins St,
    Dublin) 111f., 139f., 143,
    146, 154, 156, 158f.
Theatre Royal (Manchester), 140
Theatre Royal (Melbourne), 81,
    83, 88
Theatre Royal (Sydney), 79
Thessaloniki, 169
Tóibín, Colm, 56, 59, 65f.
    Lady Gregory's Toothbrush, 65f.
Tolstoy, Leo, 36
Tomahawk (London), 153
Tony Award, 194, 207
Toome, 1f.
Toronto, 78, 87, 136, 195
Town Hall Theatre (Galway),
    198, 211
Tralee, 177, 194, 200
Trotter, Mary, 54, 65
Tuam, 58

Ulad (Belfast), 107, 115
Ulster, 4, 28, 107, 115
Ulster Literary Theatre, 107
Union Club (New York), 37
United Irishman (Dublin), 102,
    158
United Irishmen, 109
United Kingdom, 21

Valentino, Rudolph, 78
Victor, Benjamin, 95, 109
    *History of the Theatres of London
    and Dublin From the Year 1730
    to the Present (1761)*, 109
Victoria, Queen, 153f.
Virginia, USA, 205

Wagner, Richard, 103
Walker, Joseph Cooper, 109f.,
    113
Walla Walla, 44
Walsh, Phil, 76

Walsh, Townsend, 154, 159
Wardle, Irving, 21, 31
Wareing, Alfred, 29
Warrenpoint, 127
Washington, D.C., 33, 44, 89, 180, 183, 185, 188
Waterford, 119, 126, 130
Way Down East, 78
Weismuller, Johnny, 97
Welsh, Irvine, 201
Wexford, 54, 129
Whelan, Bill, 185
    Riverdance, 185
Wild Geese, 129
Wilde, Oscar, 56, 168f., 185, 215, 217
Wilkes, Thomas, 109f., 115
    General View of the Stage, 109, 115
Wilks, Robert, 110
Williams, Emlyn, 168
    Night Must Fall, 168
Williams, Kenneth, 202
Williamson, J.C., 71, 75f., 85
Willison, John, 78, 87
Wilmer, Steve, xiv, xviii
Wilson, A.P., 70f., 73.

Wilson, Robert, 47
Windsor, Barbara, 146, 202
Wodehouse, John, Earl of Kimberley, 143, 146, 154
Woodham-Smith, Cecil, 45
Woods, Vincent
    At the Black Pig's Dyke, 201
Wordsworth, William, 2
World War I, xii
Wright, Udolphus 'Dossy', 73f., 90f.
Wyncote, Pennsylvania, 44

Yeats, W.B., ix, xi, 2f., 12, 17, 19, 28, 30, 32, 37, 39, 40-42, 51-66, 70-75, 79, 86, 89, 92, 101-107, 114, 164, 179, 215, 216
    Diarmuid and Grania, 57
    Hour Glass, The, 32, 62
    Where There is Nothing, 57
Youghal, 15
Ypres, 71, 87
Yugoslavia, 168

Zagreb, 169

CARYSFORT PRESS

The Press aims to produce high quality publications which, though written and/or edited by academics, will be made accessible to a general readership. The organisation would also like to provide a forum for critical thinking in the Arts in Ireland, again keeping the needs and interests of the general public in view.

The company publishes contemporary Irish writing for and about the theatre.

Carysfort Press was formed in the summer of 1998. It receives annual funding from the Arts Council.

The directors believe that drama is playing an ever-increasing role in today's society and that enjoyment of the theatre, both professional and amateur, currently plays a central part in Irish culture.

Editorial and publishing inquiries to:

CARYSFORT PRESS Ltd

58 Woodfield, Scholarstown Road, Rathfarnham, Dublin 16, Republic of Ireland

T (353 1) 493 7383 F (353 1) 406 9815
e: info@carysfortpress.com

www.carysfortpress.com

NEW TITLES

IRISH THEATRE ON TOUR

EDITED BY NICHOLAS GRENE AND CHRIS MORASH

'Touring has been at the strategic heart of Druid's artistic policy since the early eighties. Everyone has the right to see professional theatre in their own communities. Irish theatre on tour is a crucial part of Irish theatre as a whole'. *Garry Hynes*

ISBN 1-904505-13-9
€20

SACRED PLAY

SOUL JOURNEYS IN CONTEMPORARY IRISH THEATRE BY ANNE F. O'REILLY

'Theatre as a space or container for sacred play allows audiences to glimpse mystery and to experience transformation. This book charts how Irish playwrights negotiate the labyrinth of the Irish soul and shows how their plays contribute to a poetics of Irish culture that enables a new imagining. Playwrights discussed are: McGuinness, Murphy, Friel, Le Marquand Hartigan, Burke Brogan, Harding, Meehan, Carr, Parker, Devlin, and Barry.'

ISBN 1-904505-07-4
€25

POEMS 2000–2005

BY HUGH MAXTON

Poems 2000-2005 is a transitional collection written while the author – also known to be W. J. Mc Cormack, literary historian – was in the process of moving back from London to settle in rural Ireland.

ISBN 1-904505-12-0
€10

SYNGE: A CELEBRATION

EDITED BY COLM TÓIBÍN

Sebastian Barry , Marina Carr, Anthony Cronin, Roddy Doyle, Anne Enright, Hugo Hamilton, Joseph O'Connor, Mary O'Malley, Fintan O'Toole, Colm Toibin, Vincent Woods.

ISBN 1-904505-14-7
€15 Paperback

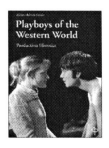

PLAYBOYS OF THE WESTERN WORLD

PRODUCTION HISTORIES
EDITED BY ADRIAN FRAZIER

'Playboys of the Western World is a model of contemporary performance studies.'

'The book is remarkably well-focused: half is a series of production histories of Playboy performances through the twentieth century in the UK, Northern Ireland, the USA, and Ireland. The remainder focuses on one contemporary performance, that of Druid Theatre, as directed by Garry Hynes. The various contemporary social issues that are addressed in relation to Synge's play and this performance of it give the volume an additional interest: it shows how the arts matter.' *Kevin Barry*

ISBN 1-904505-06-6
€20

THE POWER OF LAUGHTER

EDITED BY ERIC WEITZ

The collection draws on a wide range of perspectives and voices including critics, playwrights, directors and performers. The result is a series of fascinating and provocative debates about the myriad functions of comedy in contemporary Irish theatre. *Anna McMullan*

As Stan Laurel said, it takes only an onion to cry. Peel it and weep. Comedy is harder. These essays listen to the power of laughter. They hear the tough heart of Irish theatre – hard and wicked and funny. *Frank McGuinness*

ISBN 1-904505-05-8
€20

CRITICAL MOMENTS
FINTAN O'TOOLE ON MODERN IRISH THEATRE
EDITED BY JULIA FURAY & REDMOND O'HANLON

This new book on the work of Fintan O'Toole, the internationally acclaimed theatre critic and cultural commentator, offers percussive analyses and assessments of the major plays and playwrights in the canon of modern Irish theatre. Fearless and provocative in his judgements, O'Toole is essential reading for anyone interested in criticism or in the current state of Irish theatre.

ISBN 1-904505-03-1
€20

GEORG BÜCHNER: WOYZECK
A NEW TRANSLATION BY DAN FARRELLY

The most up-to-date German scholarship of Thomas Michael Mayer and Burghard Dedner has finally made it possible to establish an authentic sequence of scenes. The widespread view that this play is a prime example of loose, open theatre is no longer sustainable. Directors and teachers are challenged to "read it again".

ISBN 1-904505-02-3
€10

GOETHE AND SCHUBERT
ACROSS THE DIVIDE
EDITED BY LORRAINE BYRNE & DAN FARRELLY

Proceedings of the International Conference, 'Goethe and Schubert in Perspective and Performance', Trinity College Dublin, 2003. This volume includes essays by leading scholars – Barkhoff, Boyle, Byrne, Canisius, Dürr, Fischer, Hill, Kramer, Lamport, Lund, Meikle, Newbould, Norman McKay, White, Whitton, Wright, Youens – on Goethe's musicality and his relationship to Schubert; Schubert's contribution to sacred music and the Lied and his setting of Goethe's Singspiel, Claudine. A companion volume of this Singspiel (with piano reduction and English translation) is also available.

ISBN 1-904505-04-X
Goethe and Schubert: Across the Divide. €25

ISBN 0-9544290-0-1
Goethe and Schubert: 'Claudine von Villa Bella'. €14

GOETHE: MUSICAL POET, MUSICAL CATALYST
EDITED BY LORRAINE BYRNE

'Goethe was interested in, and acutely aware of, the place of music in human experience generally - and of its particular role in modern culture. Moreover, his own literary work - especially the poetry and Faust - inspired some of the major composers of the European tradition to produce some of their finest works.' *Martin Swales*

ISBN 1-904505-10-4
€30

THE THEATRE OF FRANK MCGUINNESS

STAGES OF MUTABILITY
EDITED BY HELEN LOJEK

The first edited collection of essays about internationally renowned Irish playwright Frank McGuinness focuses on both performance and text. Interpreters come to diverse conclusions, creating a vigorous dialogue that enriches understanding and reflects a strong consensus about the value of McGuinness's complex work.

ISBN 1-904505-01-5
€20

THE THEATRE OF MARINA CARR

"BEFORE RULES WAS MADE" - EDITED BY
ANNA MCMULLAN & CATHY LEENEY

As the first published collection of articles on the theatre of Marina Carr, this volume explores the world of Carr's theatrical imagination, the place of her plays in contemporary theatre in Ireland and abroad and the significance of her highly individual voice.

ISBN 0-9534-2577-0
€20

THEATRE OF SOUND

RADIO AND THE DRAMATIC IMAGINATION
BY DERMOT RATTIGAN

An innovative study of the challenges that radio drama poses to the creative imagination of the writer, the production team, and the listener.

"A remarkably fine study of radio drama – everywhere informed by the writer's professional experience of such drama in the making…A new theoretical and analytical approach – informative, illuminating and at all times readable." *Richard Allen Cave*

ISBN 0-9534-2575-4
€20

HAMLET

THE SHAKESPEAREAN DIRECTOR
BY MIKE WILCOCK

"This study of the Shakespearean director as viewed through various interpretations of HAMLET is a welcome addition to our understanding of how essential it is for a director to have a clear vision of a great play. It is an important study from which all of us who love Shakespeare and who understand the importance of continuing contemporary exploration may gain new insights."

From the Foreword, by Joe Dowling, Artistic Director, The Guthrie Theater, Minneapolis, MN

ISBN 1-904505-00-7
€20

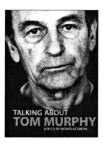

TALKING ABOUT TOM MURPHY
EDITED BY NICHOLAS GRENE

Talking About Tom Murphy is shaped around the six plays in the landmark Abbey Theatre Murphy Season of 2001, assembling some of the best-known commentators on his work: Fintan O'Toole, Chris Morash, Lionel Pilkington, Alexandra Poulain, Shaun Richards, Nicholas Grene and Declan Kiberd.

ISBN 0-9534-2579-7
€15

THEATRE TALK
VOICES OF IRISH THEATRE PRACTITIONERS
EDITED BY LILIAN CHAMBERS & GER FITZGIBBON

"This book is the right approach - asking practitioners what they feel."
Sebastian Barry, Playwright

"...an invaluable and informative collection of interviews with those who make and shape the landscape of Irish Theatre."
Ben Barnes, Artistic Director of the Abbey Theatre

ISBN 0-9534-2576-2
€20

THE DRUNKARD
TOM MURPHY

'The Drunkard is a wonderfully eloquent play. Murphy's ear is finely attuned to the glories and absurdities of melodramatic exclamation, and even while he is wringing out its ludicrous overstatement, he is also making it sing.'
The Irish Times

ISBN 1-904505-09-0
€10

THE IRISH HARP BOOK
BY SHEILA LARCHET CUTHBERT

This is a facsimile of the edition originally published by Mercier Press in 1993. There is a new preface by Sheila Larchet Cuthbert, and the biographical material has been updated. It is a collection of studies and exercises for the use of teachers and pupils of the Irish harp.

ISBN 1-904505-08-2
€40

THREE CONGREGATIONAL MASSES

BY SEOIRSE BODLEY,
EDITED BY LORRAINE BYRNE

'From the simpler congregational settings in the
Mass of Peace and the Mass of Joy to the richer
textures of the Mass of Glory, they are
immediately attractive and accessible, and with
a distinctively Irish melodic quality.' *Barra Boydell*

ISBN 1-904505-11-2
€15

IN SEARCH OF THE
SOUTH AFRICAN IPHIGENIE

BY ERIKA VON WIETERSHEIM
AND DAN FARRELLY

Discussions of Goethe's "Iphigenie auf Tauris"
(Under the Curse) as relevant to women's issues
in modern South Africa: women in family and
public life; the force of women's spirituality;
experience of personal relationships; attitudes to
parents and ancestors; involvement with religion.

ISBN 0-9534-2578-9
€10

THE STARVING
AND OCTOBER SONG

TWO CONTEMPORARY IRISH PLAYS
BY ANDREW HINDS

The Starving, set during and after the siege of
Derry in 1689, is a moving and engrossing
drama of the emotional journey of two men.

October Song, a superbly written family drama
set in real time in pre-ceasefire Derry.

ISBN 0-9534-2574-6
€10

SEEN AND HEARD (REPRINT)

SIX NEW PLAYS BY IRISH WOMEN
EDITED WITH AN INTRODUCTION
BY CATHY LEENEY

A rich and funny, moving and theatrically exciting collection of plays by Mary Elizabeth Burke-Kennedy, Síofra Campbell, Emma Donoghue, Anne Le Marquand Hartigan, Michelle Read and Dolores Walshe.

ISBN 0-9534-2573-8
€20

THEATRE STUFF (REPRINT)

CRITICAL ESSAYS ON
CONTEMPORARY IRISH THEATRE
EDITED BY EAMONN JORDAN

Best selling essays on the successes and debates of contemporary Irish theatre at home and abroad.

Contributors include: Thomas Kilroy, Declan Hughes, Anna McMullan, Declan Kiberd, Deirdre Mulrooney, Fintan O'Toole, Christopher Murray, Caoimhe McAvinchey and Terry Eagleton.

ISBN 0-9534-2571-1
€20

UNDER THE CURSE

GOETHE'S "IPHIGENIE AUF TAURIS",
IN A NEW VERSION BY DAN FARRELLY

The Greek myth of Iphigenie grappling with the curse on the house of Atreus is brought vividly to life. This version is currently being used in Johannesburg to explore problems of ancestry, religion, and Black African women's spirituality.

ISBN 0-9534-2572-X
€10

URFAUST

A NEW VERSION OF GOETHE'S
EARLY "FAUST" IN BRECHTIAN MODE
BY DAN FARRELLY

This version is based on Brecht's irreverent and daring re-interpretation of the German classic.

"Urfaust is a kind of well-spring for German theatre... The love-story is the most daring and the most profound in German dramatic literature." Brecht

ISBN 0-9534257-0-3
€10

HOW TO ORDER
TRADE ORDERS DIRECTLY TO

CMD
Columba Mercier Distribution,
55A Spruce Avenue,
Stillorgan Industrial Park,
Blackrock,
Co. Dublin

T: (353 1) 294 2560
F: (353 1) 294 2564
E: cmd@columba.ie

or contact
SALES@BROOKSIDE.IE

*FOR SALES IN NORTH AMERICA
AND CANADA*

Dufour Editions Inc.,
124 Byers Road,
PO Box 7,
Chester Springs, PA 19425,
USA

T: 1-610-458-5005
F: 1-610-458-7103